fractal

a novel of chaotic suspense

KATHRYN EBERLE WILDGEN

iUniverse, Inc.
Bloomington

fractal
A novel of chaotic suspense

This is a work of fiction. All of the characters, names, incidents, organizations, and dialogue in this novel are either the products of the author's imagination or are used fictitiously.

Cover art: © Melinda Nagy | Dreamstime.com

iUniverse books may be ordered through booksellers or by contacting:

iUniverse
1663 Liberty Drive
Bloomington, IN 47403
www.iuniverse.com
1-800-Authors (1-800-288-4677)

Because of the dynamic nature of the Internet, any Web addresses or links contained in this book may have changed since publication and may no longer be valid. The views expressed in this work are solely those of the author and do not necessarily reflect the views of the publisher, and the publisher hereby disclaims any responsibility for them.

Any people depicted in stock imagery provided by Thinkstock are models, and such images are being used for illustrative purposes only.

Certain stock imagery © Thinkstock.

ISBN: 978-1-4502-7804-1 (sc)
ISBN: 978-1-4502-7803-4 (dj)
ISBN: 978-1-4502-7802-7 (ebook)

Library of Congress Control Number: 2010918790

Printed in the United States of America

iUniverse rev. date: 01/10/2011

For
Marjorie Forstall Eberle
The best mother ever…

We become so accustomed to disguise ourselves to others that at last we are disguised to ourselves.

François, duc de La Rochefoucauld

Main Entry: frac·tal
Function: *noun*
Etymology: French *fractale,* from Latin *fract*us broken, uneven (past participle of *frangere* to break) + French *-ale* -al (n. suffix)
: any of various extremely irregular curves or shapes for which any suitably chosen part is similar in shape to a given larger or smaller part when magnified or reduced to the same size
Merriam-Webster Dictionary On line

2 February 2004
From: fractal@netconnect.net
To: gold.digger@netconnect.net

You'll never believe what's happened. My mother has come back into my life—by dying… I got a call last night from the Covington police. She died of a heart attack and had apparently been in precarious health for quite a while. The telephone and her medications were right next to her bed but there was no 911 call and no indication that she had taken, or attempted to take, her meds. Death wish maybe… I'm leaving Flagstaff day after tomorrow to check out the situation. I don't know how they found me. I didn't think Mother thought or cared about me any longer. They must have found my number in her house somewhere. Dad's so out of it I don't know if I should bother to tell him. I probably will. Even if he understands, he won't give a damn.

I was really interested in your find at Autun and hope you can get back online soon. Have you dated the skeletons yet? Write as soon as you can.

M

4 February 2004
From: gold.digger@netconnect.net
To: fractal@netconnect.net

Sorry about your mom. Even though you weren't close, those blood ties are strong no matter what the circumstances. Take care of yourself and watch out for relapses into old problems…

Finally found an internet café so will be back in contact with some regularity. Project director realizes how hampered we are by lack of regular access to 'net and plans to get a community laptop to address the communications problem. We'll see… To answer your question first, no, the skeletons have not been dated with any certainty. We know they are 12th-c. because of certain aspects of artifacts (won't bore you with details) at the site. We have much more to do before getting this find into the public eye. The site is so secret I can't even tell YOU the details. The *flics* are guarding it zealously but also trying to appear casual about it so as not to arouse suspicion or curiosity. We really have discovered a gold mine. For once, my sign-in ID is more than just an expression of hope. Later…

Please send more info about previous e-mail; also your whereabouts.

W

6 February 2004
From: fractal@netconnect.net
To: gold.digger@netconnect.net

I hesitate to write a lengthy mail because I know your on-line time costs many euros but the story is so grotesque, like everything else in my family, I have to fill in some background. You already know I've had to have extensive therapy—for depression, horrendous dreams, etc—involving the death of my uncle Buddy and the changes in my mother after the accident in 1950. When we were kids, I didn't say much about this part of my life—too fresh, too painful. I spent most of my time in high school making up stories to explain my weird parents. I was especially concerned about you, what you'd think of me. I didn't want to lose you as a friend and I thought if I told you what my parents were like, you'd find me and my family pretty repulsive. Remember how seldom you came to the house? I still see far too little of you. Amanda remains adamant about my avoiding contact with other women, especially ones she suspects I'm in love with. Irony on the way—I'm playing a CD as I write and Fred Astaire is singing "The Way You Look Tonight." I recall so vividly the way you looked the last time we were together. Enough… I'm trying to behave.

I think I'm now ready to give up more information about the accident that defined my childhood and adolescence, and, to a certain extent, my self. Uncle Buddy and Mother were driving at night and Mother slammed the car into a tree. I was only eight at the time and asleep in the back seat, so I wasn't hurt too badly; Buddy died on impact and Mother was so mangled, it took three years and multiple surgeries to get her close to normal. Thanks to Daddy's millions she underwent extensive therapy, both physical and psychological, and when she finally returned, she was bizarre in ways I can't quite pin down. She spent sixteen months in California and returned to a facility in Covington for the rest of her makeover. To a child, that seemed like a lifetime. When she returned home, she was kept in a part of the house I rarely visited, so I saw her very seldom. Most of the time, she looked like a mummy, face and hands swathed in bandages. The curtains were always drawn and the lights were kept dim, so she really was the invisible woman, forgetful and emotionally distant as well. She and I had been as close as a mother and son could be, and she tried so hard to be that way for me again. But life with Dad and me was a constant struggle, as if she were trying to become again who she had been.

Uncle Buddy had lived with us since before I was born; but as far back as my memory goes, my parents fought about him constantly. I was too young to discern the details and they never quarreled in front of me, but I can remember hearing them fighting while I was in bed trying to sleep.

2

All I could pick out of the conversation was "Buddy" this and "Buddy" that. I know Mother wanted him to leave and Dad wanted him to stay, odd because he was Mother's brother, in fact her twin. I also picked up hints that there was something wrong with him, something that made him incapable of coping. But that's it. I also wanted him to leave because I saw him as the cause of my parents' dissension and I was afraid they'd split up. So when he died, I was glad, which produced feelings of guilt as if I had willed him to his death. Once I got that fixed in my head, it took years of shrinking to get it out. After Mother came home finally repaired and refashioned, they STILL fought about dead Uncle Buddy and eventually Mother left in 1960. Dad moved to Flagstaff because he had always wanted to live in the west whereas Mother loved the south, and she then took the house as part of her settlement. She lived there until her recent death. She didn't seem to want me around, so I went to Flagstaff too. I got the parent who was rich, but missed out on the one I adored. Oh well, such is life. Actually, Mother died in that accident too because the pieced-together creature who came back from various clinics was not the mother who adored me in return but a stranger who looked vaguely like her and had her memories. Her soul was gone.

More of my saga after I've had a chance to revisit and explore my childhood home… I'm in Flagstaff now and leave for NOLA 2/8.

M

6 February 2004
From: fractal@netconnect.net
To: Cletus.Hardin@psychnet.org
Dear Cletus,

It's been a while, too long in fact. I'm still on an even keel but miss our sessions. I may need you again; my mother has come back into my life in an odd way. She died and, after what seems like a lifetime of ignoring me, has left me all her worldly goods, including the house where I lived till I was eighteen. Even though the dreams stopped many years ago, I dread their starting up again. I just can't face sleepless nights, terrified of falling asleep for fear of reliving that horror. I still dream of Uncle Buddy once in a while and for a long time, I was afraid he wasn't really dead and would come back to blame me for his death. I have to go to Covington to take care of affairs and I'm almost certain I'll fall back into old habits of thinking and feeling. I expect the dreams…

The bottom line is this: I can't come back and forth to Jerome for therapy and wonder if I can use the 'net as a lifeline so to speak. Just knowing you're a click away would assuage my fears, which are overwhelming at the moment. I can't even use Amanda's shoulder to cry on. She's been very distant and suspects an affair. Do emotions count in the fidelity department? I feel, frequently, that I ought to just indulge my inclination to tell Winifred how much I love her. Why bother with being faithful when I'm accused constantly of the opposite?

Thanks for reading and if the answer is no, I'll understand.

M

6 February 2004
From: Cletus.Hardin@psychnet.org
To: fractal@netconnect.net
Dear Malachi,

Of course, you may write anytime. But treatment via e-mail is tricky at best. Assume that all will be well. If you expect trouble, you'll find it. No drugs of any sort except your usual prescriptions, NO booze. Use relaxation tapes to help you fall asleep. If I find you need treatment, I have some excellent connections in New Orleans, about forty miles from Covington. I'll give you a list of contacts with their specialties and some info that should help you choose. Do NOT seek hypnosis without asking me and without consulting one of my contacts. No voodoo, no crystal-gazing BS, no alternative stuff of any kind. In some ways, New Orleans is like Sedona, full of palm-readers and the like, eager to separate you from your $$$. Be careful. And stay positive. From age eight to eighteen, you lived in hell, perhaps even before that time span. Remember the endless parental bickering… You are in no way responsible for what happened to any of the monsters that surrounded you in childhood. You can't repeat that to yourself often enough.

Cletus

7 February 2004
From: fractal@netconnect.net
To: Cletus.Hardin@psychnet.org

Thanks. I'll keep you posted. At the moment, I'm restless, edgy, filled with nameless dread and eager to put this reconnection with Hell House behind me. I want to take care of business in Louisiana and return to AZ ASAP. I promise not to do anything foolish.

I'm not sure what I'll do when I return to AZ. Amanda wants to keep trying to hold us together and I suppose it's unwise to divorce after such a long marriage. But the phoniness of it all makes me want to gag at times. We just go through the motions. There are still good times, I suppose, hikes in the canyons, concerts, movies… But I find myself wanting more and more to be by myself, on my own. I may have married Amanda too soon after Winifred turned me down. You know, the rebound thing. Perhaps separate vacations would help. I'd like to go back to Europe. Amanda and I visited there a few times, did a sort of grand tour as a honeymoon. But there are places off the beaten path that intrigue me. I'd especially like to visit Winifred in France. She's willing to allow us to be friends and she's in one of those intriguing places. What do you think?

M

7 February 2004
From: fractal@netconnect.net
To: gold.digger@netconnect.net
Cletus has agreed at least to read my mails. He says he can't "shrink" over the 'net but will refer me to someone if need be.

I leave for New Orleans tomorrow and will keep you posted.

Any news from Autun? Let me know if you unearth any more literary gold. I know e-mailing is hard; just write when you can.

M

8 February 2004
From: Cletus.Hardin@psychnet.org
To: fractal@netconnect.net
Dear Malachi,
I think a visit to your friend would be a good thing, but do be cautious. You're not certain yet if you want a divorce, are you? And you don't want yet another rebound thing. After you take care of business in Covington, see if you can manage a trip to France. You're resourceful enough to amuse yourself and stay out of Winifred's way if necessary. I think it would do you a world of good. As for Amanda, don't make any decisions until you return to AZ and the three of us have a chance to thrash things out. Expect her to be angry at the idea of your trip; perhaps it would be wise not to mention it. No harm in having her think you're in Louisiana.

Cletus

8 February 2004
From: gold.digger@netconnect.net
To: fractal@netconnect.net

Sounds like you'll get to NOLA in time for Mardi Gras! Wish I could crash. It's an anthropologist's dream. My colleagues here are very jealous!

I can tell you now that the dig is at the Roman amphitheater at Autun. It's just vaguely possible that we've dug up a guy who worked on the famous Romanesque church of St. Lazarus there. On the site there were tools of the sort used by sculptors and/or masons. One of the skeletons is decidedly peculiar and was almost certainly that of a VERY deformed person. IF the skeleton turns out to be such, and was somehow related to at least one of the other two, then we have a couple who harbored a wretch who would most certainly have died without the intervention of the couple. That explains why they were holed up in ruins rather than in a more conventional dwelling. The freakish person would have had to remain hidden. I don't know if we'll ever puzzle all this out. DNA tests may not be possible and will take ages, if we can get any material to test. The freak had a broken neck and one or both of the others may have killed him. Or he may have offed himself.

I'm really pleased that this project has taken me back to Burgundy, specifically Autun. I've been interested in the motif of the suicide of Judas as depicted on capitals in a cluster of churches in this area: Autun, Saulieu and Vézelay. I wonder why that theme was so popular here in the twelfth century. There's a *Suicide* at the cathedral of Strasbourg, but it's a restoration and who knows how well it reflects what was there originally? There's a painted version of the scene at a small church in Berry, brilliantly treated in a book by Marcia Kupfer. I doubt that I'll get a book out of this, perhaps a lengthy article. I've been thinking about titles. How about "Hanging around with Judas in Burgundy"? That's sure to get published in a really prestigious scholarly journal ;-))

Perhaps I can squeeze in some research in my spare time, of which I have almost none. Good excuse to come back...

How's Amanda? Is she going to NOLA with you?

Back to the salt mines.

W

10 February 2004
From: fractal@netconnect.net
To: gold.digger@netconnect.net

You aren't the only one wishing you were here. I'm doing a sort of archaeological dig of my own. But first things first. The flight to New Orleans was uneventful and my rental car was waiting for me. If I have to stay for any length of time, I'll lease something. Apparently I'm suddenly very rich. The coroner is still curious, almost suspicious, about Mother's death but the cause was quite obvious and there was no hint of foul play. They're still curious about why she didn't call for help, but I can only imagine that death was so sudden, she didn't have a chance to do so. It's also quite possible, even likely, that she wanted to die. Celestine convinced them Mother was given to eccentricity—she was in her late eighties—and there was no way to figure out her motives for bizarre actions. The coroner decided that a more than perfunctory autopsy wasn't necessary, especially since she was under a physician's care, so he released the body for whatever. Celestine is an old black woman, a little older than mom, who had been living with her forever. I sort of remember Cel from way back when. Mother depended on her very much since her own mother died when she was very young. She was spooky then and she's spooky now. She was very upset that any sort of post mortem was done; she claims Mother instructed her to do whatever it took to prevent anyone from doing an autopsy, showed the coroner Mother's will, which did indeed state that. Mother was always prissy about nudity and always locked the door when she was in the shower. This was after the accident. I imagine she was pretty scarred up and didn't want anyone to see what she must have considered disfigurement. So Cel had a funeral parlor cremate her at once. I wonder what the hell I'm doing here! Claiming my inheritance, I guess... I'll be glad when I can clear out. I'll have to decide what to do with the ashes.

I arrived at the house late in the day and, since Cel is still living here, all the utilities were on. She offered to leave but I could use some help going through the mountains of stuff Mother accumulated through the years. The house is fantastic in more ways than one. It's on the Bogue Falaya, one of Louisiana's more beautiful waterways, between the river and a swamp. Hence the name Mother gave the house years ago, Cypress Shadows. It's hemmed in by immense trees, mostly southern pine, but there are a quite a few cypress, water oak, magnolia, and river birch in the mix. I guess Mother thought cypress shadows were classier than pine shadows. She had notions about what was classy and what was not. Celestine tells me the land is subject to catastrophic flooding, hence the house is about eleven feet off the ground on pilings. Every inch of wall space is crammed with art: paintings, sculptures, candle holders, gewgaws. Some of the sculpture is miniature copies of capitals that look like the ones at St Lazarus. I can see much of Autun's art at art-roman.net and on other websites; visiting them is a way of connecting with you. Apparently it's quite a gem of a church. (In case you didn't pick up on this, I miss you very much.) In fact, I was thinking of coming for a visit once I get affairs in order. I promise to stay out of the way and you'll see only as much of me as you wish. I really want to see that church and as much of the dig as permitted. Be frank and let me know if I'd be a pest. Back to reality…

One odd thing: the house looks immense from the outside but is actually quite modest inside. Coming upon an old armoire in Mother's bedroom was a shock. I once got accidentally locked in it and it seemed like hours before they found me. I think I was hiding but haven't a clue from what. I had forgotten all about that incident, but seeing the old piece of furniture brought back not memories exactly, but feelings. Feelings of what? I'm not sure.

There are enough books here to open a library. Mother's taste was eclectic: lots of French novels (I had forgotten she majored in French, lived in France for a while, went for an M. A., then taught French for a while at some local college), tons of medieval art books (yours for the taking if you ever make it here), some philosophy, and Jung by the truckload. I think she was into psychoanalytical art criticism. I found, to my surprise, that she had written some books herself. I googled her and checked her out at Amazon; let's just say I won't look for any royalty checks in the mail.

As I indicated above, the house is smaller than I remembered and Celestine takes up a portion of the available space. But the openness, the floor-to-ceiling windows and the antique French doors are exactly as I recalled. Even the furniture's pretty much the same. While I was gone, Mother's aunt must have died because the sideboard that had belonged to Mother's grandparents is now here. It used to be in my grandaunt's house. It's a fabulous piece, all burled walnut and beveled mirrors. Mother used to

talk about it a lot, wanted it very badly and hoped her aunt would leave it to her. It's mine now and I must say I could get used to living with it. It has a strange vinegary smell about it. I have the vaguest memories of visiting my grandaunt and seeing that piece. It smelled the same then. Funny what we remember and what vanishes without a trace... Of course, it looked much bigger to me as a child. Smells are supposed to be very effective at triggering memories. But no bells rang for me. I'll just have to be patient.

Since it's the dead of winter now, I can see the river through the trees. Most of the windows are uncovered, with a few exceptions such as bathrooms. At first, it's hard to get used to. But the house is walled behind a thick cover of trees so it's not as though we're on display. I've heard the egrets have moved temporarily to the south shore of Lake Pontchartrain, but will soon return. The property is immense, no neighbors visible, audible... The ground is covered with a thick carpet of pine straw and dead leaves, very damp as it's been raining for days. Sometimes there's dense fog rising from the river in the morning—gorgeous. I can remember when I was little, I'd wait for all the leaves to fall so I could see the river from my bedroom upstairs. Celestine's in my old room, so I took Mother's. It's on the first floor off the ground. I don't like the proximity of the armoire, but will get over it. I think I told you the house is raised. Cel offered to yield my old room to me, but I thought it best to let her be. Unfortunately she's a light sleeper and gets up frequently. I hear her walking the floor, going to the bathroom. As I recall, there's a summerhouse somewhere on the property and perhaps a boathouse. I'll explore the grounds when I have a chance.

Amanda will not be coming to Covington. Truth is we've been shaky and I need some time apart to sort things out. I think she'll be relieved to have some time to herself. She knows about you and, with her exquisitely fine-tuned intuition, she knows in her heart of hearts that I've never gotten over you. She realizes that emotional infidelity is the worst sort. More on this later.

It's late and I need a shower. Also want to catch Leno's "Headlines."
More to follow...
M

10 February 2004
From: fractal@netconnect.net
To: Amanda.Greene@worldcom.net
Dear Amanda,

Am using my laptop. Will do an investigation of Mother's computer ASAP. As I mentioned in my phone call, I think it best if we do all our communicating online. Glad things are going well with McClean contract.

Please do some serious thinking while I'm gone. We've been unavailable to each other for months. I know you're unhappy and have never come to terms with my relationship with Winifred. You've waited patiently for me to decide, to change, to sort out my emotions. I appreciate this more than I can tell you. I can't honestly say what my feelings are about this strange *ménage à trois* we have been living for such a long time. I want authenticity but don't know what is authentic for us. But I do know I'm not ready to throw in the towel yet. Bear with me a bit longer. Please…

M

13 February 2004
From: fractal@netconnect.net
To: gold.digger@netconnect.net

Finally had a chance to look around. I'm stirring up some memories and suspect the dreams will return along with some emotional discomfort. If only I could stay numb. The strangest thing that's happened so far is the adventure with the armoire, the one I got locked in. When I opened the door the other day, the smell that the furniture exhaled was overwhelming, a combination of Arpège perfume and Dad's cologne. I don't know why I was filled with such dread. I remember distinctly being closed up in the thing, but I don't remember any fear or worry when it was happening. Perhaps I was more frightened than I thought or felt at the time. I could hear Mother and Dad but they were arguing as usual, screaming and yelling really, about Uncle Buddy. I knew that once the ruckus died down, someone would come to my rescue. I'm going to search through Mother's stuff to see if I can get a handle on that guy. He obviously played a pivotal role in the divorce but I'm damned if I can figure out exactly what. I think I mentioned Buddy and Mother were twins—I believe Buddy was the firstborn, but I'm not sure.

I found the summerhouse. It's falling into ruin. Calling it a house is a stretch. It's a screened room with a few pieces of broken-down furniture in it. There are "Keep Out" signs plastered all over it. I guess it interested vandals a while ago, but no one would want to get in now—except me. I'm beginning to remember bits and pieces of the past, and playing in the summerhouse is one. The feeling of dread I experienced near the armoire finds its counterpart in the summerhouse; I feel nothing but warmth and peace there. I may still be in Louisiana when spring arrives. The place is beginning to grow on me. Flagstaff sucks all the moisture out of my body and I feel like a mummy. Here, I'm nicely hydrated 24/7. The birds are spectacular. There are very shy blue herons near the water, hawks circling overheard, owls filling the night air with their haunting cry, and the woods are full of warblers, chickadees, thrushes, Carolina wrens... A few of the birdhouses that hung on the porch when I was a kid are still here. In about a month, the birds will be scouting out nesting spots. The wrens and the warblers usually vie for the same birdhouse even though there were and still are at least six available. Mother and I used to watch for the fledglings to leave the nest; we managed to catch the show frequently. Birds are clever with their young. The little ones would stay in the nest forever content to let mom and Dad feed them. Mom and Dad have other ideas. Once they begin to feed the chicks, they always chirp just before poking a wriggling something down their throats. The chicks associate that call with food. When it's time for them to fledge, mom and Dad chirp but bring no food. The kids finally get the message: get out or stay hungry. I remember Mother once thought a tiny warbler had fallen out too soon and she tried to put him back in the nest. He objected vehemently. But the weather is now so cold and rainy, it's hard to imagine the sun and budding trees. I think there are azalea bushes in the yard and a massive tumbling vine called Cherokee Rose. At the height of its bloom, it's a cascade of white flowers, like a veil worn by a tree. I'm fairly sure there's wisteria on the property. I vaguely remember being delighted with its purple blooms that took over the grounds at some season, but my lack of horticultural savvy gets in my way. I don't know when to expect it. I must wait for that.

The boathouse is gone; all that remains is a slab. I don't remember much about it. Dad got a boat and built the boathouse while Mother was recuperating, and I was too traumatized to pay attention to such matters. Mother must have had it torn down. I remember she hated boats. Uncle Buddy loved them. Now that's a memory that just popped into my head as I was writing; the words almost wrote themselves. It's a bit strange that the boathouse is on a slab. All the other outbuildings are raised except the little shed around the well. I guess the boathouse was so flimsy and so hastily thrown together, Dad decided to skimp on piers. In fact, I think he had some handymen pour the concrete, didn't even have pros build it. That was against code, of course, but no one ever called my dad on anything. Since all trace of the building proper is gone, I'm assuming a flood or a storm took it down.

Celestine doesn't like me prowling about the property; she's horribly superstitious and thinks the woods fill up with witches at night. I'm not sure I trust her. I catch her looking at me through half-closed eyelids now and then as if she's trying to guess what I'm thinking. I know there are snakes but not at this season; they don't like cold either. I also don't know if she acts through concern for me or because there's stuff she doesn't want me to discover. Her excuse for keeping me close may be just that: an excuse. Perhaps she's been filling up her own coffers through the years. Who knows how much she may have stolen and pawned? The family silver seems intact, but I haven't inventoried everything yet. I also don't know what Mother accumulated while we were apart. I saw her will but it doesn't specify anything; she just left me everything with no details about what "everything" consists of. She left a handwritten addendum with her will, something about giving certain items to someone named Luke. I'll have to ask Celestine about this.

As I said, the weather sucks. Those interested in Mardi Gras must be disappointed since a lot of parades have been canceled and some have not been rescheduled. Can you imagine spending all that $$$ on a stupid costume and junk to throw at strangers, and then not being able to do anything with it? I know, an anthropologist's dream.

I need to draw Celestine out, try to get her trust. She must remember a lot because she witnessed all that went on. Problem is she acts totally out of it. But, of course, it may be an act. Every once in a while though, she comes around and I sense some lucidity. I will wait for my chance. I think she was the one who heard me banging on the inside of the famous armoire and let me out.

Tomorrow I plan to do some digging in Mother's computer in the hope it isn't password-protected. If it is, I'll just keep at it till I guess the word. Failing that, I'll hire a hacker. I know math but not really much about breaking into people's machines. Also plan to go to the college where she taught and see if anyone there has some light to shed on her. "Why, why, why?" keeps running through my head. She was the most maddeningly puzzling woman I have ever known. How could the accident disfigure her soul? Why was I so lovable before and so repulsive to her after the event?

I won't write till I hear from you. Don't want to clog up your mailbox.

M

14 February 2004
From: Amanda.Greene@worldcom.net
To:Brad.Wald@wireless.net
Dear Brad,

I've thought long and hard about your proposal. I just can't commit to anything or anyone now, either you or Malachi. What you and I had was wonderful, but so was my marriage in the beginning. Call me gun shy... I want to see what happens when Malachi returns from Louisiana. Even though he blew off the death of a mother with whom he had ceased relations in 1960, the death of a parent is traumatic. In a way, it's worse if the parent was as uncaring as Joanna. Parker is wracked by Alzheimer's and recognizes his son less and less often. Now's not the time to make any decisions. Malachi wants time apart and I respect his needs and wishes. I want to uncomplicate my life for a while, concentrate on my writing. I owe *The European Law Review* an article and I haven't even scratched the surface of the cases I'm working on. I know e-mailing you is the coward's way out, but I'm asking for space and time, not a rupture. Hope you'll understand.

Love, Amanda

p.s. Just realized I dropped this on you on Valentine's Day. Forgive me.

14 February 2004
From: fractal@netconnect.net
To: Amanda.Greene@worldcom.net
Happy Valentine's Day.
M

14 February 2004
From: Brad.Wald@wireless.net
To: Amanda.Greene@worldcom.net
Dear Amanda,

Put me on a shelf but please, I beg you, don't throw what we have away. Let's just say we're on hiatus. I'll abide by your wishes but hope so much you'll come to your senses someday. You're wasted on Malachi.

Yours, Brad

14 February 2004
From: gold.digger@netconnect.net
To: fractal@netconnect.net
Just wanted to be sure you got a Valentine… :-)))

The dig is turning spectacular. The twisted creature, who appears to have been without legs and therefore walked on his hands (have you seen the movie *Freaks*?), was apparently the tormented son or brother of the woman. The man probably protected them from those who believed the freak was spawn of the devil and would have killed him. The death remains a mystery.

Also met the Great Man, a conceited ass of course. But with all he's published on the subject, there's no getting away from his sphere of influence. At least, he can't claim the discovery. It was my thought to explore the ruins and nothing can change that.

Sounds like you're doing some digging yourself. You should go down to the riverbank and search for Indian artifacts. Bet you'll find some good stuff. We now have decent and relatively reliable internet, so write as often as you like. You're having more adventures than I am; write even if I don't answer immediately. I await your mails with impatience.

W

17 February 2004
From: fractal@netconnect.net
To: gold.digger@netconnect.net

I've been busy!

Celestine gave me a binder with old letters in it, my mother's correspondence with her family when she was living in France just before the war (1935-36 school year). Some are addressed to her father and some to Buddy. Apparently she and Buddy were on good terms until she married Dad. I think his constant presence just wore on her nerves. I'm coming to the realization that I know so little about her. I just wish I had the letters they sent to her, letters that she apparently didn't save. Uncle Buddy was the only member of her family I really knew. I guess I should count Celestine as a family member; she was Mother's mom in every way but physical. Her mother died when she was ten—they were apparently very close—and she had a falling out with her father that lasted from a few years after the accident till just before his death. I didn't like him very much. He was cold and distant and treated Mother with disdain. I see that now in hindsight; I didn't recognize disdain when I was twelve, which is when they broke relations. He especially hated Uncle Buddy and was furious that Mother and Dad let him live with us. Mother was deliriously happy while living in France. She had the best of both worlds: the child's and the adult's. The letters are newsy but not at all sentimental; there's no trace of homesickness nor does she ever say she misses anyone. As I hold these handwritten words in my hands, the contrast between them and the cursory notes that now fly through cyberspace strikes me—hard. The intimacy and the uniqueness of pen put to paper have fallen victim to the speed and convenience of what we use for correspondence today. I'm not sure which I prefer...

I wonder why Mother ceased relations with her dad. I vaguely remember him, but he came to our house only once that I can remember. Buddy, again, was at the core of the quarrel, bizarre because he was dead by then! But I overheard mere fragments of conversation and all I remember is his name in the mix. Celestine may know the cause of the rupture in relations and perhaps I can coax more information from her. Mother and Buddy shared a cat; he took care of the animal while she was in Europe, even mailed her some fur! By the way, there's a cat here now, a magnificent Lynx Siamese. Celestine swears he's cuddly but he's given me the impression that he'd prefer I disappear. He has the most expressive heavenly blue eyes I've ever seen. Mother named him Morel. Must have had some special meaning for her, perhaps the name of an old beau. Celestine has no idea where this name came from.

I've also been going through Mother's belongings. She kept a lot of Uncle Buddy's stuff, especially photographs of him as a boy with his friends. She supported an abbey somewhere around here as is evident from her checkbook. I'll have to pay a visit to the monks to see if anyone there can open a window on what made her tick.

All people are interested in here is Mardi Gras. It's February 24, right around the corner. I'll have to get Celestine to explain some of the more peculiar customs surrounding this fête. The bottom line is that I can't get any sleuthing done. I've been told the city streets are clogged with traffic and no one seems to want to do any work. The upside is that Covington isn't too busy; everyone's in New Orleans watching assholes throw trash to strangers. After Mardi Gras I'll venture across Lake Pontchartrain on the causeway and see what I can see. Some of Mother's letters were written on aerograms and have the family's former address on them. I'll go check out the house. If I'm stupendously lucky, someone will remember the family. I could go to the Bay St. Louis (remember our adventures?), but Mardi Gras has taken over that place as well. I remember Mother telling me her first love was a summer romance there. I'll just take a sentimental journey and see if anything comes back to me. I still plan to go to the college and pump her former colleagues for info.

Must run—write when you can.

M

17 February 2004
From: Amanda.Greene@worldcom.net
To:Brad.Wald@wireless.net
Dear Brad,

I've been thinking long and hard about us, and have concluded that it is best for us not to see each other for the foreseeable future. Call me foolish or deluded or whatever, I made vows to Mal and something tells me to keep trying.

I hope you understand and wish you everything good in life.

Best, Amanda

17 February 2004
From: Brad.Wald@wireless.net
To: Amanda.Greene@worldcom.net
Amanda,

I can take rejection with the best of 'em. But I won't be bullshitted. I don't suppose the fortune Malachi just inherited had anything to do with your decision... or the $$$ he stands to inherit from the Senile One once he kicks off? You never intended to leave Malachi for me, did you? He already knows about us and apparently doesn't give a damn. I ran into him at Barnes & Noble one day and told him the facts of life. He pretended not to know what I was talking about, even claimed he wasn't your husband! If he hasn't said anything, he's in clinging mode, willing to tolerate a cheater rather than be without a wife. Some men are like that, *have* to be married and can't let go of what's theirs. But you knew he was a head case when you married him.

Good luck to both you losers. I guess you belong together. Have a nice life.

Brad

17 February 2004
From: Amanda.Greene@worldcom.net
To: Cletus.Hardin@psychnet.org
Dear Cletus,

I think you might remember me; I'm Malachi Walmsley's wife and I attended one of his sessions with you several years ago. He's now in Louisiana attending to the affairs of his recently deceased mother and I'm very worried that some of the old stuff will bubble to the surface. He seemed to have put the past in the past, but this event has stirred up all sorts of junk and brought it to the fore. Can you suggest anything I might do to help him? At the moment, all he wants from me is distance. All I want is to save my marriage. I think... I'm terribly conflicted and confused myself. Each of us is suspicious and distrustful of the other. He seems obsessed with a girl he knew as a child and I frankly resent the amount of emotional energy he spends on her. They are in touch by e-mail, far too much for my taste. I have become somewhat involved with another man but it hasn't progressed to the point of no return. In fact, I recently put him on hold for a while. He wasn't happy about it, said I was wasted on Malachi. Am I?

Thanks for any tips.

Best, Amanda Greene

18 February 2004
From: fractal@netconnect.net
To: gold.digger@netconnect.net

I'm biding my time till I can go into the city. It's still raining with no sign of letting up. Even more parades have been canceled. Ironic, isn't it, that I'm sitting here unconcerned while people who've spent their lives saving for a trip to New Orleans for Mardi Gras get screwed by the weather. I assume this place floods and I'm keeping an uneasy eye on the river. There's a small johnboat under the house and I'll see that it's properly tethered in case we have to evacuate. What a contrast with AZ!

I've used the time to explore the house and am still trying to get Celestine to give up her secrets. She watches me like a hawk and thinks I don't realize it. Those beady eyes under hooded lids never leave me if she can manage it.

Mother wasn't much of a housekeeper. Celestine told me she was forbidden to dust or tidy up Mother's quarters, consisting of a bedroom, a sitting room and a bath. There are two attic areas; one is reached from a drop-down staircase and the other, from a door off the upstairs hall. The upper attic is almost empty. The walk-in attic is crammed with junk. Much of it is Uncle Buddy's and I can't figure why Mother would have kept his stuff. Celestine told me she never threw anything away.

She had a vast collection of movies on video tape and CD. Apparently she was a great fan of the movie *Angel Heart*. Celestine told me she wore out three tapes before she got it on disc. I'll have to check it out one of these days. The rest of her videos are comedies, some French classics, Carlos Saura's *Tango* (she was a great dancer as I recall). One of the French movies is Polanski's *Une Pure Formalité*. I'll have to watch that one of these days. A friend of mine says it's a masterpiece. Wonder of wonders, she has a copy of *Freaks*, the movie you mentioned in your discussion of the skeletons at Autun! She also apparently loved a Dutch film, *Character*. I know nothing about it but will watch it. I can't spend ALL my time rummaging through clothes, books and jewelry.

I've had a chance to explore more of the grounds. I'm beginning to remember things, like the boat. It was a pontoon boat and we used to have wonderful parties, cruising on the river. We had one of the first models made, a rather crude prototype of the sleek designs available today. I was about ten when Dad bought it. Apparently my mother's distaste for boats did not extend to party barges, which are essentially floating living rooms. My parents had a nice group of friends as I recall. I used to go out with them when I was in my teens. I'm going to try to find some of them and see if I can gain any insight from what they have to say. The barge is, of course, long gone.

I had my first awful nightmare last night and plan to write to Cletus with the details. If I start with sleepless nights again, I'll surely go mad…

Write as soon as you can.

M

19 February 2004
From: fractal@netconnect.net
To: Cletus.Hardin@psychnet.org
Dear Cletus,

You said I could write and I'm taking advantage. The night of the 17th-18th I had the dream again. It was the accident with the usual gory details, but this time I came closer to seeing the figure that came out of the woods. It looked like it was my father but it was Uncle Buddy at the same time. This is completely different from both facts and other versions of the dream. I used to dream that my father had been driving and that Mother was killed. This is the first time that Uncle Buddy is in the dream. The figure that comes out of the woods is covered in blood and looks at me and says, "It's the wrong one. You must never tell." The wrong what? Tell what? There was nothing to tell. I remember falling off the back seat onto the floor and then nothing till the next day when I woke up in the hospital. The hospital is still there and I might go see how far back their medical records go. I'd like to read the accident report and check out the extent of my injuries. I guess I could have had a few moments of lucidity before everything went black but I don't remember anything, at least on a conscious level. And I couldn't have seen Uncle Buddy; he died instantly. And Dad couldn't have been driving; he was out of town.

M

19 February 2004
From: fractal@netconnect.net
To: gold.digger@netconnect.net

The dreams are back. Only more gory, more inaccurate.

Worked on digging into Mother's computer. (Do you realize how similar our work is?) She was into e-mailing men, a lot of them. Her password was "password." How careless and foolish… I wonder if they know she's dead. I can't tell where they live from their e-mail addresses and that info isn't included in any of the mails. Except one. There's some guy she used to hang out with at his place on Dauphine Street. His signature, address included, is appended to every mail. I'm going to try to see him. If he doesn't respond to an e-mail, I'll just go knock on his door. The address sounds vaguely familiar...

Celestine is getting a bit more communicative. She let me see the dark corners of my old room. I remembered the loose floorboard in the closet and found some forgotten treasures: a little plastic ring I had planned to give to you; toy trucks and cars; some old newspaper clippings. One day I'll go through them to see what interested me way back when. But that will have to wait. More pressing concerns consume me now. I guess I forgot about my stash. My sophisticated teen-age self must have rejected childish things.

Hope all is well with you and that you're finding time for Judas.

M

20 February 2004
From: fractal@netconnect.net
To: gold.digger@netconnect.net

I'm still reluctant to brave the crowds in New Orleans, especially this close to Mardi Gras. So I decided to investigate this abbey Mother supported. It's a huge complex set in a pine forest; in fact, it's my yard on an even larger scale. I went to the front desk, the porter's office as they call it, and inquired if anyone there knew Joanna Walmsley. No one did, but her specific contact was Father Luke so I asked to see him. He wasn't there but I left my number and requested he call. He must be the "Luke" of the will addendum. I still have no idea what I'll say to him. I hope he doesn't think I'm contacting him to make trouble about Mother's gifts to him. I know little now about Catholic practices. The changes of Vatican II demolished my interest in my religion. And I know even less about monks, but I suspect this Luke character won't be able to tell me anything. I'll still give it a shot.

After returning from the abbey, I took it into my head to face the armoire and recreate the situation that apparently caused me such pain, pain I don't remember. I closed myself up in the thing and just waited. Nothing. Not a damn thing came back to me. All I got for my trouble was a stiff neck and a backache.

How are things in Autun?

M

21 February 2004
From: gold.digger@netconnect.net
To: fractal@netconnect.net

Fabulous find!!! A very unconventional manuscript probably dating from the 12th century and in pretty good shape. It was written on scraps of vellum, leather, even cloth, and was wrapped up almost like a body. Also found by chance a secret room, whose entrance is a narrow tunnel, a claustrophobic's worst nightmare. There we found another text, a response to various aspects of the former, which is a sort of diary or journal. The writer must have worked as a mason or carpenter or both since much of the text is written or scratched on slabs of broken or cracked stone, or on wood unsuitable in some way for framing up a building. There's also writing on the walls. He must have been desperate to tell his story. And medievalists think 12th-c. people weren't introspective or endowed with the sense of self we moderns possess... As soon as I can transcribe a decent portion of the ms., I'll send it to you as an attachment. We'll do a bit at a time; it's tedious work, this transcribing and translating medieval Latin written on unconventional materials.

It sounds as though you're wandering aimlessly around your house. What are you looking for? What do you hope to find?

By the way, Morel is the name of a character in a French novel by Marcel Proust. I mentioned your cat to one of my colleagues and she, being on the literary side of the team, recognized the name. She also volunteered the info that Morel is a gay violinist. Rather odd name for a cat...

W

21 February 2004
From: fractal@netconnect.net
To: gold.digger@netconnect.net

Looks like we're online at the same time. Your message just popped up; I'm up late and you're up early.

The short answer is: I don't know what I'm looking for, but there are some questions I'd like to have answered. My mother seemed to detest her brother but there's Uncle Buddy stuff here in places where I wouldn't expect to find it. Why has she kept his junk all these years? Since she disliked him so much, why did he live with us? (Perhaps the second part of that question provides the answer to the whole.) And then there's the whole issue of pre- and post-accident versions of Mother. I can understand the trauma and the guilt she must have felt. But how could her personality have changed so very radically? Why didn't she like me any more? She avoided me as much as possible, something in radical contrast to her pre-accident self. And why do I find that armoire both repellent and seductive?

I got a call from Luke today; that's *Brother* Luke, not *Father*. He's never heard of Mother so I have an appointment to see him tomorrow and will take along a photograph. He may know her under a different name. I know priests can't tell anything they hear in confidence; I wonder if it's the same for brothers.

Mother's papers are a mess, not in any kind of order. She apparently was an adjunct faculty member and didn't mingle much with colleagues. All her papers consist of grade sheets, old exams, term papers, class notes. There are some notes of appreciation from students as well as hate mail. My favorite evaluation of her reads as follows: "This prof is a hell of a woman." It must have been her favorite too. It dates from 1977 and is in a perfect state of preservation. She kept no diary of any sort nor any letters except the ones she wrote home from Europe. Talking to people who knew her is my only hope and if they're as uncooperative as Celestine, I'm in trouble.

I've enjoyed getting to know Covington. It's a small town with soul. The streets of the historic district are lined with art galleries and antique shops, also some very good restaurants. I can walk the streets at night with no problem. Mother's house—or my house now—is located about ten minutes from town but is nonetheless in a wilderness area, the best of both worlds. Unfortunately the area has gotten very trendy and is becoming crowded. Traffic on arterials is a nightmare.

Since I've been here, the phone has hardly rung. She had, it seems, few friends and concentrated her leisure time in the city. (I'm already talking like a Covingtonian; "the city" is New Orleans.) Mardi Gras is almost upon us and I'll be able to do some digging in likely places soon.

I'll write again tomorrow after I see Brother Luke.

M

22 February 2004
From: fractal@netconnect.net
To: gold.digger@netconnect.net

I brought a photograph of Mother to the abbey to show Brother Luke and his reaction was bizarre. He said he didn't recognize the person but I'm absolutely certain he did. When he first looked at the picture, his face was impassive. But then he began to stare fixedly at the image and he turned from bright red to white. He also began to stammer. What the hell is going on? Maybe he and Mother were fooling around, but that doesn't explain his gradual recognition of her. I begged him to tell me what he knew, but he kept insisting that he only *thought* he recognized her for a fleeting moment. I know he was lying but I can't beat the truth out of him. When I mentioned all the checks made out to the abbey signed "J. Walmsley," he indicated that many people support the abbey without ever having made contact with the monks. He said his name was on the check in the little reminder section because he's in the development office and all donation checks would be routed to him. There was no budging him on his position. I don't know what to think.

He's a very strange man, almost frightening. The most striking thing about him is his eyes, so pale as to appear colorless. He's either totally bald or shaves what little hair he's got. The face is a mask, registering no emotion except what he simply cannot hide, as when I first showed him the photo of Mother. He tried so hard to convince me he didn't know her. He gives the impression of being a person always in ironclad rigid control of himself. I wonder what the attraction was for Mother. I'd have thought she'd go for someone a bit more approachable. But he docs not impress me as the Romeo type. I can't see him in a passionate embrace with anyone, certainly not my mother. But he has a strange attraction for me. I find myself thinking of him a lot. I feel that I'd like to talk to him, find out what makes him tick. God knows why. He's mysterious to the point of creepiness. Maybe that's why. I've always gone for the inscrutable types. I have no excuse whatsoever to call on him again so I guess he and his enigmatic ways will remain just that, an enigma. Unless I can invent something...

I've found evidence of male companionship in the house. Besides Uncle Buddy's memorabilia, there are men's clothes in one of Mother's closets and guy's toiletries in the bathroom. But no one has called the house. I guess word of Mother's death got around; and either no one knows me or that I'm in town. I'm going to look in the phone book for the few names I remember and see if any of my parents' friends are still around. I recall that their crowd sided with Mother at the break-up; that was one of the reasons Dad moved. Mother got custody of the friends and Dad got me. I wonder if the owner of the clothes will ever come to claim them.

I look forward to reading the medieval ms. when it's ready.

Write when you can.

M

22 February 2004
From: Amanda.Greene@worldcom.net
To: Cletus.Hardin@psychnet.org
Dear Cletus,

I just received an e-mail from someone who calls himself Fred Wilson. It's a pure and simple request for involvement and is probably just spam that found its way into my legitimate mailbox. It's from a wildmail address, meaning it could be anyone. I suspect it's from Malachi. What should I do?

Amanda

22 February 2004
From: Cletus.Hardin@psychnet.org
To: Amanda.Greene@worldcom.net

Don't respond. If it's from Malachi, you don't want to encourage a fantasy persona. It may very well be spam or someone with malicious intent trying to infiltrate your machine. If it's really a guy hitting on you and you're serious about shoring up your marriage, you certainly don't want to encourage this other man. Malachi may be testing you again. You must understand his ability to trust has been shattered time after time throughout his life. If you love him, you will have to be patient while he works out these problems. He's in a home that was the site of his abandonment and the locus of his loss of self. He feels that he was banished from the house in Covington, and now he must be struggling with the reopening of that wound. Don't ever forget that the Malachi you know and love may not be aware of what this "Fred" is doing. Fred may go away quickly. Encouraging him will only cause him to hang around.

You're my patient also. How are you doing?

Cletus

23 February 2004 (Lundi Gras)
From: fractal@netconnect.net
To: gold.digger@netconnect.net

I'm betting you don't know what Lundi Gras is. It's the day before Mardi Gras and New Orleans has turned it into a pre-Mardi Gras. It didn't exist when we were kids and you may not have kept up with developments in the Big Easy. There are almost as many events today as there will be tomorrow. At least, that's the "new" tradition. This year it's been raining for days and today is especially soggy. At times the rain comes down in sheets.

I stayed in and took a break from sorting out trash and treasures, and watched the two films that Mother seemed fascinated with. I think I told you that *Angel Heart* obsessed her. It's a Mickey Rourke vehicle, a wonderfully intricate story about a guy who uses voodoo to escape his pact with the devil. He eats another guy's heart and steals his soul. But old Nick can't be fooled and, in the end, the deception lands him in hell. This is shown rather neatly in a seemingly endless elevator descent while the closing credits roll. The infernal scene that opens the movie is also great. I'll probably watch it again to pick up some details I missed the first time. It's a very complex story, but it's given me a great reintroduction to New Orleans. A lot of it takes place here. Charlotte Rampling's character takes a streetcar ride that makes me want to ride the car downtown. I'll do that on Ash Wednesday. The sanitation department starts shoveling people and detritus out of the French Quarter at the stroke of midnight tomorrow night. The song "Girl of my Dreams" runs throughout the film. That would be a good way to describe you. I dream about you sometimes. It's an antidote to my nightmares. In fact, "girlofmydreams" is my password. We're two kids again, a team of two nerds against the world. I think the paths we chose, math and archaeology, are indicative of our personalities. I'm analytical and driven by patterns. You're digging up the past. Wish you could dig up mine...

The other film is *Character*, a Dutch movie about a guy whose father is a monster and whose Mother won't talk to him. It's my biopic!! The father tortures him to build his character and then tries to get the son to kill him. It's beautifully filmed and the scenes of Rotterdam under the rain are spectacular. The mood evoked is the one I experience when I look out the windows here and see the river through drizzle. It doesn't look the same but the feelings I get are similar. I haven't seen *Une Pure Formalité* yet but I will for sure, and I'll let you know what it's like.

I'm eagerly awaiting the ms. attachment. Take your time with your dig; I'm taking my time with mine.

M

24 February 2004
From: gold.digger@netconnect.net
To: fractal@netconnect.net

Happy Mardi Gras! If I understood you correctly, this is the big day.

Be very careful about what you throw away. I wouldn't toss any written material unless I was absolutely certain it was of no interest. The attached ms. transcription will make my point for me. It is a treasure whose worth is beyond telling. Faded black marks on whatever was at hand—chunks of stone, broken pottery, scraps of vellum—that are literally priceless...

What you're about to read is a medieval version of point-counterpoint or, to express myself in medieval monastic mode, an antiphonary narrative. The responses seem destined for a third party to whom the respondent appears to be making what amounts to a confession. Perhaps the respondent had arranged for its intended reader to find the text in the secret room. As far as we can tell, the diarist, a sculptor or stone carver, was a scoundrel, almost a sociopath, and the respondent punished him in some way as yet undiscovered. He considered the act of punishment to be a great sin and was explaining the situation to a priest (?), a monk (?), or perhaps just to himself. Right now, there are more questions than answers, but we're working on them. When we get more of the text deciphered and translated, we may find out. But we also may be left in what would be unbearable suspense. Stay tuned... One other thing, the diarist dated some of his material by the saint honored on that day. For clarity's sake, I added *The Feast of* to the ms. We may be able to go back and get an exact date for some of the entries.

And how about some news from the USA? All we get from the French press is anti-US diatribes and I don't know how much to believe.

W

Attachment to mail dated 24 February 2004:

The Feast of Saint Augustine, 1134

The journey to Autun was arduous. The heat, even at dusk, was intense. I long already for the coolness of the stones of Saint Hillary's. My mother cried a little when I left although my departure means one fewer at a crowded table. My father was not there, but I know he would have liked to give me still more instruction in carving stone, following me all the way to the route to Burgundy, filling my head with details and warnings. He would especially tell me to observe carefully the one called Gislebertus, Master of the Work and reputed sorcerer. They say his miraculous carvings may be the result of witchcraft but no one has yet been able to prove it or catch him engaged in the black arts. At the very least I will be able to take back some new techniques or new ideas to Poitiers. Notre-Dame-la-Grande will surely need my services when I return. Then Clémence and I will be able to marry.

While passing through Argenton, I saw a hanged man. He had been executed three days previously and was in an advanced state of rot.

Everyone else was turning away in disgust, but I walked boldly up to the corpse and observed him carefully, as my father had recommended to me. "If you wish to sculpt," he said, "pay closest attention to the work of the Divine Sculptor that is God. Imitate His creations as perfect models." The stench nearly discouraged me, but I knew someday I might be required to portray Avarice or even Judas. The man's hands were tied behind his back and his sins were exposed on a plaque hung round his neck. He had debauched a child. His neck was cleanly broken, as the hangman had been expert at his work. His mouth was agape though no sound could have been uttered by one dying such a death. People scolded me from afar for taking such interest in another's misfortune. But they did not know the purpose of my observation, that someday my work will be the cause of much praise and glorification of God.

My eyes are heavy; I have scarcely the strength to scribble these marks. Tomorrow I meet Gislebertus and perhaps begin to practice my craft. God grant me rest.

The Feast of St Giles

I am lodged in the street of the Thistle, quite close to the new church, with the family of Blaise the weaver. His wife, Marthe, puts me in mind of my own sweet mother and my Clémence. They have one son, Gérard, already like a brother to me. He also labors at the new church, dedicated to the holy Lazarus, hewing stone and showing great promise of one day becoming a master carver, which is his great wish. Gislebertus is so occupied with his own craft he scarcely has time for anyone in need of instruction. So I allow Gérard to assist me whenever possible, that he may learn by doing and not just by observing. We labor from sunrise to sunset, which in this month of August is a long day. Once winter is here, work will diminish as the days grow shorter and our hands, numb with cold. How strange it is to think of cold! It has been hot as the breath of hell since my arrival. Appropriate that it is hellish; Gislebertus seems to think of nothing else. Everywhere I look, a wild-eyed demon is staring at me. The master works with singular abandon, hardly stopping for refreshment. But what glorious things he fashions! I understand why there are those who believe him in league with Satan himself, but I have as yet seen no evidence of mischief. Nothing seems to touch him. No one knows anything about him, not even where he lodges. Perhaps his rooms would yield a clue to his skill if he owes it to the powers of darkness. I had a dream last night about a man stung by a scorpion. If Gislebertus is a wizard I must be careful not to be injected with his poison. I would rather be virtuous than virtuoso. That must be the meaning of my dream. I will be on guard against the treachery of any scorpion in our midst. I will hide from Gislebertus my ability to read and write so he will feel safe leaving secrets around that I might decipher. I will also pretend to be hard of hearing while listening intently to what he says to those in his confidence. If he thinks me illiterate, deaf and none too bright, his guard will be down. He and his work are of stunning beauty, but he is troubled in spirit. What sins does he harbor in his breast?

My new mother Marthe is constantly struggling against the fine dust from our labors that blankets everything in the house on days that are not entirely still. I have no doubt that we sometimes eat powdered stone. Perhaps I will become as hard as Gislebertus. He never has a word or even a look for me, choosing to give me my orders through another. But his works are so beautiful I will forgive him anything.

My eyes are heavy. God bless this household.

The Feast of St Stephen

Gérard shows astonishing progress. His sweet, simple nature enables him to absorb instruction without balking or arguing or insisting that his way is best or that another's way, though tried through the years, is wanting. His hand is responsible for a portion of what I give to the foreman, who would find fault if he knew that an untrained chisel had limned the stone. "Gérard is paid to mix mortar," he would say, "and you to carve." That was the attitude at Ligugé where I was sent as a sickly child to learn a trade lest I burden my parents with my dependence on them. I learned to read and write—I stole those skills—under the very noses of the monks, who no doubt thought me good for scrubbing vegetables and naught else. How the foul memory of those days stays with me. The Father Abbot never even looked at me, never knew my name. Then I kept the truth of my skills from my family. How useful it can be to appear useless! I must be careful lest anyone see me at this document. I will hide my ability even from Clémence. The less a wife knows about her husband the better. Perhaps I will tell her of my talents in due time.

Today for a brief moment, Gislebertus glanced my way. He seemed to be pleased with the wings I was carving. He favors winged creatures, if not angels then demons. Some of his images are quite nearly scandalous. However, no one dares say a word to him for fear he will leave and go to one of the many others clamoring for his work. I must make him think me a dolt. How else will I unearth his secret? I have seen no hint of spells or amulets, but what magician ever reveals his craft? Soon he will begin work on his Adam and Eve. Some claim his Eve will have very pronounced breasts. Surely the canons will step in and refuse any work, splendid though it may be, that inspires lust in their hearts. The next few weeks will reveal more and more of what I want to know.

Peace.

The Feast of the Nativity of the Blessed Virgin

Gérard is not the son of Blaise and Marthe. Last night, when all believed me asleep, I arose to piss and heard voices in the larder, a low murmur but loud enough for me to hear. Gérard is a serf, well into his term of a year and a day separated from his master. I could profit from revealing this to the proper authorities, but never would I betray my friend and brother. What else could he be when Marthe calls me "son"? He is progressing so well, even Gislebertus commented favorably on carvings he had done with my mark on them. Of course, I cannot yet reveal that the hand is not mine—all in due time.

Another great discovery… every night Gislebertus leaves the lodge at sundown, travels west until he thinks no one is observing him, and then exchanges his garments for the raiment of a beggar, which he hides in the sack he always carries about with him. He then returns past the church on the next street over and turns north, following the ancient Roman walls. Two can play at deceit. As soon as I develop a suitable disguise I will follow him straight, I wager, to the lair of his wizard. He must require daily visits to whoever bewitches his hands. He must also request a spell be cast on the canons, for how else would they tolerate his Eve? He must have looked at and fondled a woman with extreme diligence to produce such a figure. I wonder if his hands are foul with the smell of her when he carves his virgins and angels. The hypocrite… Here am I, toiling for a fraction of his wages, too exhausted in the evening to glance at the whores hanging about the work yard while Gislebertus sneaks off, in disguise yet, to visit God knows what den of iniquity. And still barely a nod to me.

There was a terrible accident today. Two men in the treadwheel were raising a load of stone blocks to the vault of the nave when one of them fainted and the other was unable to maintain his footing. The blocks came crashing down while the two men were tossed about like apples in a tumbling barrel and had many broken bones and one a broken head. His cheekbone was protruding from the side of his face, poor creature. I watched Gislebertus to see if he would produce some potion or ointment to get them on their feet again, but he kept his magic to himself. He must be made of the same stone he carves. Or perhaps people of his own creation are all that matter to him. One day I saw him kissing his Eve's stone-cold forehead. I am watching; he must give himself away soon.

I went to look at the man with the broken head. Again, those present chided me for my cold heart, but how else might one learn of the marvel that is man except by observing him in all his conditions. If only a sculptor could see the bones beneath the skin! Then would his creations resemble more closely those of the Heavenly Father. Gislebertus' creations are full of soul, but their bodies shriek artifice. Jesus the child looks like a doll, not a lad. He grabs at the gift of the Kings, more like the urchins that hang about the streets than like a docile son, and Mary his mother permits this. At least Joseph seems properly chagrined, sitting off to the side, his head in his hand. If I were the master here, God would have manners. Someday I will be the master. It is rumored that Abbot Suger wishes to reconstruct parts of his church at Saint-Denis Abbey. Now there is one who will permit no stone carver to run amok. If Gislebertus is to work for Suger, I must be careful not to betray my knowledge until the perfect moment. I will go to Saint-Denis and, at the proper time, inform Abbot Suger of what sort of master he has hired. Gislebertus will be dismissed and perhaps I may step into the breach. In the meantime, let me learn all I can from him who is now, for good or for ill, my master.

Saint Lazarus is a masterpiece. I thank God I am associated with its beauty.

The Feast of Saint Gorgonius

Bishop Étienne came to the work yard today to see our progress and was pleased. Gislebertus had covered Eve, planning, I suppose, to set the stones in place and then dare the canons to force him to remove her. I wonder if one of the whores who hang about the yard was his inspiration. Today in preparation for the bishop's visit, all the women were chased away from the church grounds, as if his Excellency were unaware of their existence. There is one in particular who seems uniquely capable in her profession. I have caught her several times looking at me in a most unchaste manner although she pretends to be interested only in my craft. I wonder if Clémence will give me pleasure, if not at first then after she has had a chance to perfect her skill. I too needed practice before I wielded a chisel—or my own tool—cleverly. The women I have had seemed content with my efforts.

Gislebertus can do no wrong in Etienne's eyes. The bishop was utterly bewitched by what he saw. We could cover his church with pagan gods if they were at the hand of the master. He noticed my work and that of Gérard. Soon I will be able to reveal the true creator of some of "my" carvings. There are rumors that some of Gislebertus' men will soon accompany him to Cluny to study his sculpture there with an idea to copy it here. If I am in that group I will know that Gislebertus values my talent. I wonder if he can function that far away from whatever magic he uses. They say he is on the best terms with Abbot Pierre, and whoever goes to Cluny will enjoy the best the abbey has to offer. I have also heard that Cluny is the most beautiful church in Christendom, far outshining Saint Peter's in Rome. Perhaps my dreams will have an answer for me.

The Feast of Saints Protus and Hyacinth

I have him! Last night I saw his demon. While I was sculpting his capitals, Gislebertus was dining with Bishop Étienne. Just as I was quitting the work yard, Gislebertus took leave of his host and headed down the street with nary a backward glance at me. I followed him, curious to see if he would disguise himself as is his wont before reversing direction. But he continued on his way, heading for the northeast side of town towards the ruins of the Roman theater. I then realized that he usually headed west, so he was going straight to his lair sans disguise and without the ploy of changing direction. As we traveled, he, at a brisk pace, and I, attempting to keep apace without revealing myself, we were gradually joined by a whole throng of most accursed wretches, some on crutches, all in rags, many smeared with blood and stinking most foully, but all laughing and jesting as if their infirmities were a great joke. Some glanced at me, but most ignored my presence. I soon realized that these were the halest blackguards of Burgundy, courtiers of the King of the Court of Miracles, *le Grand Coesre* as he is called, frauds, cheats, swindlers of consummate skill at wheedling coins from a trusting populace. Gislebertus was known to all; they greeted him as one of them. He finally arrived at a hovel cleverly situated in the very walls of the ruins. The old theater walls form the back and one side, while the front and the remaining side are of nearly matching stone, as if some Roman had taken up residence there and never left. I hid till the throng of thieves had passed and then I crept up to the narrow windows. The vines and branches behind which Gislebertus had hidden his abode also served to hide me and I watched undisturbed. Inside all was as new and clean as the exterior was old and crumbling into ruin, or so it seemed. A woman greeted him with a kiss; she looked familiar to me, but I still cannot remember where I have seen her. Her face was plain, but her hair was a wonder to behold, all shiny and coppery in color as tree leaves in autumn. They sat down and began to speak when the devil arrived, emerging from a cleverly concealed hole in the wall. Hideous he was, more like a spider than a man, with four legs splayed out from a tiny body on which was perched a huge head. He crawled over to them moving like a crab, and they petted and fondled him fearlessly. Their commerce with him must be a usual event. I was so transfixed with fright that I pissed my breeches and would have cried out, but my voice was taken away by terror. How he did not sense my presence I do not know, for the devil is nearly as aware of us as is God in heaven. When my legs became able to run again, I departed in great haste and arrived home drenched in sweat and piss. If the devil knows I was there, he will find me. Perhaps he will tell Gislebertus. I will be able to determine tomorrow if Gislebertus knows anything. God help me.

The Feast of the Holy Name of Mary

Gislebertus seems unaware that I have found him out. Before I confront him, I must go back to his den with witnesses. I do not know whom to approach in this matter. All the imagers worship the master. No one will believe me, not even Gérard. Gérard says that the evil one is not nearly so puissant as we think. I must take him with me and then he will see what a hypocrite is Gislebertus, weeping and swooning over his handiwork. "Before Jesus was a man, he was a little boy," he loves to remind us. As if he knew him personally! I must move quickly in all this. Soon Gislebertus will select those to accompany him to Cluny; I mean to go there and will insist on being one of the chosen. If he spurns me, then will I reveal my knowledge of his terrible secret. If I am chosen, I will store it up for later use.

The Feast of the Triumph of the Holy Cross

Gérard came with me, back to that hellhole, grumbling all the way about my obsession with Gislebertus. All I want is justice and recognition that I have some share in Gislebertus' reputation for genius. After all, I have no help from demons. We made our way to the ruins of the theater, once again passing through the territory of the Grand Coesre. After Gislebertus had been inside for a while, we crept up to the window through which I had first spied him and his whore. For what else can she be? Gislebertus has never mentioned a wife or a sister and he obviously keeps this woman carefully hid. And there they were, he and Mathilda or Bathilda or whatever her name is. I could not understand him when he said her name as he was always turned away from me. There was no sign of their monster, but they kept looking towards the hole in the wall whence he emerged the last time. Gérard was becoming impatient and sleepy, and we were on the verge of departure when it showed itself again. My God, how can anything so hideous be alive? Surely no one but these two can have seen this creature else he would be dead. I say "he," but perhaps this thing is female—or nothing. Gérard was transfixed with terror at first. But then he became fascinated with it, watching it scuttle across the floor. What I took for four legs is actually two legs and two armlike protuberances with large hands at the ends having in turn very long fingers or claws. It seems to be all head, and such a head: a mass of stringy matted hair above a face hideous enough to cause any honest woman with child to give birth to a monster. It has some sort of voice, and emits more of a croak than any words. But the two, Gislebertus and Casilda, as I came to understand her name, understand it and listen carefully to what it says and pet and fondle it as if it were a cherished dog. And so Gérard is finally convinced. He believes we should confront Gislebertus and make him confess to Bishop Étienne that he is in league with some unholy creature to produce his marvels. But I have prevailed upon him to wait until the time is propitious to make use of our knowledge. With this, if Gislebertus is called to Saint-Denis and thinks to leave us behind, we can force him to take us to what will surely be a glorious and lucrative work yard. The great, holy, mystical Gislebertus, living with a whore and a demon! He has decided to take Gérard and me to Cluny and we will be watchful of his commerce with the monks there. It is said that Gislebertus and Abbot Pierre are close friends, that the abbot is like a father to him. I wonder what Pierre would do with such information as I have. Gérard and I returned home late, after Gislebertus and Casilda had put the monster to bed. Gérard wanted to watch the lovers as they prepared to take to their bed; but my eyes were fast closing and I wanted to record as much of this as I could, while these terrible visions were still fresh in my memory. I dare not take this journal to Cluny, so I will hide it and continue this narration upon my return. We leave day after the morrow.

End of attachment.

25 February 2004
From: fractal@netconnect.net
To: gold.digger@netconnect.net

Ash Wednesday… What an appropriate day for things medieval. I couldn't stop reading your text till the very end. What a superb find! I hope you find and decipher the rest of the text so we'll know what becomes of this lot of characters.

Today I went into New Orleans for the first time since I was a kid. Saint Louis Cathedral was my starting point, as it is for so many tourists. The smell of incense and candle wax really brought back memories. My parents were married there. Did I tell you my parents were Catholic? Dad quit going to Mass after the accident; since Mother was giving to an abbey, I assume she continued her practice. I've been indifferent to such things for quite a while, but I must admit that the sight of all those people with black stuff smeared on their foreheads was impressive. To think they all left to return to work or whatever with that mess on their faces.

After my visit to the cathedral, I stopped at the address in Mother's e-mail address book. A most peculiar man answered the door. He was short and rather pudgy, altogether unprepossessing. He denied any acquaintance with Mother but seemed startled when I showed him a photograph of her. However, he still claimed not to know her. The odd thing was my reaction to his house: it was almost the same as the one I had to the armoire. I recognized the smell!! I've been there before, I just know it. He reluctantly allowed me to come in and I was struck by the shabbiness of the decor and the beauty, though faded, of the building. French Quarter houses are right on the sidewalk, no yard, nothing but a stoop and then a front door. The front door is all that stands between the occupant and the sidewalk, it's really like living in the street. The living room was small but beautifully proportioned. A pocket door was partially open and I could see straight down a hall to a beautiful patio surrounded by high walls. The patio walls were salmon pink, like the rest of the building. The front was accented with dark green shutters, very Caribbean in aspect. There must have been several rooms off the hall but they were out of my line of vision. Every growing thing in the patio was brown, awaiting warmer weather to bloom. When I walked in, that smell and that feeling of dread hit me again, almost like a physical blow. The smell seems to combine perfume, cologne and tobacco, and something I can't identify.

The man—he never told me his name—seemed anxious for me to be on my way, so I obliged him, but not without asking some questions first. Such as: why was his address in Mother's address book? He responded that it must have been for a previous occupant. When I return home, I need to check the dates of the letters containing the address. I seem to recall they were pretty old. He could be telling the truth. The place is a rental and turnover is apparently pretty frequent. He said the roof leaks, the toilet doesn't flush properly, there's no dishwasher, no washer/dryer hook-ups, so people tend not to stay long. The landlord is not keen on repairs and tends to evict people who complain. But the rent is low. I asked him if he planned to move anytime soon. He took my number and said he'd let me know. If he moves, I might take the place just to try to jog some memories. I know that house, I'm sure of it. It's a small and compact masterpiece of the French Quarter style. The Covington house is what I would call "rural Louisiana." I think the official style designation is "Acadian."

Write soon. M

26 February 2004
From: gold.digger@netconnect.net
To: fractal@netconnect.net

I "did" Ash Wednesday too. I decided I could do the ashes routine, so I paraded up to the bishop (remember Saint Lazarus is a cathedral) to get my forehead smeared. Why should I look different from everyone else in town? These French won't be back in church till Good Friday, if then.

We're still hoping to find some more text. As I said, Thomas and his respondent wrote on durable surfaces, but also on scraps of materials that may not have survived. I am quite caught up in this saga as I am in your adventures. Too bad your mother didn't leave many clues. Any help from the letters?

The big cheese is bellowing... must fly.

A bientôt, W

28 February 2004
From: fractal@netconnect.net
To: gold.digger@netconnect.net

You asked a while back about news from the US... Mel Gibson's *Passion of the Christ* is causing much angst in lib circles. The "elite media" are gang-banging him. John Kerry has the dem nomination sewed up. The governor of Louisiana is in a brawl with the legislature. And the murder of Laci Peterson absorbs the news.

On the personal side, I'm beginning to think Mother was over the edge. I'm finding vast quantities of hormone replacement medications around, along with men's clothing too small to fit the average male. I wonder if she had gender issues but find that hard to believe. Of course, my memories of her are sketchy. I lost contact when I was eighteen and am now almost sixty-two, so heaven knows what she was up to in all that time. The letters did not help at all. They all date to the period before she was married and, while interesting as commentary on Europe of the late 1930s, have no bearing on the situation at hand. One interesting aside... Mother's aerogram letters with the address on them indicate a house on the same street as the pink house I recently visited. The house number, though, is different. I did look for the former family home, but found no such address. In fifty-four years and counting, some residences may have merged into one or the street numbering may have changed.

I went to the college where Mother taught and spoke to some colleagues. No one seemed to know her very well. She was pleasant, well respected and apparently well liked, but a woman of mystery. She never socialized with anyone there as far as I can tell but, judging from her clothes, she must have socialized with someone. Her clothes verge on the flamboyant. Really high heels that must have been difficult for a woman her age...IF she wore them in her later years. Sequins, fringe, frou-frou galore. She had large breasts, slim hips and dynamite legs if I may trust the photos of her that are scattered about the house. And skin to die for. Very few wrinkles, didn't look her age. Of course, hormones are useful in that department.

Amanda has called a few times, against my wishes, so I've begun letting the machine pick up. I don't want to talk to her yet.

Leap Day

Celestine's son Ruben came over to celebrate Feb 29 with us. I knew him vaguely while growing up; he's a nice fellow, about my age. He has a party barge similar to the one I recall and Mother had been letting him use our dock. I told him I'd continue the favor and he was very appreciative. The alternative is hauling the thing around behind his car. We all decided to go for a cruise after lunch. Ruben had a bit of trouble getting the engine started, but finally prevailed. The river is gorgeous and there are hints of delights to come. Some trees and bushes are putting out tiny flecks of green in anticipation of the warmth of spring, which comes early here. Ruben promises cascades of Cherokee Rose growing in profusion along the banks, some wild azaleas and some cultivated ones both in our yard and in those of the manicured mansions that dot the river. But it will be another month or so before this promise if fulfilled. The trees, mostly pine and cypress, are draped with Spanish moss; this is real Uncle Remus country, a veritable cliché. Mother's house is on the Bogue Falaya, which meets the Abita River about a mile downstream. At the confluence of the two sits a huge garish mansion, the concoction of someone with more money than taste. It would be ostentatious in Beverly Hills; here, it's totally out of place, an eyesore and an embarrassment to all except those who should be embarrassed. I don't remember if I told you that our house is what's called a Cajun cottage with large porches and a swing, a steep metal roof, dormers, and wonderful pine floors. It's nestled among the trees in perfect harmony. Louisiana has grown on me. Even if Amanda and I get it together, I'm not leaving this place, not permanently. She'll have to join me here. But I must build a gazebo. Then life will be complete.

We went down the Bogue Falaya till we met the waters of the Abita, then turned east and went up that river as far as we could. There were several large trees that had fallen into the water and made the river almost impassable in places. There are wonderful houses of all shapes, sizes and styles in that section of the vast waterway that drains Saint Tammany parish. Then we returned to the confluence and continued downstream on the Bogue Falaya to the place where it meets and merges with the Tchefuncte River. At this spot, Interstate-12 crosses the river, scarring the properties on the banks, places where generations must have enjoyed what they thought would be a peaceful, rural retreat forever.

We were all relaxing and having a fine time until I spied a house that, once again, brought back those feelings of deep distress, dread and anxiety. Celestine and Ruben were uneasy as well but pretended not to be. Since Celestine won't tell me anything, I'll try to buttonhole Ruben and see what I can dig out of him. The mystery house is quite different from the rest of the places on the river. Most are very open, with tall windows offering as much view of the river as possible. This one is dark, shuttered and seemingly abandoned. When I asked Celestine who lived there, she said she didn't know but I think she does. Again, I have that feeling of having been there before.

M

1 March 2004
From: fractal@netconnect.net
To: Cletus.Hardin@psychnet.org
Hi, Cletus,

Just checking in. No dreams I can't cope with yet, but an odd one last night. No context at all, just a noise like a beeping sound that would come from a wristwatch alarm. I awoke in a cold sweat and had to take an extra pill to get back to sleep. It's been raining and the swamp that covers about half the property is full of horny frogs who sing "I'm in the mood for love" all night. There's even a couple of frogs that inhabit Ruben's party barge. Ruben is the son of Celestine the housekeeper. He's a very nice man who wants to tell me more than his mother will permit—at least that's my gut feeling. At my urging, he's moored it at an abandoned dock on the property and is working on getting the dock into shape. He may even rebuild the boathouse that used to be in the vicinity but will have to put this one on piers. The previous one blew, or was washed, away. All that remains is a slab of concrete. Birds wake me up in the morning along with the sun that streams in my bedroom windows. I could cover the windows though it would be a shame to block the glorious view. Perhaps I should change rooms... I'll think about it.

I'm working on trying to remember why my negative reaction to an old armoire in my room is so strong; ditto for a house we passed during a river cruise. I *know* Celestine knows but won't tell me. In fact, there's a lot she won't tell me, but there's no coaxing it out of her. I occasionally hear her and her son having heated discussions. I can't make out what they're saying but I'm fairly certain my name is mentioned. It's peculiar, especially considering how Celestine doted on me when I was little. It's so frustrating how the accident changed everything, ruined so many lives. They say tragedy either draws a couple closer or rips them apart. My parents followed the latter path. I wish I had talked to my father when I had the chance. He always seemed so reluctant to discuss anything but the present with me, no going back, no reminiscing—and no answers.

I'm sitting on the riverside porch as I write. It's begun to rain gently and I'm beginning to remember how much I loved this place. I tried crushing my emotions to get over my mother's decision to abandon me to my father, but they're all coming back. I'll never leave, I'll die here. Neither Amanda nor anything else can separate me from this tranquility.

I'm planning a trip to Bay St. Louis in Mississippi, the site of another maternal ancestral home. I usually don't call the town by its full name; it's "the Bay" to all who know and love it. My mother sold it years ago and I'll be interested to see what's become of the old place. It is, or was, little more than a shack. Yet of all the houses connected with my past, it's the one I love best. They say you can never go home, but I'm going to try. I haven't seen it since Hurricane Camille flattened the MS Gulf Coast. I wonder if the house is still standing.

As we've discussed, I dream a lot about houses, not any specific one, just houses. A recurrent motif is that of finding new rooms, ones I didn't know existed when I entered the dream house. This theme has intensified since my arrival here. This house looks bigger from the outside than it is inside and this may have triggered these dream patterns.

Thanks for listening,

M

p.s. I may want a name of someone in New Orleans; someone in Covington or its environs would be even better.

2 March 2004
From: Cletus.Hardin@psychnet.org
To: fractal@netconnect.net

Pay close attention to "house" dreams. A house may symbolize the Self and the dreams may indicate new aspects of you, waiting to be discovered. More on this later...

Cletus

3 March 2004
From: fractal@netconnect.net
To: gold.digger@netconnect.net

Yesterday I went to our former family home at the Bay. I almost wish I hadn't. Our summers at the Bay remain my most treasured memories. It was a magical time, before all the mess of later years. And even the little time we spent there after the accident seemed to wash away the dirt of ordinary life. My visit was like finding a beloved toy in tatters. But I'm getting ahead of myself.

One year—I think it was before we met—I went to Camp St. Joseph, the summer program of a school there, and made a sign that said "Camp St. Joseph" out of tin by pounding the letters into the metal with a hammer and nail. I mounted it and gave it to my parents. When the house was sold, I'm sure the plaque was tossed. But it's one of those icons of my youth I'd love to have.

The property is as large as I recall. They say everything looks smaller when you go back to visit childhood places; not so for the Bay house. The only difference is the absolute dearth of pine trees, all knocked down by Camille. Have you been there since the storm? If so, how did your house fare? I'd have looked, but I forgot exactly where it was. There was one tree on our property—not a pine—that we used to call the butt tree: it had an odd protuberance that looked just like a rear end. I was about twenty-seven and living in Flagstaff when the storm hit; but that house was always important to me and I worried about its fate. Now I know. The garage, with a *garçonnière* on top, was demolished, but the house came through OK. It's still a house of bedrooms unless the current owners have done some remodeling. When we lived there, the front porch, with its swing, and the screened-in back porch passed for living and dining rooms. There was an over-rigged sailboat in the yard that Dad and Buddy used to take out in the bay. The street, Leonhard Avenue, meets the water at right angles. Dad used to take me crabbing at the seawall. Remember how in the summer, the street would get so hot, little bubbles formed in the tar and we'd pop them? The two mid-town theaters, the Star and something else I can't recall, are stores now and have been replaced by multiplex mall theater complexes in areas that used to be woods. We were watching a Judy Canova film at one of the downtown theaters when the railroad bridge burned in '50-something. Remember? In fact, I think you and I were there together. Everyone ran out to watch the bridge burn and there was mass confusion since the whole town eventually gathered along the seawall. We got separated and my dad eventually found me. He had heard the sirens and come to town looking for us. I wanted to go to your house to make sure you had gotten home safely, but Dad said no, that you could walk home, you lived so close to the theater. Then we went right back to Covington and I didn't see you again till school started. But we wrote when you were at the Bay and I was stuck in Covington. I still have your letters. They're in Flagstaff and I shall retrieve them when I go there to collect my belongings for a move here.

Holy Week at the Bay was special. We'd troop to all the services at Our Lady of the Gulf church. I remember especially the procession to the tabernacle on Holy Thursday. I also remember the intense, insistent ringing of bells during the Gloria, a sound replaced by that of a wooden clapper for the remainder of the service. Mother detested the changes brought about by Vatican II but eventually came to terms with them. I didn't. When I moved to Flagstaff with Dad, I ceased going to church altogether. Still, to this day a whiff of incense takes me back to the Bay.

Easter Sunday was defined by hats and candy, lots of it. The huge yard with its many trees was a perfect site for an Easter egg hunt. Uncle Buddy would take me around as I looked for every gooey chocolate egg I could find. If Easter was late, the weather was warm and most of the candy melted, at least the chocolate. I especially liked the gummy bunnies made of gelatinous paste covered with sugar. I wonder if I want to know what was in that stuff... A huge part of my guilt at his death resulted from my subconscious realization that he loved me very much coupled with my desire for his disappearance from our lives. I loathed him yet used his affection for my own purposes.

Do you remember the Bay? And was it as important to you as it was to me?

On the whole, I suppose I had a happy childhood until I became fully aware of how tempestuous my parents' marriage was... After the divorce, Dad never was tempted to remarry but preferred to hang out with a group of men, mostly divorcés and widowers he met at AA meetings. Oh yes, he was a lush. He fell off and climbed back on the wagon many times. But he was never a mean drunk, just a sentimental one. He'd come home loaded and I could hear him mumbling to himself and crying through the walls. He'd ramble on about Mother and Uncle Buddy. I'll never know why he didn't call her once in a while. Once they parted, they seldom spoke again. I'm sure the binges contributed to the state he's in now. I wish I could get some answers out of him. I still don't know if he's aware of who I am or that Mother is dead. I left it up to the authorities to contact him. I'll eventually go back to Flag for a visit with Amanda and will see Dad as well. He's in a super posh assisted living residence in Sedona. Then I'll return here to finish going through this mountain of stuff and think seriously about what life would be like here year 'round. I understand the summers are horrendous and begin in late April! I don't think Amanda and I will make it. I can't stand the lying, the pretense that there's nothing wrong and that the distance between us is a phase or a normal transition we're going through. She's acutely aware of you; you're like the elephant in the room, like Camilla when Charles and Diana were together. Forgive me. I can't stop myself. And it pains me because I know it distresses you.

I'll probably also see Cletus. The dreams are getting more intense and I don't want to go back to dreading nightfall and bedtime. It was so wonderful to be able to sleep normally when I finally got rid of whatever demon was haunting me. Just to be normal… Is that so much to ask? In the meantime I'm seeing someone in Covington, recommended and contacted by Cletus. I'll let you know how that goes.

And you must keep in touch as well. M

5 March 2004
From: gold.digger@netconnect.net
To: fractal@netconnect.net

Yes, the Bay was important to me also. But I haven't returned there since I was ten. Our old house survived Camille and is still on de Montluzin Street. If you visit again, let me know its condition. The house number was invisible from the street and probably still is. The house was set back from the road and a wall of foliage kept it nearly hidden from view. There was a high wrought iron fence around the property and a creaking gate; I nicknamed it the Inner Sanctum after the old radio show. My mother still lives there. I should write to her more often but it's such a pain having to deal with folks who don't use e-mail. Shame on me!

As for your dreams, an ancient text recommends that the names of the Seven Sleepers of Ephesus (don't ask!) be written on communion wafers, that an incantation be sung into the right and the left ears and above the head of someone suffering from nightmares caused by goblins, and that the wafers be hung around the sufferer's neck by a virgin. So now you know what you must do to sleep soundly and dreamlessly. I've been meaning to give you this pearl of wisdom but have been forgetting.

We found more text of even greater import. A wall collapsed, revealing another room deep within the recesses of Gislebertus' dwelling. There is text is written all over the walls and another skeleton is at the base of one of the walls. It looks as if he was writing when he died. The text is a response or commentary on Thomas' text by a person we THINK is Gislebertus himself. Oh, Mug, this is the most wonderful result we could have had, a find beyond all price. I'm sending a transcription of what we've found so far of Gislebertus' self defense, for Thomas is very hard on him. Let me know what you think. W

Attachment to mail dated 5 March 2004:

How I wish I had the magic power Thomas imagined in me! Then would I restore us all to this point in his story. How many lives would have been spared ruin had I not journeyed to Cluny in such company. But first things first. There will be plenty of time to regret the pain that I, in my ignorance, inflicted on Abbot Pierre and his monks. I feel that I nourished a viper and loosed it in their holy midst. How I came to have Thomas' diary in my possession will be explained in due course. I beg you to accept my commentary on portions of it as my heartfelt confession.

Thomas' father should have warned him to look after his soul as much as after his skill, for he was prodigiously skilled. His notion that I did not notice him or respect his work is grotesque. I did notice. I just did not praise him with sufficient ardor. 'Neath all that venom and bravado was a sick heart that all the love of which man or woman is capable would not cure. Poor Gérard's fate was the result of such unnecessary envy. But this is supposed to be my confession. Forgive me, Father, I forget myself and what I am about. I sometimes wonder if I was envious of Thomas, if I resented one so young farther along than I was at his tender age. I should have seen the signs. When I was sculpting Judas... Enough! I will take things in order.

Thomas claims to find my carved demons oppressive, but he was nearly bewitched by them. He observed me as a hungry hawk watches a fat mouse while I was at work on their ugly faces. I thought that was all he needed in the way of instruction. I suppose the first item I must formally confess is a failure to encourage my young apprentice. But he seemed so sure of himself, so lacking in self-doubt and having no need of my guidance. In fact, he seemed more concerned with Gérard's progress than with his own. I was at all times aware of Thomas' tender solicitude for his young friend, his brother as he called him, and I was aware that Gérard was doing rather more than he should have, but I thought it good for both men: one was learning by doing and the other was learning by teaching, the best way.

Perhaps what I should concern myself with at this point in my story is what Thomas learned about me, and what he inferred from that information. The truth is so much more prosaic than the fantasies he imagines, but it is also more beautiful. You will be the only one aside from the principals— and me—to know of this affair. Casilda wanted it that way. The story is hers, truly, hers and Mallory's.

In 1114, when Casilda was eighteen, she and her parents lived in Paris. She was the only child of Jehan and Margery. Jehan was the victim of an accident at the tannery where he was working in 1096, an accident which rendered him incapable of fathering any children after Casilda. She was born but a few months before this accident. Jehan was a good and gentle man, but somewhat slow witted, whereas Margery was an intellectually curious and gifted woman, if not a brilliant or learned one. As the years passed, she became more and more enticed by all the learning going on around her, living as she did in the shadow of the Mont Sainte-Geneviève. She started to listen to the debates you yourself staged in public, not understanding a word, but fancying herself a scholar nonetheless. The poor woman, whose husband had, you recall, been almost castrated by his accident, fell under the spell of one who cast himself in the role of devoted disciple of the master of the Mont—you probably did not know him—and the usual result of such goings-on was born nine months later. This occurred a few months before Casilda's nineteenth birthday. The fruit of this adulterous union was as monstrous as he was unwelcome. As you may have guessed, the pitiful creature Thomas mistook for one of Lucifer's minions is this ill-begotten spawn of Margery and a lecherous clerk, whose name no one save Margery ever knew. Jehan of the generous heart believed his wife when she alleged her lover had bewitched her and that she had given birth to Lucifer's child. It was easy enough to believe. Mallory—that was the name so appropriately given him by Casilda—was so freakishly misshapen that it was difficult to imagine that he was human or even capable of eating, drinking or breathing. He had, in effect, no body. Or one so small as to be nearly invisible under the huge head perched on a short, thick neck. His arms, of disproportionate length when he was born and destined to grow even longer, sprang, or so it seemed, directly from his neck. When Jehan and Margery first saw this unfortunate creature, their first reaction was to kill him. He could not be human, so where was the sin in disposing of him as quickly as possible? Casilda had helped with the birth, so no one outside of the immediate family knew of his existence. Margery was a large woman. No one realized she was with child. No one need ever know there had been a birth. Whatever possessed Casilda to intercede for this child remains a great mystery to me. Her charity must have been boundless. She looked upon Mallory's hideous face, framed already in thick, coarse, black hair, and was moved to pity. Three days she spent begging Jehan and Margery not to kill her brother. Mallory's sex was difficult to determine, his member being proportionate to his tiny body. Casilda finally prevailed, upon condition that she would take him away and never seek to rejoin her parents so long as he was alive. She departed and always kept her part of the bargain.

Thus in the year of Our Lord 1115, at age nineteen or thereabouts, Casilda left Paris with this "ill-omened one," Mallory, and settled in Burgundy, not far from the Abbey of Saints Peter and Paul at Cluny. There she would go to attend Mass as often as she dared, carrying Mallory wrapped in a shawl, terrified that his cries would betray his presence and someone would see him. For if anyone had seen him, surely he and his sister would have been driven away if not stoned or burned as accomplices of the devil. Like Our Lord Jesus, Mallory grew in wisdom and in God's grace if not in that of man. The pitiful creature was blessed—perhaps I should say cursed—with extraordinary intelligence and character, even a winsome disposition and a most delightful sense of humor. Casilda was obliged, almost from his birth, to teach him to hide, for his very life depended on it. How does a loving sister tell her brother that his hellish looks would frighten the stoutest man on a sunny day? He lived in the innermost recesses of their little house, venturing out from a windowless room only when all openings of the house were covered or closed. When Casilda left to deliver the lace she made to support them both, he hid behind a false wall lest some stranger wander into the house and discover him. Fire would have most certainly been fatal—he would burn or be slaughtered in the street when he escaped.

It was about the time that Casilda was beginning to explain his condition to Mallory that Pierre de Montboissier, that font of charity, became abbot at Cluny. Casilda looked upon him and realized that she had a friend, a confidant, an advocate if need be. She had baptized Mallory herself, but had never been able to procure the Eucharist for him. Abbot Pierre came to their home, bringing Our Lord's body and blood with him, which he gave to Mallory after instructing him in the faith of our Church. This, however, was a rare occurrence, one that threatened to divulge Mallory's existence to a populace avid for scandal as well as to expose both Casilda and Pierre to unseemly gossip. All three were severely vulnerable to being compromised by Pierre's holy zeal. Former Abbot Pons was incessant in his machinations to regain his abbacy, taken from him by the Pope himself, and his followers—there are some at the Abbey to this very day—were always lurking about, waiting for Pierre to betray even a small portion of the venality that had characterized his predecessor. I regretted that I had to leave Cluny just as Pierre badly needed a friend who was not involved in Abbey schemes. As it happened, Casilda and Mallory had to find new lodgings in the town of Autun for there was not enough demand for her skill and talent in the village of Cluny. And I had been hired to be Master of the Work at Saint-Lazare. This was in 1124. Casilda was twenty-eight, I was thirty-five, Mallory was a lad of ten. So Casilda and I left Cluny at the same time, but as strangers to one another.

How can I relate in mere words my first encounter with Casilda? I had begun work at Saint-Lazare and my joy was intense, as I had been given carte blanche, complete control of the entire project. I was under no obligation to follow anyone's dictates, to adopt anyone's program. I had never been more content in my work. And then my life was up-ended and shaken, my bones turned to water, my heart filled with such a perpetual ache, a yearning so intense I thought I would faint with desire. And all because of a look, a glimpse of a miraculous face. Casilda is not beautiful. And yet there is no visage in heaven or on earth on which I would rather gaze. What would I not give to capture such a one in stone? Beauty can be rendered in my sculpture, but nobility, courage, piety, generosity, charity... All this and more shines forth in her glaucous eyes, the color of the sea on a cloudy day.

I first saw her at Saint-Lazare just after I had begun work there. It was on the feast of Pentecost. She was there to pray and I, to observe the areas of the walls and those column capitals that first catch the rays of the sun on its journey westward. But I could not keep my eyes from her. A lock of her hair was visible 'neath her shawl; it was of a color I had never seen before, a burnished coppery red. Her eyes were closed, her lips scarcely parted, moving ever so slightly in silent prayer. Her glory eclipsed the very sun I had come to observe. When she left, I followed her, intent on devising a plan to make her acquaintance, determined to possess her or die. Sunlight, columns, capitals...all forgotten in my pursuit of such radiance as I had never imagined.

My method of gaining knowledge of her was the same as Thomas' in his curiosity about me; I followed her without her realizing it. But such was her need to keep hidden her abode, which was Mallory's also, that she lived in a state of perpetual flight from whoever might be in pursuit of her. I lost her almost at once. My desperation was unspeakable. I kept watch at Saint-Lazare, with one eye on my carving and one on the only door to the church unblocked by construction. She finally returned and I determined that the only way I would ever know this woman was to be forthright about it. I approached her without the slightest idea of what I would say or do. For a few moments I just stood there and looked at her with what she described later as utter anguish on my face. What a pair we must have made, she, seated on a bench with her face turned upward over her right shoulder and I, standing there, clenching and unclenching my fists and babbling nonsense about wanting to use her as a model. She knew full well what I was about as a woman does when she senses desperate love in a man. She stared into my face for a few seconds and then said, "Why are you telling me lies, Gislebertus?" I was so astonished, I did not even think to ask how she knew my name. When she spoke, all trace of discomfort left me and I looked into her face and said, "Because I was afraid that you would spurn me if I told you the truth." So I did tell her the truth and she did not spurn me. She did, however, keep me waiting for what seemed like an eternity before becoming my lover. Hiding Mallory's existence was not merely for his protection, but also for her own. She knew that both their lives were lost if he were to be discovered by the wrong person. We courted in the streets, at the market, even at the old Roman theater long before I knew how close we were to her abode. Mallory would peep out at us from a corner of a window, careful to hide behind the curtains. She came to Saint-Lazare often to watch me work and share the noon meal with me. It took little time for me to decide to make Casilda my wife, but ages for her to consent. First she had to reveal her brother to me. As much as I adored her, my first sight of Mallory nearly stopped my heart. How readily I understand Thomas' conclusion that he was dealing with spawn of hell, for Mallory is monstrous to behold. He does appear to be a human spider, walking on his hands, which have become large and disproportionately muscular. Had he a normal body, he could strangle any man with them. His face is appallingly hideous and the crow has a beautiful voice compared with his. The lack of correspondence between the soul and the body in that one is marvelous to contemplate, for Mallory is both intelligent and good. Casilda's mother taught her to read and write and she fulfilled the same task for her brother. Mallory loves to argue, espousing a position he abhors just to confound an adversary. But I am straying far from my purpose here. Casilda accepted me as her husband at last; Pierre, now abbot at Cluny, heard our vows. Our marriage was a secret; even Bishop Étienne, my employer, was unaware where I spent my nights. Would that Thomas had remained so also…

It is the moment now to return to his text. He discusses the treachery at Cluny, which I will further elucidate at the right moment.

End of attachment.

5 March 2004

From: Cletus.Hardin@psychnet.org

To: ruth.blanchard@psychnet.org

Dear Ruth

I'm going to fill you in on some background for a patient you'll be seeing in the near future, Malachi Walmsley. When he was eight, he was asleep in the back seat of a car driven by his mother, who slammed into a tree, killing her brother and doing some serious damage to herself. Malachi escaped injury of the physical variety but the accident, the fact that for various reasons he wanted his uncle out of the picture, and the eventual abandonment of the family by the mother all took their toll. The problems didn't show up until Malachi was almost thirty and were triggered by his wife's supposed infidelity, the first in a suspected string of affairs. I have, to this day, no idea if Amanda was truly seeing other men or not. I do know Malachi has been obsessed with a woman he knew as a young girl in his childhood and with whom he is still in touch. Whether he's ever had any physical contact with her since a very young age is anyone's guess. He refuses to discuss it with me. He began having horrendous dreams that were so bad, he started avoiding sleep altogether and finally landed in a hospital in a state of nervous exhaustion. His dreams consisted of variations on this theme: his uncle and his father, who was out of town at the time of the crash, come out of some woods together, laughing and embracing while his mother's body lies in the road; the two men then throw the body into a ditch and cover it with leaves.

Malachi escaped into another personality for a while, but finally confronted his alter ego and has been doing well. His mother recently died and Malachi's return to the scene of the accident has reinvigorated some of his problems, especially the dreams. He was able to face and overcome his fragmentation and alienation only within the last five years. I don't believe he has fragmented again, but if pushed hard, he could succumb. He still resists realizing *he* is all the figures in his dreams, so the belief of his dream ego that his uncle survived the accident is his manner of dealing with his unassailable feelings of guilt about his death, which he desired as a child. He saw him as a cause of friction between his parents. I'm sure he'll fill in some gaps in this sketchy narrative. He's a sensitive and intelligent person born into a family that is the stuff of nightmares—literally.

Thanks for seeing him and call if you have anything you want to discuss.

Best, Cletus Hardin

8 March 2004
From: ruth.blanchard@psychnet.org
To: Cletus.Hardin@psychnet.org
Dear Cletus,

Thanks for sending me the most interesting "patient" I've had in ages! After a fairly lengthy session with Malachi, I've decided to start from scratch with him. He doesn't seem to mind my lack of official credentials; he seems hungry for someone to talk to. There's far more to his story than first meets the eye. I've lived in this parish forever and know where all the bodies are buried. I knew his father and the cronies who were in charge of investigating accidents and the like in the '50s. Some of what he says doesn't add up and I plan to dig, even on my own time, until I unravel the threads of this bizarre event.

According to Malachi, there was almost no investigation of this accident, which resulted in one death and one lengthy hospitalization, effected in another state. Charity Hospital in New Orleans is not pretty or luxurious, but is and was excellent for trauma cases. We also have two university hospitals, and more than adequate specialists in reconstructive surgery. So Parker Walmsley's haste to send his wife, or what was left of her, out of state for so-called therapy smells. And then Joanna's abandonment of a son she adored and protected demands explanation. By coincidence, you have sent me a patient whose family I knew. I'm between generations, younger than the parents, older than Malachi. I don't recall any interaction with him in his early years, but my parents knew his parents fairly well, and my mother told me Malachi and his mother were very close, too close as I recall. Malachi had an almost mystical affection for Joanna; he became very upset when he thought he had done something to displease her. After the accident, Joanna became more and more reclusive, and everyone in Covington who had been her friend lost touch with her. Malachi wanted to contact his mother's former friends, but I explained the pointlessness of that exercise. Joanna cut off relations with all her friends when she returned from California. I remember seeing her in town occasionally, but she avoided my family and me. Celestine, the maid, did everything that required contact with the outside world except teach Joanna's classes for her.

There's much about this case that intrigues me. Since I'm retired and have some time, I'm going to get to the bottom of this. Most of the principals in this drama are dead—the police chief (in Parker's pocket), the coroner (ditto), probably the surgeon(s) who operated on Joanna. The funeral parlor in charge of John's (aka Uncle Buddy) cremation went out of business ten years ago, but their records should be stored somewhere as should the hospital's. As for the police records, who knows? If something was covered up, the records will be useless but some of the younger deputies may remember something. I'll keep you posted on my finds. In the meantime, I'll continue working with Malachi. Even though he feels his head's been shrunk to the size of a pea, he may want to do something about the dreams. He questions whether therapy will intensify them. I've explained that buried or suppressed traumatic content will fester until it is confronted and dealt with, if not now then at a later date, and that the longer he waits to examine his past, the less he'll have to draw upon to help him. I've also explained that I'm not a therapist, but an amateur sleuth of the mind and the tricks it plays on us. I think the fact that I'm not a credentialed shrink will help him to relax and not feel that his every word and movement are being scrutinized for hidden meaning.

As I said, I'm going to start from scratch and will send you transcripts of our sessions, which I plan to tape. You will undoubtedly have very valuable insight and I encourage you to comment anytime you wish.

Best, Ruth

10 March 2004
From: fractal@netconnect.net
To: gold.digger@netconnect.net

You called me "Mug"! You remembered our names for each other, dear Wump. I hadn't thought of that in ages. I guess dredging up childhood memories makes all sorts of stuff bubble to the surface. I wish we could be those kids again, walking on the beach at the Bay with tan faces and sun-bleached hair, holding hands and telling secrets. Oh well, back to the dreary present…

I think I've found a friend, or at least someone who'll take seriously my concerns, my pain, without assuming I'm a chronic malcontent or just a nuisance. Cletus recommended that I see a woman who grew up in this area, knew my parents and all concerned in their drama, and is a naturally inquisitive person. She's not a pro but an "amateur detective of the mind," as she styles herself, and seems intent on ferreting out solutions to the mysteries of my life. She lives in a small cottage in Covington, a real plus. I dreaded trips into New Orleans. The city's fascinating but dirty and dangerous. And I hate to drive. I especially hate to cross the causeway. Driving over water gives me the willies. You may recall my intense fear of drowning. Each time we went swimming in the bay, I'd stick to areas where I could put my feet firmly on the bottom, even if the bottom was slime.

Ruth is a widow in her late sixties, recently retired from teaching, with two cats that sit in on our sessions much to my delight. She scheduled me for one hour and I ended up staying at her place for almost three. I felt immediately as though I'd known her all my life and found her very easy to talk to. She didn't ask many questions, just listened to what I had to say. The only time she probed deeply was when I was discussing my memories of the night of the accident. But of course, those memories are sketchy at best. And I don't even know if they're memories, dreams or fantasies. With her help, I'll find out. With all the $$$ Mother left me, I'm going to finance some travel for her. She's going to attempt to talk to my father but also check hospital records in CA where Mother had her surgery. Police records such as they are will be perused. I feel good about her. She laughs easily and listens well. I like her. I can also e-mail her with anything that pops into my mind without feeling that I'm an intrusive bother.

I'm very tired after today's marathon talkathon so will close.

Love, M

11 March 2004
From: ruth.blanchard@psychnet.org
To: Cletus.Hardin@psychnet.org
Dear Cletus,

Malachi and I spent most of yesterday getting acquainted. I'll send you a transcript of the session as soon as Gladys can get it word-processed. At times, I'll use initials so as not to be indiscreet or risk betraying a confidence. Some of the people Malachi discusses are dead, but some may still be alive. Plus there are the characters he's run into—in the Quarter, at his mother's school, at an abbey Joanna supported. Celestine and, to some extent, Ruben hold many keys but will not talk. I'm going to ask Celestine gently if she will relinquish Malachi's former bedroom; I don't think Malachi's sleeping in his mother's bed in the room where the armoire is situated is conducive to healing. That piece of furniture is of great importance in unlocking the mystery of Malachi's recurrent and increasingly disturbing nightmares. They've progressed far beyond bad dreams and Malachi is exhausted. Furthermore, his mother apparently had a colorful sex life with Dad and it's possible Malachi witnessed some of the goings-on at far too young an age to understand. He may have mistaken enthusiastic sex for violence.

Item #1 on my agenda is to stabilize Malachi's sleep. If Celestine puts up a fuss, then we'll do some furniture rearranging: get rid of the armoire and buy a new bed.

Next I'll try deep relaxation techniques to try to bring up more of the past.

I also plan to contact this friend of his in France. They were childhood friends and Winifred may be able to fill in lots of gaps. I'd be curious about her take on Malachi's parents.

Last, I'm seeing someone. I knew you'd be pleased, you've been urging me to get out more. I happen to have a date tonight and will fill you in on the details soon.

How are you?

Best, Ruth

12 March 2004
From: Cletus.Hardin@psychnet.org
To: ruth.blanchard@psychnet.org
Dear Ruth,

Glad Malachi isn't a pain. I've worked with him for years and he seemed to be making good progress. I just hope all this mess with his mother's death isn't too much for him to handle now. He has always professed an aversion to the woman; her apparent abandonment of him hurt him beyond all telling. Of course, Joanna's startling lack of love for her son was probably a result of the trauma of the accident. But how can anyone be totally indifferent to his mother? I would have loved to contact her but: 1) I didn't know how to get in touch with her and; 2) Malachi would not have permitted it. Working with one half of a dysfunctional pair is tough. Malachi's relationship with his father did not bother him, or so he said.

Furthermore, by the time Malachi contacted me, Parker was beginning his slide into dementia, so talking to him would have been pointless. I understand that he has moments of seeming lucidity, so make a list of talking points and I'll seize the opportunity to interview him for you if you wish.

How am I? I'm OK. Jerome is beginning to thaw out and soon the searing summer will be here. We've had a rough winter and hope the tourists are plentiful; that will see us through next winter. I'm semi-retired and see only former clients from Prescott, Sedona and Flagstaff, and then only in the summer. No one wants to tackle Mingus Pass in the winter. Malachi used to telephone from time to time, but we haven't had any deep work in years. And I hesitate to do anything but the most cursory chat online because of privacy issues. I sense that he will need a steady hand and that's why I urged him to see you.

I also am seeing someone, a fellow shrink from Sedona who got tired of the vortices-seekers and crystal-gazers. I did explain the flake factor in Sedona, didn't I? It's worse than California! Some place offers "metaphysical" services. So just for the heck of it, I went in and asked what metaphysical services were. The guy hadn't a clue. But the place does have some great massage therapists and it's a lot closer than Flag. I don't know where this "seeing someone" will go. For now, it's very casual and will stay that way for a while.

I'll be interested in the transcript of your sessions with Malachi. Send it at your convenience.

Best, Cletus

16 March 2004
From: ruth.blanchard@psychnet.org
To: Cletus.Hardin@psychnet.org
Dear Cletus,

I had a productive session with Malachi. There's a long way to go, but with patience and some sleuthing—perhaps you'd help with a visit or two to Parker sick as he is, to feel him out and soften him up—I think we can make some progress. I'd really like to see Parker myself; sending you a list of questions would be too cumbersome. Besides, the form and scope of question B would depend on the response to question A. And I have a hidden agenda. I'd love to see both you and the west. If you'll have me, I'll wait out Parker's lucid moments—unless they're months apart—interview him, then set out for some tourism.

Here's the transcript of the session sent as an attachment. I had a pro type it up so there will be a lot of material you already are familiar with. I thought that was simpler than editing out the background stuff. Skim over what is superfluous. I also deleted last names and used initials where possible. I trust Gladys completely; the internet is another matter.

Best, R

Transcript of 8 March 2004 meeting of Malachi G.
and Ruth Blanchard:

R: Hi, Malachi. Let me tell you something about me before we begin our discussion of you. First, I am not a psychiatrist, a psychotherapist or a social worker. I have a doctorate but it's in English lit, not psychology. I've done a lot of reading of books and papers dealing with psychoanalysis, mostly of the Jungian variety, and I've been friends with Cletus Hardin for ages. I've also done my share of psychoanalytical literary and art criticism for scholarly journals, but I'm not licensed to treat mental or emotional illnesses. All I have is a smattering of learning and a lot of common sense. I think I can help you, but there are no guarantees. I'm keenly interested in the workings of the human soul and I'd like to get to the bottom of a problem that has obviously plagued you for a long time. For a while it's lain dormant but seems to have flared up again. Cletus has gone about as far as he can go, especially since he's in Jerome and you're here. But so, I believe, is the key to your hurt. I'm also willing to do some sleuthing of the sort therapists and counselors don't do. If all this information doesn't send you straight out the door, I'll ask you to sign this statement indicating that I've disclosed everything I've just said, and stating your willingness to accept me and my work with you on these terms. I also don't charge Cletus Hardin's sorts of fees. My sessions are $50 per hour plus any expenses incurred in my investigation. I do this sort of work because I find it fascinating, but my time is worth something and $50/hour is it. And I may find it necessary to travel to Arizona to consult with Cletus and to try to glean some information from your father. Do you want time to think about this?

M: No, I made up my mind once I spoke to Cletus. He thinks very highly of you and your unorthodox methods. [M was smiling throughout this exchange so I assume you don't think I'm a total crackpot. Also, pardon the wisecrack about your fees.] I trust him and his suggestions, and have no problem putting myself in your hands.

R: Remember, I'm neither a physician nor a person protected by any confidentiality laws. What you divulge to me may be demanded by law enforcement in the event that any sort of crime is brought to light in these sessions. And should I determine that you or anyone else are or may be guilty of some sort of criminal activity, I must report it. This does not include confessions of pot-smoking or other such minor lapses in judgment.

M: I must be the only person my age never to have touched the stuff or any other controlled substance for that matter. I was prescribed Paxil and

53

Diazepam, but use neither at the moment. I keep Diazepam around for help with sleep if necessary.

R: Do you have trouble sleeping?

M: Only when the dreams come.

R: What triggers dreams, unpleasant usually I assume?

M: Yes, they're horrible. And I don't know what brings them on. When I suspected my wife of cheating, they were frightful. Since I've been in Covington, they've been getting worse and worse. The armoire in my mother's bedroom really provoked some terrible nightmares.

R: I think the best thing is to begin at the very beginning. Go back in your mind to the earliest memories you have. Omit nothing, even stuff you may consider trivial or meaningless. Treat your memories as if they were paintings or short narratives. Often an artist or a writer puts in a detail of whose significance he is unaware or whose meaning becomes clear to him years after the event of creation. Or sometimes never. But a clever critic who knows the artist well may discover the meaning of a detail, often to the discomfort of the artist or the writer. Sometimes your memories may be inaccurate, but those very inaccuracies may be meaningful if we can tease them out and *recognize* that they are inaccurate. As much as possible, connect your dreams to what was going on in your life at the time. Dreams are useless to us unless we can put them in context. An element that is significant to one person may have a totally different importance to another. Begin with your earliest memory and go from there.

M: My first clear memory is of the backs of people's knees at the level of my eyes. How odd is that? Then I remember getting my stomach pumped because I had ingested roach poison. I remember the ether mask coming down on my face when I had my tonsils out. Ever since then, my fear of suffocation or drowning has been intense. I'm highly claustrophobic, perhaps another effect of the memory of the ether mask. I remember missing my bus stop and my mother's frantic attempt to catch up with me. I do not remember how she and I finally connected.

R: How old were you when you missed the bus stop?

M: About five.

R: Your parents let you ride the bus alone at that age?

M: I think it was a school bus. Yes, it must have been because I was coming home from school.

R: What sort of child were you?

M: Docile, eager to please…. I was rather well liked by adults but not by my peers. In first grade, there was a girl I liked so much and I wanted to be her best friend. But she didn't like me especially. I gave her an enormous fancy valentine, the sort with a huge satin heart slightly plumped out with foam or fabric, and paper lace all around it. I was sure no one could resist loving the giver of such a splendid gift. But she was best friends with somebody else and I remained on the fringes. I guess that's a good description of me, always with my nose pressed up against the glass. Until I met Winifred. She and I were both fringe people and when we found each other, we became lifelong best friends. We were in different homerooms so it took a few months for us to discover each other. When we did, it changed my life…. I was also sexually precocious.

R: Explain the latter characterization of yourself.

M: I entered puberty really early, before I was ten. My teachers—nuns— thought I was oversexed. But I was also repressed, I suppose. I thought a lot about kissing, necking, that sort of thing. I had my first sexual encounter when I was about fifteen but Winifred, who wanted to keep me at arm's length, always interfered with my enjoyment of other girls' company. I wanted every girl I interacted with to be a replica of Winifred. I sometimes wonder if I'm obsessed with her, if all my problems exist because I can't let her go.

R: We're getting too far forward into your memory bank and concentrating too much on Winifred. If she's involved in your troubles, we'll dig that out eventually. Usually family—early family stuff—is at the root of neurosis. You need to concentrate on pre-accident memories. And you must concentrate on this piece of furniture, the armoire that seems to be playing such a large role in your current situation. Let's take a moment for some deep relaxation techniques that may allow you to piece together its significance in your distress. Lie back, close your eyes, and breathe as deeply as you can, hold it for as long as possible, then exhale very, very slowly.

[Pause of about fifteen minutes.]

Now, give me every detail of getting locked in the armoire—what you heard, what you saw, what events or sensations now evoke that episode.

M: I used to play in the armoire. I'd go there not so much to hide as to be completely alone, to escape from my life for a while. It's a vast piece of furniture and I could move to the far side of the clothes and feel very, very safe. I was totally hidden. There was a crack in the side, a tiny slit, that I used to peer out of, but of course my field of vision was very limited. I could see only what was directly in front of that fissure. My mother used Arpège perfume and her clothes smelled of it. Now, that scent is very evocative of my childhood.

R: You said you felt safe. What did you want to be safe from?

M: From the bickering, I guess. Mother and Dad fought a lot about Uncle Buddy. He was Mother's fraternal twin. In fact, his given name was John, I think, and Mother's was Joanna. Corny, right? He lived with us against Mother's wishes; I could never figure that one out.

R: Aside from the bickering, what else do you recall about your parents' relationship?

M: Not much. They met in New Orleans in 1937 after Mother returned from France. She was working in an antiques store in the French Quarter and this rich handsome older guy came in one day. Her mother died when she was ten and she was never close to her father. She was seduced by my father's charm but also married him to please her dad. Dad and Grandfather were friends, close friends, and also business associates of some sort as I recall. The rest is history.

R: You're an only child?

M: Yes. Mother used to say she put all her eggs in one basket. As I look back, I suspect she eventually wanted as few ties to my father as possible.

I have no children by choice. But the downside to that is, when you get to be in your 60s and mortality forces itself on your consciousness, death has a finality to it that it doesn't have for other people. At least, not for people with offspring.

R: Some people have a child or children who don't reproduce, so childlessness doesn't have quite the baggage you ascribe to it. If you felt you weren't cut out for fatherhood, then your decision was prudent. Having children to create a sort of legacy for oneself is very foolish and sometimes backfires in unpleasant ways. Get past regretting something you can't control now and move on. There are other ways of achieving immortality.

M: I'll try...

R: Let's continue with childhood stuff. Any inkling at all as to the state of your parents' union aside from the conflict over your uncle's presence in the house?

M: I sensed, as a child senses, tension, a lack of warmth or closeness. My father is so wealthy—and was then also—it would have been difficult for any woman to walk away from that. Mix in my mother's Catholicism and the times in which they lived... Divorce was not an option. I think my mother was severely depressed. Of course, no one talked about depression in that era. The only time my mother smiled was when we were doing something fun together. We did a lot of things together. I think I was by far more important to her than either Dad or Buddy. In fact, as I said, she didn't like Buddy and wanted him to leave.

R: And you have no idea why?

M: Buddy was very... needy. He'd have been on the street without my parents' intervention. His mother, my grandmother whom I never knew, died when he and Mother were about ten and Buddy was much more affected by her death than Mother was. He was the quintessential mama's boy. He could never focus enough to get educated or even properly trained to make a living. My grandfather tolerated this for a while, then tossed him out. That may have been the cause of the rift between him and my mother; she felt that Buddy had been imposed on her. If her dad had allowed Buddy to live with him, Buddy wouldn't have come to stay with us. As I look back from the vantage point of my sixty-two years of living, I see enablers of

57

Buddy's sloth all around—his father and then mine. Of course, *enabler* is newspeak along with *depression*. My mother could have put her foot down, insisted that the house wasn't big enough for her and her brother. But she didn't. She just didn't... And I think she put up with him to hang on to my father's money. And perhaps just to hang on to a husband. Some women have to have a man. They'll put up with anything to that end. Sometimes I feel that way about Amanda. I've suspected her of cheating and decided to be deaf, dumb and blind. All the signs were there and I ignored them, pushed them away. I think I know how my mother felt.

R: Let's go back to the armoire. I'm convinced your secret is locked in it and once we find the key and can open the door so to speak, we'll have a clue as to how to proceed with other stuff you may have buried in that mind of yours. You're not remembering because part of you doesn't want you to. But you must, or the dreams and the depression and the exhaustion will continue and consume you. I think I'm distracting you from the very deep relaxation you need to allow what we need to resurface. Let's end our session today. I want you to take at least an hour this afternoon to lie down, breathe as I've instructed you, and let your mind go blank. Use this relaxation tape with earphones. If you dream before our next meeting, write down as many details as you can recall the moment you awaken. Keep pen and paper by your bedside. Omit no detail, however trivial it may seem. Now I want you to give me the address of the house of the man in your mother's e-mail address book. And do you recall the name or location of the antiques store where your mother worked?

M: Celestine would know. Perhaps I can get her to tell me.

R: Speaking of Celestine, one of these days I'm going to want to talk to her.

M: Good luck. She plays dumb with me. But I'm sure it's an act. I catch her and her son Ruben having murmured conversations that stop when I come upon them. I can't imagine what she wants to hide and why.
[End of transcript.]

So there you have it. The rest of our session was inconsequential small talk, not worth recording. My next stop will be the Dauphine Street house of the mysterious man. I'll report on what I find as soon as I find it.
    Best, Ruth

16 March 2004
From: fractal@netconnect.net
To: gold.digger@netconnect.net

Here we go again. Oh, Wump, if my head gets shrunk any more, I'll be fit for a museum of anatomical freaks. I'm so sick of repeating the same shit over and over to People Who Can Help Me!! Childhood, mommy stuff, daddy stuff, why can't I just xerox my life's story and hand it out; or better yet, post it on the internet? That's it, I'll post it on the 'net and ask for comments. I could have a contest to find the most outlandish explanation of my situation.

The woman Cletus sent me to is nice enough, not a pro so easier to talk to. She doesn't seem to take herself too seriously. And she apparently has nothing better to do than listen to me. She's going to investigate the little house in the Quarter, the one where the guy weirded me out. If she can find out why and when he knew my mother, that alone would be worth the pittance I'm paying her.

The azaleas are beginning to flower and the birds are finally showing up, hunting for real estate. Two of the birdhouses have attracted attention. Warblers and wrens, I think. This cheers me up.

Please write and tell me what you're up to. You're the only one keeping me sane at the moment. Thanks for your support.

Love, M

20 March 2004
From: Cletus.Hardin@psychnet.org
To: ruth.blanchard@psychnet.org
Dear Ruth,

I'm delighted at the prospect of seeing you again and showing you "my" west. That's assuming you'll let me tag along... I have a guest room waiting for you whenever you think it opportune to come and an itinerary all planned in my head. Please let me do this. Of course, if the someone you're seeing objects, I'll understand. The someone I was seeing... Well, notice the past tense.

Let me know what you think.

I've printed out the transcript and look forward to reading it at my leisure. It will have my undivided attention.

Cletus

20 March 2004
From: ruth.blanchard@psychnet.org
To: Cletus.Hardin@psychnet.org
Dear Cletus,

Thanks for the kind offer. I hasten to accept although I have no clear idea of a time line. The someone I was seeing is also in the past tense so no complications in that quarter. And of course you may tag along; I was hoping you'd offer. Traveling alone can be depressing. I know. I've tried it. When Liam died, I did everything I could to dull the pain before I figured out I'd just have to let time do its work. I'm sure you understand, having been through the same trials.

Back to Malachi. I finally had some luck with his mysterious French Quarter house. I didn't quite know how to get into the Dauphine Street place and was wondering what story to concoct when I spotted a "For Rent" sign in the window. I wonder if Malachi's visit scared off the man he talked to... I called the number and got a person, not a machine. The person agreed to meet me there but I had to kill a couple of hours. And I use the word *person* advisedly. On the phone, I didn't know if it was a man or a woman.

A stroll through the French Quarter is not the thrill it used to be. The place used to be full of elegant shops, expensive private homes, and swell people on their way to chic places. Now, it's filthy, smelly, and populated with the grossest street people you can imagine. I walked to Jackson Square and went to the cathedral for a quiet moment. All Catholic churches have a most distinct smell, a combination of incense, flowers, and candle wax. Liam used to say French churches smelled of garlic, stale cheese, and mold, a combination he called "Eurodank." Then I decided to play tourist and visited the Pontalba apartment, now a state museum. The living looks so gracious, but what must it have been like in the summer without A/C? That and some beignets kept me amused until 4, at which time I was walking through the front door of 39 Dauphine Street. It's a typical French Quarter dwelling—a stoop, then a door leading right into the living room. No front yard, no walkway, just a door on the sidewalk. The living room had a small window with bars disguised as a discreet, decorative wrought iron grill, through which waft the sounds and smells of the street. There's a long hall from which one enters all the rooms of the house; the rooms also connect with each other. The last room is the bedroom; it gives onto a lovely patio.

The (male) owner's reaction to me was peculiar, as if he couldn't believe I might want to rent the place. It was cheap and he accepted a month-to-month lease with 30-day notice, so I took it. I plan to take Malachi to it for a session or two to see if it jogs anything. Places tend to keep their odors, and you know what powerful stimulants of memories odors are, even deeply buried memories. It won't take much to furnish it; I'll go to a thrift store and then sell the stuff when I tire of French Quarter living. This could be an adventure I'll enjoy and remember for a long time.

My next plan is to try to worm something out of Celestine then head to AZ. Seeing you again will be such a treat.

Best, Ruth

20 March 2004
From: Cletus.Hardin@psychnet.org
To: Andrew.Smith@ysu.edu
Dear Andy,

Hope all is well in academe. I'm still enjoying retirement, being out of academic politics. Health is holding up even if a few other things aren't. I still take on a few patients, one of whom is a fascinating case, Malachi W. I've written you about him, I believe, and he's back on the front burner so to speak. I had gone as far with him as I could: years of therapy, medication, hypnosis. But I knew things were just covered over, not settled. Lately his mother died and Malachi returned to the "scene of the crime," the house where he grew up and where he was living when his mother and her brother were in a car crash that killed the uncle. Now the insomnia, nightmares, anxiety are back and getting worse. He asked me for advice via e-mail, which I reluctantly and hesitantly agreed to, but with many caveats. And there's a further complication…

As you may recall, I met a woman in graduate school, dated her a few times and got the distinct impression I was wasting my time. She was head over heels with a good friend and I didn't want to muddy the waters. They eventually married as did I and we were all reasonably happy, I suppose. We remained in touch through the years, first with cards at Christmas and occasional notes, then through e-mail. I recently put Malachi in touch with her; it happens that she lives a short distance from Malachi's newly inherited house. Now Ruth and I are both widowed. I'd let sleeping dogs lie, but Ruth may be coming to AZ for a visit soon. She's coming to see Malachi's father in what I consider a vain attempt to get some info out of him. He's wracked with Alzheimer's and what he says even in moments of apparent lucidity is suspect in the extreme. I don't know what to do in the romance department. I'm afraid if I broach the subject, she'll laugh me out of the room. I guess I'll just play it by ear and see if I can feel her out.

Hope all is well with you and yours. If you have any advice for an old college buddy, let me know. And if you ever come to AZ, stop in Jerome. You'd love it. It's hot in the summer and freezing in the winter, but the rest of the time, it's paradise.

All best, Cletus

22 March 2004
From: Andrew.Smith@ysu.edu
To: Cletus.Hardin@psychnet.org
Go for it, ole' buddy! As I recall, I met Ruth once and thought the two of you were a match. I always wondered what happened there; now I know. Ask yourself what you've got to lose and what you've got to gain, then weigh the two. Go for the one that's the heaviest. I think you can guess what I'd do in your place. Vera and I are just getting old and fat—beats the alternative. I've now got only one foot in academe, officially retired but still slaving away on projects, mostly other people's. The current one is for a former colleague. And I thought retirement would mean relaxation. Ha! It's tough to be indispensable. But it sounds as though you've had the same experience.

Don't get too wrapped up in other people's problems. I remember too well how it almost killed you.

Take care of yourself and let me know what happens with Ruth.

All best, A

22 March 2004
From: ruth.blanchard@psychnet.org
To: cmartin@psychnet.net
Dear Catherine,
Forgive the long silence. A combination of the weather and other factors too boring to delve into has brought back the blues. However, a guy I knew in grad school, Cletus Hardin, recently asked me to try to help one of his patients, a man in his early sixties with a horrendous past and a not too cheerful future unless someone can unlock some pretty nasty memories. Malachi's a very pleasant fellow and it doesn't hurt that he's easy on the eyes, tall and lanky with very blue eyes and a graying beard. Very distinguished… Back to my real subject lest I reveal how much I've become a dirty old woman. I think that just because I'm a senior citizen, I can flirt with younger guys with impunity. Of course, he's not *that* much younger.

It's funny that Cletus should pop back after a few years of silence. We had kept in touch casually when Liam was alive and I thought nothing of it.

But now that Cletus and I are both single again, something strange is going on in me. I had a huge crush on Cletus when we were younger but he never gave me a second glance and I just put him out of my mind, determined to be a good wife to Liam. Now, I'm in a bit of an emotional dither since I'll be seeing Cletus in a short while, as soon as I can piece together some info on his patient's past, vital to solving the puzzle of his anguish. And I don't use the word lightly. This is an unhappy man. Something awful happened to him so long ago, I wonder if I'll ever get at the truth. I just hope I'll be able to concentrate on the work I have to do. I have gone so far as to rent a place in the French Quarter, one associated with Malachi. The address was in his mother's e-mail address book. When Mal visited the man living there, he denied recognizing the photo of his deceased mother that he'd brought along, but he was certain the guy was lying. In fact, he seems to be surrounded by people who refuse to tell him what he wants and needs to know. This, coupled with the fact that I don't know if he remembers events or dreams of events, is making my task quite difficult. I'm going to take Malachi there in hopes something will get jogged. He thinks he remembers the place from his childhood, but who knows?

All else is well in Covington. I'm so happy here in this lovely town. I'll probably miss the spring art openings, when all the galleries downtown stay open till ten, and music and the smells of great food fill the air. But I need to work quickly with Malachi and, I must confess, I'm anxious to see Cletus again. I wonder if my feelings will be written all over my face. I don't want to look like an old foolish man-hungry broad! I also don't know if I want another man in my life. Liam and I had our ups and downs, like every couple I suppose, but the downs were really awful and there were times I swore I'd never let this happen to me again, that if I found myself single I'd stay that way. Liam's family and friends were amazed he married. It was many years before I understood their concern and I myself sometimes wondered why he chose to attempt connubial bliss.

Enough kvetching! It's not as though I'll arrive in AZ and have to make a decision on the spot.

Write when you can. R

24 March 2004
From: Cmartin@psychnet.net
To: ruth.blanchard@psychnet.org

Follow your heart and soul, girl! Do I have to tell you love is a risk? What's to lose if he's not interested—except every shred of your dignity and pride? Just kidding, but you know that! And you have total control of your life, if not your emotions. But you can choose what to do with them. Remember that.

All is well here. Classes are chugging along, I'm swamped with papers to grade, students are fairly cooperative.

Keep me posted on your case. Do you suppose I could use some of the material if all names are changed? If I totally disguise the circumstances?

Toodles, Cath

24 March 2004
From: ruth.blanchard@psychnet.org
To: Cmartin@psychnet.net

I must say no to your request and I do so regretfully. Too bad because Mal's story would make a great novel. It's possible he may have dreamed or imagined some of the stuff he's talking about, but it's also possible a serious crime was committed and I don't want to compromise any investigation. I'm going to try to have him do some active imagination work during the twilight period between being fully awake and falling asleep. I also have to disentangle dreams, memories and imaginary events. That's going to be a job especially if there is more than one persona inhabiting his body.

More later, R

29 March 2004
From: ruth.blanchard@psychnet.org
To: Cletus.Hardin@psychnet.org
Dear Cletus,

I include a transcript of my last session with Malachi. It took place in the house on Dauphine Street. I got some good info but not exactly what I was hoping for. The significance of the house itself remains a mystery, but I did learn more about Malachi. The relaxation and active imagination work I had asked him to try either are not working or his mind is so determined to block what he needs to remember, we're doomed to failure. I'm going to wait till Jerome thaws out before heading west to see you and Parker. I had forgotten I'd promised a paper to NSPC and will need to devote some time to it. In the meantime, Malachi seems content to putter through his new house, hobnob with the servants and continue to try to pry info out of them. I tried talking to Celestine and Ruben, but neither seems inclined to give up anything although I have the sense that Ruben might cooperate if I could get him alone and loosened up. I'll work on that. Here's the transcript:

Transcript of 27 March 2004 meeting of Malachi W.
and Ruth Blanchard:

R: Instead of concentrating on your past, let's talk about the present. How
are things in Covington?

M: Very good. I love the place more each day and plan to stay there, at
least part of the year. I hear the summers aren't so great and summers in
Flagstaff are irresistible, cool, dry except during monsoon, filled with
fun events. But winters are awful and I'll probably divide my time pretty
evenly between the two. But I keep changing my mind about these matters
and much depends on Amanda and our relationship.

I'm bonding with Morel, my mother's cat. And, no, I haven't a clue why
she named him Morel. She was a French prof and Morel is a character in
some French novel I've never heard of.

R: Or maybe she was crazy about mushrooms.

M: Pardon?

R: Never mind, lame joke. Tell me about your friends. Are you bonding
with any humans?

M: Aside from my wife's associates and a few people at work, I have no real
friends in Flagstaff. In fact I have few friends period. Winifred H..., has
been my dearest friend since the summer of 1950 at the Bay. And you're the
only person I've talked to in any depth since I got here. Winifred is it.

R: Wasn't 1950 the year of the accident?

M: Yes. The accident happened in April and my father decided we needed
to maintain as much normalcy as possible. So we went to the Bay as usual.
Mother was in California and Dad left me at the Bay a few times while he
went out of town to see how things were progressing. Celestine took care
of me.

Wump—I'll explain the name in a moment—and I went to the same
grade school but didn't really become friends until we realized that our
summer homes were in the same town. At some point during grade school,
she and I began calling each other "Mug" and "Wump," in an attempt to
feel like siblings. One of us heard the word *mugwumps* in the course of

some conversation among adults and we decided it was the funniest word we'd ever heard. So we started calling each other "Mug" and "Wump" instead of "Mal" and "Winnie." You are the first and only person I've revealed that to. We always use the letters "M" and "W" because they could stand for our real names. But for us, it's "Mug" and "Wump" that are meant. We were both fairly bright, and not very popular with the other kids. Wump especially suffered from being bright. A smart boy is OK but you know what little bitches girls can be, especially to those who aren't pretty but are really smart. Wump is a genius; she's fluent in most of the western European languages. We went to grade school and high school together, and began college at LSU. I had to quit when my father took me to Flagstaff with him in 1960 and most of my contact with Wump since then has been through phone calls, mail, then e-mail. Moving away from where she lived was traumatic, almost as bad as the accident. I guess that's another reason I hated my mother so much for turning on me and deciding she didn't want me with her any more; she separated me from Wump. I simultaneously lost the two most important women in my life.

R: May I have your permission to contact Winifred?

M: [A long pause…] I don't see what harm could come of that. Yes, okay, I'll give you her e-mail address and tell her to expect correspondence from you. She's in France now and may take a while to answer you. Her field is art and archaeology, and she's working on a fascinating project. They're excavating a Roman theater and discovered that some people who used a portion of it as a house in the middle ages also left behind some written material. The text is a combination diary or journal and a commentary on that journal. Wump can't get online too often so she e-mails me sporadically; but she sends me transcripts of the text as it is deciphered. The other night characters in her transcript got mixed up in a dream I had about my family. I was dreaming about Uncle Buddy and all of a sudden he turned into Mallory. Mallory is a freak, the brother of a woman named Casilda; both are protected by a sculptor or stonemason named Gislebertus. Casilda and Gislebertus have to keep Mallory hidden or he'd be killed. He's so misshapen, people would think he was a diabolical presence in their midst. The two have nothing in common so I can't imagine why they got confused in the dream. I suppose I might have dreamt of Mallory because his name is so similar to mine. I'm rather self-absorbed these days. Both Mallory and Buddy were repulsive, but for different reasons. And I feel a great deal of self-loathing at times. Mallory, Buddy, Malachi… we all have elements in common. My dreams involving Wump are usually pleasant, but too infrequent. Since she's always on my mind, *girlofmydreams* is my password on all my e-accounts… It describes her accurately and, heaven knows, I can't forget it.

R: That reminds me, I think I should have your e-mail address in case we're in different places and I can't get you by phone.

M: It's fractal@netconnect.net.

R: Now that's an odd one! Reminds me of *fracture*. How did you choose that?

M: Fractal and fracture are semantically related. They both carry the weight of brokenness. When I began my study of math, chaos theory was a gleam in Benoît Mandelbrot's eye. Chaos theory is still a corner of math looking for an application. For now it is mostly an intellectual curiosity; the buzz words are *strange attractors* and *phase-space. Phase-space* is used to describe attractors, and chaos theory has some promise in cosmology. I'm no expert in the field and I've only played around with it. But then I learned about fractals, extremely irregular curves or shapes for which any suitably chosen part is similar in shape to a given larger or smaller part when magnified or reduced to the same size. They remind me of mirrors that, when placed at proper angles to each other, send the same image bounding back and forth to itself. Chaos and fractals were good metaphors for aspects of my life. *Chaos* was a bit too trite for my ID; and I was almost certain it was taken. *Fractal* seemed to fit me better. And, as you point out, it resonates with the notion of fragments, fractures, broken things, things in small pieces, some infinitesimally small.

R: I had no idea your ID was of such an intellectual nature. And I won't pretend that I understand it fully. But, as you say, certain aspects suit you well.

Back to the mundane—and easily grasped. When did you last see Winifred?

M: I haven't seen her since we moved to Flagstaff. I began college at NAU and Wump's work took her out of the country so often, we never seemed able to hook up.

R: What did you do when you finished at NAU?

M: As you may have gathered, my major was math. I worked at an accounting firm, mostly with computers. Amanda used to say I lived in cyberspace She and I married in 1970. She's a prof of Law at NAU and does a bit of law practice with cases that interest her. We've both had issues with fidelity and trust. I guess it would be fair to say we don't trust each other and are both suspicious of infidelity on the part of the other spouse. Now that I've inherited a wonderful house here and will soon have my father's fortune to play with, I'll travel to wherever Wump is in order to renew our friendship. In fact, I don't really need to wait for Dad's millions; Mother died a fairly wealthy woman and I suppose I'm free to do as I please. I have yet to trace the source of her wealth. Her bank account indicates a sizable sum deposited each month but it was always in cash. I wonder if she was blackmailing someone…

R: Do you seriously consider that a possibility?

M: It's hard to say. Who knows what changes occurred in her life and mind after Dad and I left for the west? Even before she and my dad divorced, she had weirded out.

R: How did your father make his fortune?

M: I haven't the foggiest. He used to give me vague statements about investments, brokering deals, stuff like that. But nothing specific. For all I know, he was a narc.

R: Do you think he could have been into drug trafficking?

M: No, not really. Although he had a reputation for ruthlessness that was legendary. One of the reasons mother waited so long to leave him, I think, was that she was afraid of him, of what he might do to her.

R: How did he treat you?

M: He didn't. He scarcely seemed to notice me. When we moved to Flagstaff, I think he took me because he had to. I wasn't yet able to be on my own. Also, he knew how close mother and I had been and I think he thought her lack of interest in having me around was an act designed to get custody of me in order to extract money from him. He probably figured that foisting me off on her was just what she wanted so he kept me close. In any case, if either one was playing a game, it backfired on both of them. If they were sincere, they were spectacularly successful. Dad kept mother from getting more than a pittance. And mother was all too glad not to be responsible for me. Even when I was quite able to take care of myself, I stayed with Dad to save dough. Cowardly, I know, but I was always looking to save a buck whenever I could. Must have been my old man's greediness that rubbed off on me.

R: Tell me about life in Flagstaff with your father.

M: As I indicated, we moved there when I was eighteen, in 1960. At first, we lived in town. Flagstaff has the most charming downtown, full of the atmosphere of old Route 66. Today it's practically an artist colony but then it was a town. There are two old and historically significant hotels and lots of buildings that date from the turn of the century or close to it. After I finished college, Dad moved to the most exclusive part of town, Forest Highlands. Our house was enormous and very elaborate, but cold as ice and utterly without charm. When I say "cold," I mean the atmosphere, the decor, although Flagstaff can of course be very cold in the winter. The

subdivision butted up against one of the more colorful areas, Kachina Village. In fact, it touched the trailer park area and Forest Highlanders constructed a wall that actually crossed a street in order to ensure that none of the riff-raff invaded their territory. I eventually got tired of life with Dad, even if it made great economic sense, and I rented a place south of the railroad tracks but close to town, the low-rent district. Trains come through all day and most of the night, so the closer one lives to the tracks, the lower the rent because of the infernal racket. I finally got used to it and no longer heard them. They were just part of the background noise of life. Even today, the sound of a train takes me back to my bachelor days in Flagstaff.

As I said, I worked for an accounting firm there. The pay was good and the work was interesting. I also did volunteer work assisting a woman who used art as therapy for troubled kids. I guess it should have prepared me better for handling my own difficulties. You know, "Physician, heal thyself." But somehow it didn't. When Amanda and I married, I made sure we lived in Kachina Village. It just had more soul, if you know what I mean. It also pissed off my father, who hated to tell his hoity-toity friends his son lived on the wrong side of the barrier. There was, and still is, a huge meadow at the entrance of the village where Pumphouse Wash begins and elk come to graze in groups ranging from four to twelve. In fact, they've visited our yard from time to time. It was, and still is, a hodge-podge of mansions and single-wides, sometimes cheek-by-jowl. I've heard that prices have skyrocketed lately. When we bought our house for $76K, we thought it was an extravagance. It recently sold for $237K. Amanda and I were quite happy for a while. We stayed in the Village but moved to a grander place on a huge lot with a canyon view. KV is very hilly. Some houses sit at the top of a hill, some, at the bottom. Those at the top command top dollar. My house in KV was the fulfillment of a dream of long duration. I love it, especially the surroundings and the elk that wander through the yard. Then Amanda's eye began to wander and it all started to fall apart. I take solace in my land. In fact, it's incorrect to say I stayed with Amanda. I stayed in my house. Our Kachina Village backyard is a mountainside, full of wild flowers in the spring and summer. There's red hot poker season, always eagerly awaited by residents. The flowers—I guess they are flowers—are so strange, sort of rubbery and not very flowerlike. But they are colorful. There are rock outcroppings I yearned to explore but I was afraid I couldn't make it back up the mountain once I descended. I've never been much of a climber. I once scrambled down to Walnut Canyon and thoroughly enjoyed my visit. But then I looked back up to where I'd come from and realized I'd have to make the climb. It almost killed me! So the possibilities of Grand Canyon were wasted on me. I always saw it from high on the rims, south and north. I vastly prefer the north rim but it's an overnight journey from Flagstaff and Amanda was usually too busy to travel much. We lived surrounded by national parks and visited very few. I insisted on seeing Canyon de Chelly, even on descending to thebottom of the canyon in a very strange vehicle with an Indian guide. Unforgettable… Another great place near Flag is Jerome where Cletus lives. You should visit him just to see the town. It's one of Arizona's premier old mining towns, in many respects a ghost town. Some of the houses are perched so precariously, you wonder why they don't just come crashing down the hillI have frequently fantasized Amanda's death or her departure, imagining life alone or with Wump. Please don't misunderstand, Wump insists that our relationship be strictly platonic. I abide by her rules but I do love her and believe she loves me back in a unique way. We're in a relationship that cannot be pigeonholed. What I want more than anything is to be able to explore all the wonderful places near Flagstaff with Wump, just the two of us, with no cares or concerns or schedules. I'll have to wait for her to retire but that shouldn't be too far down the road. She's my age after all. In fact, we both have birthdays in the same month and were born in the same year. If I'm rich enough, maybe I can talk her into living with me, letting me take care of her.

R: Tell me more about your relationship with Amanda. I know Winifred is important to you but Amanda is still your wife and not subject to the idealization you're able to bestow on Winnie. You'll have to decide between them before there's any possibility of living with Winnic.

M: We had a wonderful courtship, full of fun and shared interests. But after our marriage, very gradually, her work consumed her to the point that there was no room for me. She was no longer available. She returned home later and later; midnight was normal. Colleagues, students, friends and especially clients were all ahead of me in line. I frequently felt suicidal. I wanted to find a way to get her attention, I mean, *really* get her attention and not lose it. I thought of throwing myself down the stairs, but worried that I'd be incapacitated and she still wouldn't pay me any mind. Hopelessness overwhelmed me, and much pain. And to think we courted for two years… I've concluded that we all marry strangers no matter how long the engagement, even if people live together. Marriage changes lovers, usually the guy. But this time it was the other way 'round. If I had my life to live over, I'd remain single. And if Amanda and I divorce or she precedes me in death, I'm not sure I'd even date. I may indeed be idealizing or romanticizing Wump and I'd hate for that glorious image to disappear. Remember, I haven't seen her for a very long time.

R: You remind me of someone else I know. But she's decided to take a chance, let things happen, see what life brings. I suggest the same for you. Do you know Keats' poem, "Ode on a Grecian Urn"? It touches on the very subject of the destructive aspects of consummating love. If you don't know it, you may want to google it. I'm sure it's online. My favorite lines, and the ones pertaining to your situation, are: "She cannot fade, though thou hast not thy bliss, For ever wilt thou love, and she be fair!" But this is the case only if the beloved is an image, an artifact, not a flesh-and-blood woman.

Let's get back to the present. Tell me more about the post-accident Joanna. Can you be more specific about the differences in her?

M: I've been trying to pin down exactly what I noticed as much for myself as for you. But all I can come up with is a vague and generalized sense of otherness. The impression that struck me the hardest was that she was always afraid, but I have no inkling who or what frightened her. She seemed to be constantly on guard against a slip of the tongue, a wrong move. There were things she had forgotten, but I chalked that up to amnesia caused by the accident and subsequent surgery. Oh, and she smelled different. I don't mean she changed perfume. She still wore Arpège. Her unperfumed skin had a different odor to it. Very strange...

R: It's possible her whole body chemistry changed as a result of what happened in the aftermath of the accident. Is it possible your father substituted someone else for her, had some other woman surgically turned into your mother? I know that sounds preposterous, but stranger things have been known to happen. I don't know if you're familiar with the movie *Shattered*, but you might do well to watch it. It concerns an amnesiac who is literally turned into another person to satisfy a grasping, sociopathic woman. The plastic surgery is a bit too perfect to be completely realistic, but the movie works, and it works beautifully. Watch it if you have the chance.

M: I will, but I don't think your scenario is possible. Mother remembered enough that I was satisfied that she was who she purported to be. There were things she referred to of which my father was ignorant; he couldn't have coached a stranger to that extent. And she talked about her childhood, reminiscing about events my father could not have known about. No, Mother was herself, no doubt about it. I wouldn't put what you're suggesting past my father, but he wasn't capable of providing anyone with the information my post-accident mother had. She was different but not an entirely different person.

R: What about your father's family? You haven't mentioned your paternal grandparents at all.

M: Neither did my father. Of his parents he spoke nary a word, except to say that they died when he was very young. He was raised by an aunt, and she too died when he was in his early twenties. I don't even know if she was his father's or his mother's sister. And he never spoke of any siblings. I've always assumed he was an only child. Knowing what I know now, I wouldn't be surprised to learn that he had poisoned them all. His inheritances from these people formed the nucleus of his wealth. What little I know of his nature leads me to believe he is hopelessly vice-ridden.

R: You may well be correct. I'll see what Cletus has to say about this. So, on to another topic. What do you make of this house? Are any bells ringing?

M: No. I don't think I've ever been here before. But it does remind me of the place where my parents met. Mother used to tell me the story of her meeting Dad and it must have been in a house very similar to this one. A lot of French Quarter businesses are located in former residences. And many of these buildings go back and forth between commercial and residential use.

R: So your reaction to this place was based on what exactly?

M: It was based on the smell. I couldn't place it but it evoked the same feeling I had when I got a whiff of the armoire. And then there was the reaction of the man who opened the door. I know he was lying when he said he didn't recognize my mother's picture.

R: Can you be more specific about the smell? What is it like?

M: Like old wood that's been in New Orleans humidity too long.

R: Does the armoire smell like this house?

M: Yes. As a matter of fact, it does. But there's an overlay of mother's perfume and Dad's cologne in the armoire. I used to like to move to the far end, beside and behind the clothes. I felt completely alone and safe, as I said.

R: Yes, from the quarreling. Anything else?

M: Sometimes I didn't like the way Uncle Buddy looked at me. But he never did anything untoward, so I guess my reaction to him was very subjective.

R: Most reactions to people are. We tend to recoil from people who display elements of ourselves we find unattractive. But I doubt this was in play in the dynamics between you and your uncle.

M: I hope you're right... I'd hate to think I was anything like him.

R: I think we'll end today. I'm going to come to your new digs in Covington and try to squeeze Celestine and Ruben. Frustrating to have so much information at hand and not be able to get at it.

M: Thanks. I'll enjoy showing the place to you. It's really nice.

R: I'll also get Winifred's e-mail address from you. I'd like to contact her soon.
[End of transcript.]

29 March 2004
From: gold.digger@netconnect.net
To: fractal@netconnect.net
  We found more text! It's gets more wonderful every day. It's cold and rainy, perfect weather for poring over ancient docs, trying to decipher letters, etc. Here's a transcript of the latest; it's a continuation of the last portion of the ms. The medieval names for countries/territories have been changed for the medievally-challenged. The text/commentary on the text pattern remains.

Attachment to mail dated 29 March 2004:
The Feast of Saint Thomas

On this day, my own saint's feast day, I again take up this journal to relate the events of the past three months from memory, since I left this text at Autun for fear of being discovered as a literate man. How I wanted to preserve all the details of my sojourn at Cluny as they occurred... Perhaps I will forget or neglect something. No matter, I must try to reconstruct the events. If ever anyone discovers what I did, I will have some record of causes and effects with which I might defend myself if the need arises. Should Gislebertus threaten me, I would show him how much I know of his scandalous liaison with that woman and her infernal familiar. If Abbot

Pierre ever learns of my deeds, this will be the record of who enticed me into sin.

The Feast of Saints Cornelius and Cyprian

We set out at daybreak. There were Gislebertus; Gérard, whom I warn often not to give away our secret knowledge; Gianni, an apprentice from Lombardy seeking new skills to take home with him; Anselm from England; and Marcel from Tours in addition to me. Gislebertus leaves Autun from time to time to work on the new church at Cluny; he wanted us to observe what he has done there so we could imitate it at Autun, and he needed the assistance of skillful stone carvers. This means that we were the best, the most skilled at his disposal at that time. Would that I could convey this to my father. But I must spend Christmas here in Autun this year. The weather is unexpectedly mild and we must profit from it. Moreover Gislebertus wants us to put what we observed at Cluny to use before it fades from our memory. But enough of the present…

The weather was still very warm when we set out in mid-September. Since all we could possibly need for our trade awaited us at Cluny, our bags contained little more than clothes and some provisions to sustain us on our way. We encountered no misfortune en route; robbers, wild animals, all sources of danger seemed to be elsewhere. No one had much to say. Gérard was uneasy, concerned lest he be found out and returned to his master before freedom was in his grasp. I know that he was torn between fear of discovery and pride of achievement. Thanks to my tutelage, he is quite competent now. How could he have contemplated foregoing such an honor and an opportunity? I could not reveal that I was privy to his secret, for then he would know that I had been listening at doors. I feigned belief that he was nervous about travel in general and about testing his skills at Cluny. Gislebertus tried to engage the others in conversation, but Gianni speaks little of our language, as does Anselm. Moreover, the Master knows us as wielders of chisels and picks, hardly as men. When he tried to converse with us on the way, he realized that we shared no language universal among us and he shared nothing of our experiences. All he knew were our hands, not our hearts, not even our heads. His people of stone are more real to him, and more important, than are we. So we traveled in silence.

Gislebertus has made this journey often enough that he knows where to stop for the night. The first day's travel took us to a farm at Le Creusot where we were warmly received, especially Gislebertus. The wife seems willing to offer him unlimited hospitality, including her bed, and she would not make a trifling bed companion, lusty and full-bodied as she is.

Gislebertus seems disinclined; he must assume that the infernal hordes of his wench's familiar watch him constantly and report any misuse of his tool.

On the second day, we departed our hosts soon after sunrise. Gislebertus has another favorite halt between Montceau and La Guiche, near Saint-Gengoux. There we would find lodging for this, our second night en route. The forest we traversed was quite beautiful, teeming with game we did not need since our sustenance was to be provided. The floor of the forest was dappled with sunlight, but the air was cool as little heat was borne on the constantly shifting luminous shafts. Each tree must have seemed to our leader a column with the most perfect capital. At Autun, he urges us to imagine the capitals we rough hew in preparation for his touch as growing naturally out of the stone as branches grow from the trunk of a tree. I have observed him weeping on several occasions, no doubt from the tension involved in sculpting the beauty of God with the help of Satan. How can he carve Jesus' face, look into his stony eyes, then go home to his whore and that evil monster? It will soon be time to take that matter in hand. But enough of the present...

We saw no beasts of any sort save birds; they were high enough in the trees to find us no threat. Our strange, nearly wordless march did not cause much alarm in the woods among any of the forest-dwellers. Gérard and I exchanged some thoughts, but the exertion of our walk left us with little wind for idle conversation. Gislebertus is so perpetually preoccupied, ruminating sculptural compositions and God knows what else, that he seldom speaks even when he is not out of breath. Gianni, Anselm and Marcel would have had to converse with the three of us in Latin or the language of Burgundy, and the effort was no doubt too great. All three are with us to learn, to perfect their skill, to look at stone, not to listen to words. The product of Gislebertus' hands is more important to them than what issues from his mouth.

On the second night, we were roused from a sound sleep by soldiers demanding lodging. They claimed to be soldiers of the Duke, and Eustache, our host, had no desire to argue with them. We got up from our beds, eyes nearly sealed shut with sleep, and moved to the small barn where Eustache and Agathe store provisions for their pigs. I could find no comfortable spot and spent the rest of the night awake. The next morning, an acorn was imprinted on my cheek. The soldiers had already left when we stumbled out of our lodge and, judging from Agathe's satisfied look, one of them at least had found his way to her side of the bed. Women are an untrustworthy lot and I will have to find some way to keep my Clémence faithful to me.

All of our adventures were reserved for the third day, the greatest of which was our arrival at the marvelous Abbey. En route, we had cause to wonder if we would arrive whole! In mid-morning, our nostrils were assailed with the stench of rotting flesh, an animal, we assumed, whose carcass had been left undevoured, or which had simply died in that spot. The actual cause of the odor was a man's left hand lying in our path, the middle finger separated from the rest of the appendage and tossed a few inches from it. Brigands had obviously accosted a solitary traveler in these parts, one with a ring worth stealing, and had cut off his hand when the ring would not budge from his finger. There was no blood on the ground save a few drops from the finger, severed no doubt on this very spot. The man must have been accosted some distance from here and the robbers carried his hand to what seemed a safe place. Gislebertus told us there were no huts, no work sheds, no dovecotes anywhere close by, and the robbers could have done their work undisturbed. We buried this putrid morsel of the poor wretch and continued on our way.

An hour later, we came upon a hut and, in mortal fear that it was the robbers' lair, crept through the bushes, careful not to step on any more branches than necessary. Ordinarily the sounds of the woods pass by our ears unheard, so accustomed to them are we. In our extraordinary state of terror, our very breath seemed to exit our nostrils like the mistral, our hearts beating in our chests seemed the gongs and cymbals of the charivari. The birds flying from branch to branch were winged behemoths and their chirps, the blasts of trumpets. But the noisiest offenders, those determined to announce intruders in the woods, were those accursed squirrels, whose scurrying in the face of our arrival sounded like the yelping hordes of Attila crashing through the underbrush in search of booty. How could something so small make such a racket? Fortunately, our fears were soon allayed as the denizen of the sylvan hut made her appearance. If Agathe had been obviously willing and eager, what words are at my disposal to describe the vision that greeted us now? Gislebertus need look no further for inspiration to depict the vice of lust; here was a walking occasion of sin. Her body spilled out of clothes designed to display her wares rather than cover them, especially her breasts. Her face was not beautiful in the ordinary sense, but she had a look about her that indicated an extreme sensitivity to and desire of sexual pleasure. Even if I could draw, I would not be able to represent the lustful excesses of her face, particularly of her nostrils and her mouth. She was made for fucking, there is no other way to say it. Our relief that the hut was not a robbers' den but rather the dwelling of such a slut caused us all to burst into laughter, which did not seem to frighten Jehanne—for that was her name—at all, but rather to cheer her. She seemed half-witted, poor thing, and all the more appealing to Anselm and Marcel for it. Gislebertus conceded to these two, who were ready to abandon their mission to Cluny for ten minutes with the wench, that we four—Gianni, Gérard, and he and I—could afford a leisurely pace until such time as the two could rejoin our group. I claimed a sense of loyalty to Clémence although in truth I am not tempted by idiots, spawn of Satan, I say; Gérard could not bear stench and the woman stank; Gianni also invoked loyalty to a sweetheart, but I suspect him of the Greek perversion; and Gislebertus made the most outlandish excuse of all: fornication is a sin! So we four continued our journey to Cluny, while Anselm and Marcel tarried along the way.

We had been walking for about half an hour when we were again affrighted, this time by sounds of crashing through the bushes, sounds that were approaching rapidly. We quickly climbed trees that were fortunately nearby and suited for our purposes. Our surprise was great to see the amorous twosome and we dropped from our sheltering branches. At first, Anselm and Marcel, red-faced and confused, refused to discuss their adventure. When they finally confessed, it became obvious that the harlot Jehanne's hovel was indeed the robbers' lair, that she was a lure for their victims, and that she was crafty, not stupid. It was furthermore clear to us that Anselm had gotten nothing and that bare-assed Marcel had had to flee with his breeches around his ankles, so suddenly did the brigands pounce upon them. Their very poverty saved them. When the robbers discovered my colleagues' penury, in their rage they turned their fury upon Jehanne and her cries were echoing in my friends' ears as they made their escape. I do believe neither Anselm nor Marcel will ever wear a ring.

But these events of this third day were as nothing when, at sunset, we first caught sight of the wondrous Abbey of Saints Peter and Paul. Gislebertus' hand is everywhere evident. The glorious tympanum of the church brings tears to my eyes. Can Christ Himself be more beautiful than his image on this façade? I was desperately anxious to advance into the church for a glimpse of Gislebertus' capitals, but he insisted that we await Abbot Pierre, who hastened to greet us with the Brother Almoner. The Father Hosteller would have seen to our needs, as befitted our status, but he was grievously ill and unable to leave his bed. Gislebertus and the Abbot fell upon each other's neck as long-lost brethren who had not conversed in ages. Gislebertus makes a trip to Cluny every two years ostensibly to advise those now responsible for the *œuvre*, but clearly also to see his great friend Pierre.

From the church we were conducted to our room in the lay brothers' quarters; I would have liked to linger, but Brother Almoner Germanus needed to show us to our lodging in time for him to chant Vespers with his fellow monks. And Abbot Pierre had to leave us for the same reason. He scarcely had time to invite us to dine with him in the Abbot's palace before he was off to his prayers. Our quarters were quite comfortable. The lay brothers' dormitory is long and wide; there is a decent space between beds and adequate room under them for our possessions. Construction has been going on here for so long, there is a shed filled with the finest in masons' and stone carvers' equipment that is now a permanent fixture of this Abbey. The storehouse is just across from our quarters, near the Abbot's palace and not too far from the church. So we were well situated for our task. We were also housed very near the latrines, which did not stink too much.

The beckoning of sleep causes me now to cease writing. Blaise and Marthe are visiting her sister for the Christmas season. They are able to continue their work there, for Marthe's sister, Clothilde, is also a seamstress. This means I am alone in the house and can write without fear of discovery. I must replace the store of candles, for at times I write far into the night and Blaise would not understand why his store of candles is so diminished. Until tomorrow…

The first night we spent at Cluny was taken with feasting with the Abbot. The dinner he had ordered for us was fit for a king, with two kinds of meat, fowl and pork, and even a sweet dessert at the end. Abbot Pierre's dwelling is most fine, all of stone like the rest of the Abbey, and hung with beautiful tapestries and all sorts of treasures given him by various grateful clients. To my astonishment he keeps about the place a freak worthy of Gislebertus and his woman, a hunchbacked dwarf who serves his table and is obliged to hold dishes on top of his head so that people at table can serve themselves. Pierre explained to us that Steven the dwarf was left on the church steps and, like all the other foundlings, was simply incorporated into the life of the monastery. Many of these abandoned children eventually join the ranks of monks, but some leave and others stay as lay workers. Steven had become so attached to the abbot, voluntary departure was unthinkable and ejecting him would have been cruel beyond the abbot's capability. As Steven is both dim-witted and ill-tempered, Pierre keeps him about as a penance. His face will grace a church someday—as that of the devil! Pierre also told us that soon the abbey would have to refuse any further oblates and try to place abandoned children with families as Cluny is running out of space for all those the charity of Cluny attracts. Steven's parents must have been sorely tempted to rid the world of such as he. I wonder if he wants to exist or if at times he sees what God has denied him and wishes to do away with himself. How loathsome to be a burden to others…

The first full day we spent at Cluny was occupied with learning our way around, where we could venture and what was forbidden territory to us, what we were expected to accomplish and where the instruments of our labors were stored. I was yearning to return to the glorious tympanum. When we arrived, I had gotten the merest glimpse of the most famous sculpture in Christendom and tearing my eyes from it was torture. Instead of Christ in Glory, I was faced with mere humans and their irritating mansuetude and fawning obsequiousness. After dinner with the abbot, on that first night, I was able to return to the tympanum and observe it by moonlight, but clouds kept frustrating me, hiding the face of God from my view. The next day I had to follow Gislebertus and my colleagues while we learned what was expected of us. Finally, in late afternoon, while the abbot was occupied with a group of important pilgrims who had just arrived from Normandy and Gislebertus was deep in conversation with the monk in charge of the fabric, I was able to slip away and examine the sculpture at leisure.

How immense it seemed and how brilliantly its colors shone! Christ on his throne in a mandorla supported by two angels with the signs of the blessed evangelists all around, this will be the image of the future and all sculptors will seek to imitate it. At dinner the night we arrived, Abbot Pierre expressed alarm at the intrusion of the Cathar heresy into the very bosom of the Church. Some of his brethren have shown an inclination for this most peculiar teaching that attacks the priesthood and the Eucharist, claiming that the Holy Benedict himself preferred his "brothers" to his "fathers." Pierre wants Gislebertus to proclaim these holy mysteries in his sculpture wherever possible. Jesus and his apostles must raise the right hand in blessing after the manner of priests.
End of attachment.

The material that follows the above is a commentary on Thomas' ms. I'll save that for a later mail or your mailbox will explode.

How are your sessions with Ruth going? W

30 March 2004
From: fractal@netconnect.net
To: gold.digger@netconnect.net

My sessions with Ruth are exhausting and I can't see much progress. I lie down and attempt to think of nothing, as she directed. Do you know how hard it is to think of nothing, to make the mind go blank? If I get relaxed enough, I begin to fall asleep and then I begin to dream, which is not the same thing as remembering. The text you're sending is fabulous, great for getting my mind off of my troubles. I'll read the next installment with relish. What goes through my mind as I read, especially Thomas' narrative, is how little human nature has changed in eight hundred years. We're all just as petty, just as jealous, manipulative and devious. You'd think we might have improved morally and emotionally in that time span…

Ruth is poking around in New Orleans, trying to get some answers from the house on Dauphine Street. I don't know why she thinks the guy who lives there will be any more cooperative with her than he was with me. Oh, I must let you know I've given her your e-mail address. I have no idea what she'll ask you, but it's okay with me if you open up to her and tell her anything she wants to know.

She's also going to talk to Mother's former colleagues in the hope they'll be more forthright with someone trying to help me than they were with me. If Mother was a bitch or a nut, they'll be more likely to admit it to her than to say that to my face. She may have explained her aversion to me to one of them. Somehow, though, I can't see her indulging in girl talk with any of those people. No one there seemed to know her very well. She showed up, taught her classes, and left. The woman of mystery…

I haven't written lately about the delights of my new home. I've definitely decided to put down roots here. The city is charming, and this house and property are full of peace and beauty. A while ago, the azaleas were in bloom until a fierce storm beat them all to hell. And the Cherokee Rose was as spectacular as I had been led to expect. It also fell victim to the tempest. The wisteria managed to hang on. If I remain here, the rhythm of the seasons will become part of my mindset and I'll know when to expect what delights. Ruben has been taking me out on the river with some frequency. Every time I broach the subject that's consuming me, he clams up. He's a kind man so I suspect he thinks he's protecting me from something dreadful. We pass the mystery house every time we go out. It remains as it was, shuttered, brooding, hermetically sealed to the outside world. Like my mother after the accident… Like my mind that won't give up its memories of pre-accident baggage… In the yard, there are sprouting pines and yaupon bushes and other foliage, that happen to be in the proximity of climbing vines. These vines are covered with thorns and are incredibly tenacious. Once they latch on to something, it takes brute force and a willingness to get scratched to force them to release their prey. Sometimes a pine sapling is bent nearly double since it continues to grow while the vine holds it close to the ground. When I release the little tree, I can almost hear it say thanks. I feel that way sometimes, bent and twisted, strangled, constrained by something I can't even identify. Oh, and we have fireflies!!! Or lightning bugs as they're called in the south. When all the lights in the house are turned out and I look out into the woods, it is as if a million tiny flashlights are going on and off. It's like an all-encompassing Christmas tree… Breathtaking. How I wish you could see it. The last time I saw them was at the Bay. Then along came DDT and that was the end of that. As I recall, we used to catch them and put them in jars. How cruel that was, but what do kids think about cruelty? I also used to catch mosquito hawks and once I pulled one's wings off just to see what it would do. When I think back on that, I'm so ashamed. What was I thinking? The other day, I saw a wasp chewing off the head of a mosquito hawk. I killed them both. I hate wasps and the mosquito hawk was a goner anyway, so at least I had the pleasure of destroying the wasp and putting the mosquito hawk out of its misery. Louisiana's pelicans are also back in force. We occasionally spot a manatee or two in the lake. Slowly but surely, my affection for this part of the country is returning. Now that it's not suffused with parental quarrels and frustrated hopes and dreams…

Ruth is coming here in a few days. She wants to explore my surroundings, see if she can get anything out of Celestine and/or Ruben, and check out this piece of furniture bewitching me. If I know Ruth, she's going to get in the armoire herself to replicate my experience. Perhaps she'll make a discovery, something that totally escaped my notice. Or she'll think of a question that will start a ball rolling. She's already dredged up a lot of childhood stuff I hadn't thought about for ages. I told her about "Mug" and "Wump"; I know those are our secret names but assumed you wouldn't mind under the circumstances. I need to tell her everything, as much as possible about me if she's to have any success. I feel better just having her to talk to. Of course, having you here would be better. I wouldn't have to explain so much to you. In fact, a conversation among the three of us would be most illuminating.

How are Thomas and Gislebertus and Casilda and the rest of the gang at Autun?

Love, M

31 March 2004
From: ruth.blanchard@psychnet.org
To: Cletus.Hardin@psychnet.org
Dear Cletus,

I've been doing some digging into the accident around which this entire affair revolves and will give you what details I've been able to unearth. The exact date of the incident was April 5, 1950. The police were notified by an anonymous phone call at 2:57 a.m. The call allegedly came from a phone booth at a gas station about two miles north of the accident, which occurred on River Road one half mile south of the junction of River Road and Highway 25. The caller was never identified; in fact, the call itself remains rather mysterious. There is not now, nor has there ever been, a record of this call on the police log. The officers responding to the alleged call were then Police Chief Joe Bernhardt, whom I remember as an old pirate, and a very young officer, Guy Favre, who is now seventy-six but still quite sharp. He has, or seems to have, very clear memories of the incident. He still has serious doubts about the accuracy of the official report drafted by Bernhardt, and there are numerous questions that have remained unanswered. He tried to get clarification for his own peace of mind, but doors were slammed in his face whenever he attempted to probe into the affair. His principal question is why the chief involved himself in a car accident that happened in the wee hours of the morning. This is precisely the sort of job meted out to grunts, especially since it was a one-car accident and seemed very straightforward. Favre supposes Bernhardt was involved because he was in Parker Walmsley's pocket, like every other politician in town. In any case, Bernhardt himself called Favre and asked his junior colleague to accompany him to the scene. Favre offered to meet him there but Bernhardt insisted on picking him up, an action that delayed their arrival, another peculiarity. When they got to the site, an ambulance was waiting and a medic was inside, tending to the occupants of the vehicle. The car had crashed into a tree, demolishing the passenger side and doing serious damage to the driver side, but not enough to kill the driver, identified as Joanna Walmsley. Favre had the distinct impression that Bernhardt didn't want him anywhere near the vehicle and, to that end, ordered him to stand watch for oncoming cars to prevent them from rear-ending the semi-demolished car, part of which was protruding into the street. River Road makes a sharp curve just before the accident site, and even though it was 3:15 a.m. before Bernhardt and Favre arrived, there was a possibility of traffic on the road. Favre confirms that Malachi was in the car; he rolled off the back seat onto the floor at the moment of impact and was insulated from serious injury by that fact and by the size of the vehicle, a big Buick. He saw him bundled into the ambulance but did not see the two other passengers. Since Parker was out of town, and Celestine did not live with the family at that time, no one was ever able to find a reasonable explanation for this wee-hours excursion involving an eight-year-old no less. Why Joanna would be driving around at that time and in that area with her son and a brother she didn't like remains a question that only Malachi may be able to answer, and only after a lot of delicate prodding of his memory. And of course, we have only Bernhardt's word to Favre that Joanna was driving. I must get Malachi to recall as much of the time period preceding the accident as possible and, of course, the accident itself.

In 1950, Saint Tammany Parish was very rural and very much in Parker Walmsley's control. The way Favre tells it, Parker had carte blanche in every conceivable sort of activity. He bought up huge swaths of riverbank and developed them with no care for permits or land use restrictions, if indeed there were any in his day. If what he did caused flooding elsewhere, tough luck for elsewhere. He was utterly ruthless. It will be instructive to meet him, even if his personality is gone along with most of his mind.

What remains before my trip to AZ is a visit to Malachi's house, and a grilling of the servants. Celestine and Ruben both know more than they're telling Malachi. I also plan to have him get into the armoire while I ask what I hope will be questions that jog his memory. He's already tried this on his own, but with no one to prod him, the experiment failed.

I'm feeling an increasing urgency to act as Malachi seems to be regressing—he's not sleeping and is getting quite edgy. At times, I wish Joanna had just left her house and her fortune to some charity. If she meant this bequest as a last gesture of kindness to her neglected and abandoned son, something to make up for years of emotional frigidity, she failed.

I'll let you know how the continuation of this attempt at sleuthing goes. Ruth

2 April 2004
From: ruth.blanchard@psychnet.org
To: gold.digger@netconnect.net
Dear Dr. Hauser,

I am currently working with Malachi W… in an attempt to help him overcome feelings of anxiety and depression that have plagued him since an accident that occurred in 1950. He has informed me that he's written to you, giving you permission to reveal whatever you see fit; hence, the use of initials. I assume you know of whom I speak.

It is my understanding that you have known him since that time and that he has been in sustained contact with you. The farther back we can go, the better. His memory of life before the accident, and of the accident itself, is an almost blank slate.

I realize fully that you are involved in a research project and that every minute given to me is taken from your work. I will understand if either your project or your personal preference prevents you from responding. However, any bits of information, no matter how trivial they may seem, could be extremely helpful and will be kept confidential insofar as possible. I may need to refer to what you write in order to further Malachi's progress towards recovery. References to your feelings towards him will be kept confidential. If anything you write must be kept off the table, you have only to indicate this to me and your wishes will be respected. I will attempt to use this sort of information in an oblique fashion to avoid betraying your confidence. Be aware that I am not a mental health professional and any information I receive may be required by the police should there be determination of a crime.

I thank you in advance for your assistance and will accept unquestioningly your declining to divulge information about Malachi. Please do acknowledge receipt of this e-mail.

Yours sincerely, Ruth Blanchard

5 April 2004
From: ruth.blanchard@psychnet.org
To: Cletus.Hardin@psychnct.org
Dear Cletus,

As I wrote the date, I realized it's an anniversary of the accident, the 54th.

I have contacted Malachi's friend in France and am still awaiting an acknowledgment of her receipt of my letter.

Yesterday I visited Malachi's house and managed to get a few moments with Celestine. Malachi knew what I was up to and tactfully made himself scarce so I could probe the old servant's mind in relative peace. What is obvious is that she adores Malachi and would like to help, but her memories are hazy at best. What Malachi took for hostility in Celestine is really concern with his return to the scene of so much pain, and fear that Malachi will be distressed or harmed again. Celestine is of the all too common opinion that the past, especially the evil or hurtful past, should stay buried. It took me a while to convince her otherwise; I had to relate some of Malachi's history of depression, nightmares, inability to sleep peacefully, etc. It wasn't really news to Celestine as she's witnessed Malachi's decline since she's been here. But she's also seen Malachi improve after his sessions with me and I think the old woman finally trusts me. She believes I'm here to help, not because I'm nosy or looking to stir up trouble. However, I have the same problems with her as with M: determining if what she allegedly remembers is real or a dream or simply truth distorted by the passage of time. She confirms Malachi's description of his parents' marriage as shaky and cold. But she adds considerable depth to the relationship between Parker and Buddy. She describes it as "not right." When I asked for clarification, she indicated that they liked each other the way a man and a woman like each other, "lovey-dovey like." This goes a long, long way towards explaining the dynamics among that trio. If Celestine picked up on a homosexual attraction between Parker and Buddy, surely Joanna did also. And if Joanna fussed and hounded Parker about it yet stayed in the marriage for whatever reason, she would have become increasingly difficult to live with and wretchedly unhappy. She would also have been concerned for Malachi. But from all accounts, Parker was as selfish as they come and would not have cared what anyone thought. It's entirely possible that he married Joanna for her brother! When Joanna squawked, he'd just turn the volume down and go about his business. Speaking of his business, I have yet to determine what he did for his dough.

I asked Celestine about the mysterious house further down river, the one that troubles Malachi so much. It's tied in with the rest of this mystery, I know it. What went on in this household??? As Celestine grows to trust me, perhaps she'll give up her secrets. She's protecting Malachi, or so she thinks. Perhaps Buddy molested Malachi, and Celestine believes that this realization would push Malachi over the edge. I also want to explore with you the possibility that Malachi is blocking the memory of something *he* did wrong, of some evil deed eating away at his conscience and destroying any possibility of psychic wholeness. It's been my (limited) experience that the most troubled people are those who themselves did something so shameful, they'd rather be half alive than face what they did. Malachi seems to be a charming man. Have we not seen very attractive sociopaths? We'll have to discuss these things.

I'm so looking forward to my visit to Arizona. I've been so submerged in Malachi's Faulknerian melodrama, I really need a break. And it will be good to see you also.

Ruth

12 April 2004
From: gold.digger@netconnect.net
To: ruth.blanchard@psychnet.org
Dear Ms. Blanchard,

I'll be happy to give you a hand with Malachi. I've known and loved him for a long time, and will do anything I can to help.

We met in first or second grade but didn't become close friends until the summer of 1950. I believe that was right after the accident that killed his uncle. I'm sure he's given you all the minutiae of our relationship, so I'll concentrate on him, what he's like, what makes him tick and so forth.

I remember him as a sad child. Even when he smiled, there was a depth of melancholy about his eyes; the smile didn't reach them. He spent a great deal of time at our house on de Montluzin Street in Bay St. Louis, even called my mother "Mom2." At the time, his own mother was in a hospital in California and his father was extremely preoccupied, traveling to the west coast every few weeks and tending to business in New Orleans. I have no idea what he did for a living; I only know it must have been lucrative since the family was extremely wealthy. During that summer we became fast friends. When we returned to school in the fall, we remained close. Neither one of us was particularly popular with our classmates. We were both rather homely but very bright, what you'd call nerdy today. We got picked on for showing up our less intellectually endowed schoolmates. We remained in close touch until Malachi moved to Flagstaff. Then, as these things go, we corresponded less and less. But the quality of the relationship was unchanged. I feel as though I could walk into a room, sit down with Mug—I know he's told you of our names for each other—and we could pick up exactly where we left off. He's confided to me the difficulties with his marriage, his recurrent nightmares and bouts of depression. I've talked him out of suicidal thoughts at least three times; I have no idea how many actual attempts he's made or how many times he's had to struggle with the temptation. I can also tell you he didn't like his uncle Buddy or the fact that he lived with them. From my perspective as an adult, I suppose I could suspect sexual molestation, but I never got that feeling when we were together. His complaints always centered on his mother's dissatisfaction with the living arrangements. Malachi was afraid Buddy would break up the marriage. I don't know how he felt about his father as he seldom spoke of him. Awe at his wealth and power, fear that he would leave his mother who clearly needed him, desire that he would pay more attention to his son—these are the only emotional responses I discerned. I never had the sense that he loved his father or that he felt loved by him. In fact, if he and Joanna could have survived without him, he probably would have been just as glad to see his parents split up. However, parental divorce is traumatic even when the relationship is defective in the extreme, as Joanna and Parker's was.

Malachi has indicated he'd like to come to France for a visit. Encourage this. It would do both of us a world of good. He'd be able to be in touch with you via e-mail and we do have telephones should any emergency arise. I sense that he's fairly stable now and capable of taking care of himself while I'm off digging.

That's all I have to offer now. If you have any questions about what I've written or anything else for that matter, please ask.

Best, Winifred Hauser.

13 April 2004
From: ruth.blanchard@psychnet.org
To: gold.digger@netconnect.net
Dear Dr. Hauser,

Thank you for your response. It both confirmed what I'd already gleaned from conversations with Malachi and added a bit to the big picture. I realize I'm asking you about events that took place more than fifty years ago. However, if something is dramatic or important enough, it will remain with you. Whether anything Malachi said or did fits that category for you is another question and I do know I'm seeking a miracle.

I'm wondering if I may impose further on your clear concern for your friend. A key to his emotional state seems to be an event or events he experienced or witnessed from an armoire in his mother's bedroom. If you could shed any light on that, it would be most helpful. It would have occurred shortly before the accident. However, my impression is that the event was so traumatic, he would have kept it to himself, perhaps even denied its factual element. He may have referred to it in an oblique fashion. If you could search your memory for any hint of this, I'd be keen to hear anything you have to reveal. It may be a word he said, something that startled him in school, something that would not normally cause anyone alarm, a sudden aversion to a person, a place, an object—anything out of the ordinary during that time period. We generally reveal what is most emotionally significant without meaning or wanting to, and I'm not referring solely to what is commonly called a Freudian slip. I'm looking for an involuntary and spontaneous reaction to *something* or *someone*. Anything you can offer along these lines would be most helpful and appreciated.

I will indeed encourage Malachi to visit you, perhaps while I'm in the West trying to gather information from his father. I think that would be better than having him here alone with the servants.

Again, thank you for your time and attention.

All best, Ruth

14 April 2004
From: ruth.blanchard@psychnet.org
To: Cletus.Hardin@psychnet.org
Dear Cletus,

I've written to Malachi's friend, W. H. She responded but didn't give me much more than I already had. I've asked her specifically about that damned armoire and if it figured in anything Malachi may have told her. She's eager for Mal to visit her in France. I think this would be helpful and very good for his state of mind. As the French say, travel changes one's ideas.

I'm looking forward to seeing you and making the acquaintance of the west. Have you any idea when Parker might move into a phase of lucidity? I can leave with twenty-four hours notice.

While I'm waiting, I'll spend some more time with Malachi and hope for a response from his friend.

More later when I have something to report.

Best, Ruth

15 April 2004
From: gold.digger@netconnect.net
To: ruth.blanchard@psychnet.org
Dear Ruth,

I'm up to my elbows (literally) in work but did remember one odd thing about the "armoire" episode. Malachi told me about getting locked in the thing several years after it happened and indicated his mother was screaming the name "Herbert." He asked his mother about this person but Joanna claimed to have no recollection of the event, knew no person named Herbert and didn't know what Malachi was talking about. I let the matter drop and have never brought this up again so am clueless about this Herbert. Maybe the name will jog Mal's memory. W

16 April 2004
From: gold.digger@netconnect.net
To: fractal@netconnect.net
Dear Mug,

I connected with Ruth and told her of the name "Herbert" involved in your armoire episode. Does that ring a bell with you? Ruth seems nice and I believe she will help you. Pay attention to her directives; she has your best interests at heart.

In the meantime, when you're suffering from insomnia, turn your sleepless eyes to this text of Thomas. It's quite mesmerizing:

Attachment to mail dated 16 April 2004:

It is very cold tonight in Autun as Christmas approaches. How odd it is that when I write it is as if I were sculpting. The house is very still and the night, dark. I feel alone in the world. No one will ever see this manuscript. It is for me. I am alone, writing for myself—unless, of course, I need to make public the information I have acquired about Gislebertus. When I am at work, I am creating an image for someone else according to someone else's instructions, yet the image is also mine and is of me in a way I cannot fathom. But Gislebertus does not see me in my image, just what he has ordered me to depict. I alone see myself in my images just as I alone see what I have written on these pages. All art is for the artist. If others look, they are intruders blundering onto the scene, utterly uncomprehending, gawking with amazement at what they in fact do not perceive. No one will see this text save me because I am the only one who could understand it. My text and I know each other. It comforts me. I will write my life as long as I live.

Bishop Étienne has invited all the workers to dine with the chapter on Christmas day. I will feast with the others, then return to my writing.

...

After the first two days at Cluny, which are etched on my mind since all was new and strange, all other days blend into one: a three-month stretch of work punctuated with some amusements. In the rectangle formed by the new narthex, the L-shaped stables and the Abbot's palace, we worked. It was pleasant and convenient to leave one's domicile and be instantly at the *chantier*. The sound of our hammers and chisels was in constant competition with the monks' singing, which is incessant. We were making permanent templates for others to follow should any of the sculpture be damaged. Abbot Pierre is determined that Saints Peter and Paul Abbey be eternal. Even as we were leaving the monastery—was it just a week ago?—he was instructing Gislebertus on what he wanted at his next visit, which will be no sooner than two years hence. It is as though Pierre wants Gislebertus to create unceasingly lest someone called Bernard prevail. What does anyone care what the monks do with their abbey? Why would anyone object to sculpture, especially of holy people?

Perhaps there is one day after the first two that does indeed stand out. Ghislaine of Normandy arrived. I was working on carving a bunch of grapes when a shadow fell across my hands. I assumed it was Gislebertus or one of the monks come to check on my progress or to see if I was carrying out my instructions to the letter. "You are in my light," I growled. I was hot and thirsty, and sweat was making its way into my eyes; it was still and very warm even though we were well into September. The shadow moved and I continued working. About a quarter of an hour later, when I arose from my rather cramped position, I turned to face the source of the shadow, who was still there watching me. A beauty, a marvel, indescribable, a face any imager would die to create—or recreate. This heavenly creature said, in a voice I will always remember, "My name is Ghislaine and I have been watching you work." No matter that she was older than I, I determined then and there to have her. I saw very clearly that, even were she to deny it to herself, that was what she wanted, that was the purpose of her presence in the work yard. Even terribly bored gentlewomen do not find a stone carver's work exciting. I could also tell she was the sort who needed convincing that love, even adulterous, is heaven-sent, figuring somehow in God's grand scheme of things, and that the depths of love can wash away all sin. She was apt to swoon with secret delight at the saga of Peter Abelard and Heloïse. I knew I would have her, but I had to proceed with caution. First and foremost, I had to convince her absolutely that I was uninterested, unattainable, awash in indifference. I yawned, stretched, mumbled something about the necessities of life, and headed in the direction of the latrines. They were located at the south end of our quarters. In the night, I was grateful to be lodged where we were. As it turned out, the latrines were strategically located for another purpose, but more of that later. I left Ghislaine that day standing next to a carving of grapes; when I returned from my business, she had gone. I knew she would return.

End of attachment.

It's getting late and my eyes are very tired from translating and transcribing all this material. Some of the words are so faded, I use a magnifying glass to try to make them out and sometimes I just have to infer what an indecipherable word might be.

More later—but soon. W

20 April 2004

From: ruth.blanchard@psychnet.org

To: Cletus.Hardin@psychnet.org

EUREKA!!! At last, a breakthrough, and a big one.

Winifred gave me a tip about the armoire incident, and it unlocked a major portion of Malachi's memory of that aspect of his troubled past. Apparently Malachi told W that his mother had been shouting for someone named Herbert during the episode, so I decided to try something. I had Malachi close himself up in the armoire exactly as he had that afternoon and then I came into the room screaming "Herbert." At this point, two things happened more or less simultaneously. Malachi turned and looked out through the crack by the door hinge and Celestine came running into the room. Malachi began to yell "Two mommies," and Celestine began to moan and cry about letting bygones be bygones. I pulled a trembling Malachi out of the armoire and calmed him down. He then remembered what he'd been blocking for so long: he saw two versions of his mother that afternoon. Celestine filled in the rest when she realized it was useless to attempt to protect Malachi from the truth any longer. Joanna had come upon her brother in a wig identical to her own hair, preparing to have sex with Parker and had screamed "pervert," which, to a child, sounded like "Herbert." *Pervert* was not part of Malachi's vocabulary at the tender age of eight, not in 1950 at least. Unfortunately every eight-year-old today knows what a pervert is… But Celestine did, and took in the whole scene: Joanna screaming at her husband and her brother; Parker trying to calm her down; Buddy, in full drag and make-up, whimpering, "He made me do it"; both men swearing to Joanna that it would never happen again; Joanna threatening to go to the police, get a divorce. Celestine and Buddy both made a quick get-away and no one knows what then transpired between Parker and Joanna. Malachi was in a closed-in space with his eyes shut and his hands over his ears. That, he remembers now. And all thanks to W's memory of one word. I must write to W immediately and let her know what mysteries she's unlocked, what help she's given us all.

In any case, this solves a large portion of the mystery. All of the tension, all of the negativity in the household were the result of the affair between Parker and Buddy, who was, by inclination or by economic necessity, Parker's lover. What Malachi saw through the crack was, first, Buddy pass by on his way to Parker's bed; since he was wearing "Joanna" hair, he assumed it was his mother. Since Malachi was, by his own admission, sexually precocious and, as a child, naturally curious about such things, he assumed he'd hear, if not see clearly, the goings-on of his parents. By twisting around a bit, he might have been able to get a better view of the episode. However, the lovers and their little *voyeur* were interrupted by the screams of Joanna, who was supposed to be out for the afternoon but returned for something she'd forgotten. Malachi was so terrified of being discovered, he remained in the armoire till long after things had quieted down. He was not locked in but hidden. And that's where Celestine found him when she went looking for the child at dinnertime. Celestine suspected Malachi had taken in the whole episode, but Malachi seemed normal, unaffected by it all, so Celestine and Joanna decided to pretend nothing had happened. A few months later, Buddy was conveniently killed in the accident and all was buried under a mound of silence. Neither Celestine nor Joanna ever spoke of it again.

Malachi is still shaken by the memory now so I'll let it percolate a few days before going into the episode in depth. We'll see if that's all there was or is to it. If the dreams stop and all seems well, case closed. But I strongly suspect there's more beneath this layer. Parker was evidently bisexual, probably using the "mystery" house on the river and the place on Dauphine Street as houses of assignation. Malachi may have surprised him at the river house or even actively sought evidence of his practices. As for his aversion to the French Quarter house, perhaps the sight or scent of the place was enough to make him shudder. I can't bear to think that Parker pimped out his own son although this is a possibility I'll have to face.

Despite this seeming success, a few questions remain and Malachi will decide my future course of action. There's something not quite right, not entirely settled about all this. No matter what, I'd still love to come for a visit and I definitely want to discuss this development with Parker if the occasion presents itself. Besides, I need a break from this southern gothic melodrama!

See you soon. R

21 April 2004
From: Cletus.Hardin@psychnet.org
To: ruth.blanchard@psychnet.org
Can't be soon enough for me. Look forward to seeing you. C

22 April 2004
From: gold.digger@netconnect.net
To: fractal@netconnect.net
Mug, No news, just more text. As I transcribe, I might as well send it to you.
Love, W

Attachment to mail dated 22 April 2004

It was later that day that Gislebertus gave Gérard a task that should have been mine. Gérard's progress, under my tutelage, came under Gislebertus' notice and he began using him, in my opinion, in ways far beyond his capacity. Faces are always a challenge for the chisel. To Gérard were entrusted copies of the faces of Adam and Eve on a capital in the apse hemicycle, an important image in a conspicuous place. His copies will be used should the originals ever be damaged. I wonder if Gérard asked for this charge or if the Master simply preferred his work to mine. I decided that day to bide my time and watch for signs of my being cast aside in favor of my own apprentice.

I determined that the way to information was through the Brother Almoner Germanus. Since the Father Hosteller was ill during the entire duration of our stay at Cluny, Brother Germanus saw to the needs of all guests, workers, pilgrims and paupers alike. Germanus was easy to know and easy to mine for gossip. He was pleasant, almost obsequious, on the surface, but the set of his jaw when anyone, even the abbot, gave him an order indicated to me a man ill at ease with obedience and deeply resentful of his betters. It was the simplest thing in the world to flatter him into frightful indiscretions. He had been a partisan of the former abbot, Pons of Melgueil, in his struggles with Pierre and with Rome over the direction Cluny should take in 1120 and years following. Abbot Pons, a saint according to Germanus, was ousted by Pierre on the false claim that Pons had spent too much money on the decoration of the abbey. In truth, Pons was just trying to provide work for the poor laborers of the area, including Gislebertus, who then shamefully refused to support Pons, his benefactor in former years. Ever since then, Germanus had resented Pierre, even while vowing obedience to him, and loyalty and fidelity to his abbey. For Germanus, deference to Pierre was a mask. The worst insult to Germanus was the naming of one Savin of Saint-Martin-des-Champs as Grand Prior of Cluny, a position that was rightfully Germanus' by reason of seniority, a position given to Savin solely because he was a priest and Germanus, a brother. From the moment of Savin's taking of his new position, Germanus determined to destroy him. A vengeful, jealous man is the most malleable creature on earth. I realized that his good services were mine for the taking. I could get what I wanted from him by allowing him to believe that he was using me. The first bit of useful information he conveyed was that the Duke's men were frequently billeted at Cluny; if and when the need arose, they would be quite interested in the servile status of one Gérard of Autun. Germanus was useful in another way, but I must first continue with another aspect of my existence at Cluny.

I was correct in my surmise. I had caught Ghislaine's attention. She found a thousand reasons for our paths to cross. The day after the one on which we met, she attempted to stroll casually through the work yard, which did, after all, lie right on the path between the women's guest quarters and the latrines. But I could feel her eyes upon me and deliberately avoided taking any notice of her. I would make my move the next day. Germanus informed me that she spent mid-morning exploring the choir and the narthex of the old church. What could be more natural for a stone carver than to examine the work of his predecessors? I would observe her for a while to assess correctly her frame of mind. A woman like Ghislaine must believe that she is loved, that it is fated and that God approves.

I succeeded admirably. As I had planned, we chanced upon each other in the narthex of the old church. She truly was a lovely creature, about thirty-five in years, slender with exquisite hands. She and Hugh, her husband, were on pilgrimage to Compostela on a quest for some favor or in gratitude for a favor granted. Ghislaine never told me exactly what she sought from God, but apparently adultery was compatible with supplication. Although considering Ghislaine's state, I do not believe she gave much thought to logic or morality. How impossibly easy it was to seduce her. In fact, I think the woman thought she seduced me, led me astray. The second time we met, we progressed to discreet and rather timid touching. It was all very dangerous in this closed world of the abbey. Neither Ghislaine nor I had any reason whatsoever to absent ourselves from the world of Saints Peter and Paul, which became for us a microcosm and a prison. It was very simple to hide from the monks, as they were at their chanting and praying all day, morning till night, and sometimes far into the night. The most deserted spot in all of the abbey was the exterior north side of the church, between the two arms of the double transept. We could hear anyone approaching and if we clung to the church wall, no prying eyes could see us from within the church. It was a most pleasant spot, cool and shady most of the time, the monks' hymns wafting over the autumn air. My mouth found hers and my hands strayed over her body, which seemed to me like a work of art, warm and moving. How odd it was, feeling flesh under my hands accustomed to unyielding stone. How often I had passed my hands over my carvings, which were cold and rigid. Real breasts are supple and warm, and react to my touch. No carving will ever capture and convey the response of a breast aroused by love. Describing it, as I am doing here, will help me remember what it was really like. I cannot carve it, no painter can paint it, and I am unable to write it

If such was ineffable, what will I write of the act? When union became an absolute, imperious need, a never-ending itch, all-consuming, we had to disconnect our bodies and think. We had to separate our mouths, our hands, and ponder the prosaic question of where we could fuck in safety. We each would explore the abbey for a spot and then, under cover of darkness, satisfy our longing. We needed a place where, if anyone happened to approach, we could be warned, then separate and have a plausible explanation for being there in the darkest hours of the night. The place we settled on was the deep wedge formed by the abbey wall and the latrines. If anyone approached, one of us could appear, claiming illness and not wishing to enter a latrine in a state of nausea, and the other could remain in the shadows. A night of a full moon was too risky, so for a few days Ghislaine and I had to content ourselves with frantic caresses that left us both in a state bordering madness. On the third day of unassuaged passion, we agreed not to meet until such time as we could lie together.

Germanus helped me pass the time. In a way, he was very much like Ghislaine, hovering around me, afraid of what he wanted from me but wanting it nonetheless. Ghislaine wanted my whole being; Germanus wanted my soul, or perhaps I should say "my wit." He began by pretending to examine my work as he passed by the workyard on his way to Terce, Sext or Nones. He actually had about as much appreciation of my work as the geese in the barnyard. He was, furthermore, the Brother Almoner and, as such, frequented the building almost directly opposite our lodgings and forming one of the borders of the work yard. He also had charge of the ill Father Hosteller's guests and was thus able to provide me with information useful in my pursuit of Ghislaine, who was in his immediate care. I first responded to his attentions because I knew he could be useful. Little did I know he had similar designs on me. I am skilled at dissembling; but Germanus could read my mind. My interest in Ghislaine, which he interpreted correctly as far from casual, came exploding through my words, betrayed by my face, my eyes that could not meet his scrutiny. He seemed oddly disappointed when I abandoned questions about Hugh, on whom I had fixed my attention at first to hide my true interest, and concentrated instead on Hugh's wife. I assumed that he was ill at ease with the possibility of suborning adulterous desires, but I soon found out that morality was of scant concern to him. He had thought, because of my clumsily urgent queries about Hugh, that I was one of those men who love men. He needed that for his plan. Even after he was disabused of that notion, he still harbored hopes of using me. End of attachment.

It's getting late and my eyes aren't as young as they used to be. I'm using them up fast, poring over this text and trying so hard to make letters out. I'm dying to know how all this will end but I just can't go on and must go to sleep. As I decipher and transcribe, you'll receive the fruits of my labors.

W

23 April 2004
From: fractal@netconnect.net
To: gold.digger@netconnect.net
Dear Wump,

Thanks much for the continuing tale of Thomas. I wonder if he was as wretched as I am

Well, part of the mystery of my past is solved. You provided the key to unlocking my memory of the whole episode by mentioning "Herbert" to Ruth. How to begin my sad saga…? This is as much of the tale as I can put together. I used to spy on my parents by hiding in the armoire in their bedroom. The door didn't close completely, the furniture being old and somewhat warped. By peering through the crack by the hinge, I could see a slice of the room. But I was most interested in what I heard. Most of what I heard was parents fighting about my uncle. One day, I saw, first, my father, then my mother, come into the room and begin to disrobe. I was paralyzed with fright as this was much more than I had bargained for so I kept very still. I planned to wait out their lovemaking, then escape. Shortly after they were at it, my real mother—what I had seen before was Buddy in drag—surprised the twosome and began screaming "pervert" at the top of her lungs. Mother also began pummeling both of the men as they lay in bed. I was traumatized by what I had seen and heard, and probably would have remained there for a long, long time if Celestine hadn't waited for the din to die down and come looking for me. She knew about my affinity for the armoire, found me and spirited me away. The whole event was swept under the rug and everyone pretended it had never happened. Apparently the tension became unbearable for Mother, and the night ride with Buddy and me was probably a suicide attempt. She didn't want to leave me with my dad, so she decided to kill herself, me, and the brother she hated by now. The so-called accident had totally unintended consequences, as you know. She maimed herself, killed Buddy and traumatized me. Nothing that she wanted, except for Buddy's death, was accomplished.

In any case, I thought you'd be interested in knowing that you broke the case. "Herbert" was the "Open Sesame" of this soap opera that has plagued me for so long. I just hope I can heal in peace. Ruth still wants to talk to my father and is going to see him (and an old flame I suspect she still has a crush on) in hopes of finding a few lucid flickers in his aging skull.

I'm mulling over a divorce from Amanda and will remain in Covington for the foreseeable future.

How are things at the dig? I hope you find enough text to give us an ending to Thomas' narrative. Have you noticed that treachery and deception are at the root of his story and mine?

Love always, M

24 April 2004
From: gold.digger@netconnect.net
To: fractal@netconnect.net
Dear Mug,

I couldn't put down the text even though my eyes are rebelling. Here's more, as much as I could manage. Forgive me for giving you so little news. But Thomas' life was much more interesting than mine.

Attachment to mail dated 24 April 2004:

Germanus was a Poncian, a partisan of that former abbot of Cluny who died in disgrace and excommunicate in Rome, overthrown by his monks sickened by his abuse of funds and by his notions of being designated arch-abbot and by his zealous pursuit of all the perquisites attendant upon the position of abbot of the most powerful monastery in Christendom. Pons' principal opponent during the power struggle was precisely this Pierre who now sits upon the abbatial throne, naming Savin to the position that should be Germanus'. All of this took place several years ago. How hard a death does resentment from wounded pride die.

Germanus' determination to bring down his rival knew no bounds. Since he could find no fault in Savin, he decided to invent one. Suspecting that Savin was a man who loved men, he watched him carefully and surreptitiously in the presence of various comely young men, but never saw a hint of anything untoward. Nonetheless he was convinced that Savin was vulnerable. How else to entrap him other than to do just that—dangle bait under his nose and see his reaction? Germanus hatched a plan with Brother Jacob and Father Philippe, the Hosteller, before his illness. Someone they could trust should request an audience with Prior Savin on an urgent moral question with the intention of confessing and seeking absolution, someone young and beautiful—and male. This person was to describe in graphic detail a homosexual coupling, cleverly and carefully, so contritely, so sincerely, with weeping and breast-beating, but also with such lascivious content, that Savin, were he made of stone, would succumb. That he would not succumb did not seem to cross their minds. The one they chose to tempt Savin beyond all endurance was I. I objected that I had no idea what to say, having never been with a man in that way. Germanus and Jacob told me how to go about it, described what men do with men. I asked them how they knew so much. They insisted that such is the stuff of treatises on morality and that all monks, no matter how violently they are opposed to any contact, even through the ears, with such behavior, are obliged to learn of such comportment so as to avoid it utterly in their own lives. I then objected that leading a man into sin was itself a sin, but they assured me that once Abbot Pierre should learn what sort of vile creature was his prior, he would grant me not only absolution of my fraud but also a plenary indulgence for all my sins. They told me my eternal salvation was at stake, that if I had the opportunity to rid Cluny of such as Savin, I was obliged to do it. They told me that the worse the sin I could induce him to commit, the better would be the state of my soul. I resolved to follow their dictates. But I decided to wait until such time as I had had relations with Ghislaine so as to use my actions with her as inspiration. Seduction is seduction, regardless of who is seduced. The sight of her was pricking my flesh and I found myself thinking ever more towards the day, the moment when she would finally be mine.

We settled on the feast of Saint Michael, close to the end of September. The monks arose an hour before dawn to sing their Office. The hour before that was the one in which the whole abbey was plunged into the deepest sleep. In fact, Germanus had suggested that I confess to Savin that I had had carnal relations with one of the stable boys at just that time. This meant that I would have to stay awake until then, for in no way was it possible for me to awaken from sleep without a nudge from someone. I would have to count the hours as tolled by the abbey bell, midnight, then one, then two. Two would be the signal to meet. I was to leave first, Ghislaine would count to one hundred before joining me in case some dolt was wending his way to piss at just that hour.

After waiting so long, with so much anticipation, we were both, perhaps, expecting too much. It was enjoyable but not so much as I supposed it would be. I could not see Ghislaine very well, and it was the beauty of her body and her face that made kissing her, touching her so pleasurable. How I longed to take her during the daylight hours when all my senses could be involved. Fucking her in the dark was like sculpting blindfolded, my hands fending for themselves. We had to hurry, take care not to make any sound. I could hear her muffled cries of pleasure, her face pressed up against my chest. Knowing that we could be interrupted at any moment set our nerves on edge. It was as if, after waiting so long, with so much desire for each other, we were spent before we began. She clung to me like a drowning woman, not wanting to let go. She made me promise to return the next night.

Then I knew what I had to say to the Father Prior. It was a simple matter requesting a meeting with him. Gislebertus and his workers have considerable status here. We have almost whatever we require or wish. Moreover Savin was a frequent visitor to the work yard, having a keen interest in sculpture. In fact, he even attempted it under Gislebertus' direction. The master allowed him to chisel the folds in the back of a man's cloak, an image that would have its back to the viewer and be considerably higher than eye level. He acknowledged that knowing that his handiwork would endure for all time and in the sight of God gave his soul cause for rejoicing. When I asked to meet with him privately on a spiritual matter, he seemed pleased, even flattered. It was difficult to believe that Savin was as dangerous and lascivious as Germanus alleged. I would soon find out for myself.

Savin suggested the cemetery chapel for our encounter. It is usually deserted and has but one entrance and small, high windows. I arrived early, eager to escape the midday sun. After the clanging of the hammer and shouts of workmen, the unbroken peace of the cemetery and its chapel was exquisite. The quiet was also soothing to the ill in the infirmary, close to the cemetery. I suppose this made burial easier on those putting the dead in the ground, but harder on those watching their graves dug. I thought of Father Philippe on his bed of pain and illness, and wondered if the abbey would be arranging his Requiem soon. Odd that my thoughts drifted towards the one who had sanctioned the entrapment of the one I was waiting to betray. The chapel was of the plainest construction: a tympanum of Christ not as judge or king, but rather as one awaiting a friend on the other side of the grave. There were no carvings on the capitals inside. Most striking was the dazzling whiteness of the place, which somehow did not hurt the eyes. It was not used for funerals but simply for the lying in state of the body in advance of burial.

Savin finally arrived. He looked at me with such kindness, I was momentarily ashamed of my mission. But I realized that I had been entrusted with a sacred task, bearing upon the sanctity at the heart of the abbey, and that betrayal in the name of a higher power was no sin. I avoided looking at Savin, alleging deep shame for my failings. I fixed my gaze on a crucifix and asked him to hold my hand as I stammered out a crude and graphic description of the seduction of a young man I fabricated out of thin air. In describing the fondling of his legs and thighs, I concentrated on those of Ghislaine in order to be able to say the words. Not once did Savin stop me. The pressure of his hand on mine was constant. My own fiction caused me both shame and arousal of my passions. I was sweating profusely by the time I ended my confession. I thought that if I could just bring myself to tears, Savin would be utterly convinced of my guilt. That he was convinced became apparent later.

I then looked into Savin's face and realized my success. He was white as the walls of the chapel and his eyes were bright as if he were suffering from the ague. His voice was calm as he spoke my absolution and meted out my penance. But his lips trembled as he passed his tongue over them and his eyes darted here and there, unable to meet mine. He then arose and departed, saying that he was required at nones. He was shaken badly. The Poncians and I had won.

End of attachment.

I'm exhausted, Mug, and need some sleep. I'm going to try to finish transcribing the text in one or two more mails. The end, at last, is in sight. I'm relieved in one sense but disappointed in another. You'll understand as you continue reading.

Love, W

25 April 2004
From: gold.digger@netconnect.net
To: fractal@netconnect.net
Dear Mug,

I think you should come for a visit. I can show you all the places where we found the text, including the secret room with words scribbled all over the walls, and you can explore the other sights of Autun on your own. There's lots to see here and you'll be in the heart of Burgundy with many side trips at your disposal. You may also find interesting the process of deciphering medieval writing. The text written on the wall was hard to make out, plus the textual expert was breaking his neck and going blind trying to read it all. So we photographed it, making it much easier to read in every respect. One can darken the letters in the process of photocopying and that was a great help as the text was very faded. Remember how the image of the Shroud of Turin was more visible on a photographic negative? Similar principle here.

Your latest letter was a real shocker. I guess I'm glad I could help and hope I didn't stir up stuff that would have best remained buried. I know, I know, shrinks don't think anything should stay buried.

The weather here has been cooperating, not too much rain. I just hope we can have a visit before the project wraps up. You'd enjoy seeing the dig site.

Here's an attachment with more text from the person reacting to Thomas' narrative. Enjoy!

Love, W

Attachment to mail dated 25 April 2004:

How difficult it will be for me to clarify and explain Thomas' text, for I know how it all ends and I will want to digress, discuss this and that, meddle with his story in a word. But I must not, because it is important for you to appreciate the large measure of ignorance in which I observed the events at Cluny, observed but neither saw nor understood what was before my eyes. This is my only defense. Unless you share in my former incomprehension, you will deem me irredeemably lost in the present and damned in the future.

Thomas was quite correct in assuming that I was unaware of his ability to read and write. I also believed him to be hard of hearing. But none of that made the slightest difference in what I said or did around him. There was no secret information that I kept from him, no skill of which I was jealous. You know, whatever else I may be guilty of, I am no sorcerer nor is Casilda a witch. I think that Thomas' filthy accusations of her and her wretched brother made me angrier than any of his other cant. I wished to impart knowledge, not keep it secret.

Thomas was also correct in assuming that the five I chose for this mission to Cluny were the best stone carvers at my disposal. Not only did I seek their assistance in what I had to do, I also wanted them to be conduits of my skill down through the ages. No stone will last forever. After I am dead, I want my work to endure. That requires sculptors who can copy what I have done. Thomas thought he was stealing skills from me and I was merely using him for my own artistic immortality. I suppose you could say we were each using the other for our own ends, two selfish scoundrels who deserved each other.

The journey from Autun to Cluny was much as Thomas relates it, pleasant, beautiful, perhaps the last cheerful moments I will have for a long time. We were all full of zest for the task that lay ahead. I was most anxious to reach our destination, to see again the works I had worked on and which were still in progress when I last saw the great Abbey, and to embrace our dear Pierre, a desire you understand better than most. I am sure you wonder, perhaps, why I am not confessing to him. I do not wish to break his heart. I know you will be sorely grieved by what I relate here, but your relationship to the principals in this drama is not as close as that of Pierre and you will be able to react with a certain detachment. Pierre could not. It is also the case that I am a vain man, I suppose, and I do not want Pierre to know of my sin. Because of your own history, you will understand.

It is quite clear in Thomas' text that he was obsessed with Gérard, concerned that this man, whom Thomas claimed to love as a brother, was in some way usurping his position in the hierarchy of stone carvers if not in my affections. I did love Gérard, but as any father would love a son, and I was indeed aware of his status as serf whose freedom was a matter of weeks. How could Thomas suppose that I would discuss such a delicate matter with anyone? This business of Thomas' listening at cracks in doors, what a foul situation was this! This diary of his is such an odd mixture of the cruelest, starkest self-knowledge and the most deliberate self-deception. It also contains truths about me that I do not care to confront, truths that Thomas has foisted upon my consciousness.

In the oddest way, Thomas' criticism of me echoes Casilda's; we seldom quarreled, but when we did, it was essentially the same argument repeated in myriad variations. She accused me of living for my work, and not only for it but in it. All of life for me, according to her, was a vast pageant in a frozen state of pose, unreal unless and until it had been sculpted. Thomas' claim that I spoke in images and cared naught for words is Casilda's lament also, as is his observation that I reveal little of myself. Casilda, I can silence in a trice; she loves me and has thus relinquished a portion of her freedom to deal with me as I deserve. Thomas' words are like so many darts penetrating the marrow of my self-love. I can set aside his diary, but I cannot stop the words before they are uttered as I can with Casilda, using her love for me in my own defense. It is the sort of love shared by us that is utterly unfathomable to Thomas. If he were capable of love, he would know that it is not fear of discovery that keeps me faithful to Casilda. Both the farmwife at Le Creusot and Agathe, Eustache's wife, had indicated an inclination to lie with me, but neither one tempted me in the slightest. Poor Thomas' notion that he must find some way to keep Clémence honest indicates the extent to which his feelings for her are hollow and selfish.

I know that you, Peter Abelard, have suffered immeasurably from the lack of comprehension of your motives; your love for Heloïse was a diamond that men have beaten into powder as if it were glass. That, I suppose, is another reason for my confessing to you. You understand me even before I say anything.

I have a delicious piece of gossip for you, totally inappropriate in a confession, but which I will convey, nonetheless, at the end of my commentary on this segment of Thomas' diary. It concerns the rotting hand in the forest… Be patient.

End of attachment.

25 April 2004
From: ruth.blanchard@psychnet.org
To: Cletus.Hardin@psychnet.org
Dear Cletus,

I've determined that Malachi is in a good place emotionally. The news of Buddy's cross-dressing and Parker's involvement with him came as a shock to him, but he's settled down and doesn't seem too upset. He may have suspected as much deep in his unconscious and letting it all hang out came as a relief.

As I mentioned, there's more to this than we've discovered so far; I can't get over the feeling that the roots of Malachi's problems go deeper. I've decided it's time for me to come to AZ, to see Parker and to see you. According to what you've told me, it's about time for him to have a cycle of wakefulness. And I need a break. Ever since we made plans for me to come for a visit, I've been getting more and more eager to hit the road. I'm going to talk to a travel agent about the possibility of an open-ended ticket and see what I can come up with. I'll let you know as soon as I do. Malachi has planned to be in France while I'm visiting you. We can stay in touch via the 'net.

Love, R

27 April 2004
From: ruth.blanchard@psychnet.org
To: Cletus.Hardin@psychnet.org

I'll arrive the 30th in Phoenix and pick up a car. I'll use my map software to find my way to your house. Unless the plane is delayed—in which case I'll call—I should get to your house before dark. I gain two hours heading for AZ.

Looking forward to this, R

27 April 2004
From: Cletus.Hardin@psychnet.org
To: ruth.blanchard@psychnet.org

Best news I've had in ages. Can't wait to see you again. Cletus

30 April 2004
From: fractal@netconnect.net
To: Amanda.Greene@worldcom.net
Dear Amanda,

I know it's been a while... So much has happened since I last wrote. I've been seeing a woman recommended by Cletus, an "amateur sleuth of the mind" as she styles herself. Her name is Ruth Blanchard and I like her very much. Cletus has helped me a great deal but he's so clinical, so... shrinkish. Ruth is more down to earth. She devised a crazy scheme to help me deal with "armoire" issues. You may recall my mentioning several times through the years that there was an armoire in our Covington house that gave me the willies just thinking about it. I finally know why. I was hiding in it, hoping to see what I wasn't supposed to see when a bizarre threesome presented itself to my prying eyes. Mother, Dad and uncle Buddy, the latter gotten up in a wig and make-up to look like my mother, in a free-for-all, screaming and punching at each other while Celestine tried to break things up and calm everyone down. The stuff of nightmares for a kid, I suppose. I assumed this was the end of it, that all my problems would vanish. They didn't. I still feel hollow.

I know you're wondering why I'm unloading on you. At the moment, you're all I've got. Ruth is on her way to AZ; she'll visit Cletus (I think there's more there than meets the eye) and also my father if he ever attains a state of lucidity. Celestine and Ruben are at the grocery store and I'm home alone, wondering why I don't just off myself. I think that a glimmer of hope for us is preventing that. But I don't want to treat you like a yo-yo, get your hopes up (if indeed you have any hopes), or set myself up for another fall. On one level, I know, without actually knowing, of your involvements with other men throughout the years. I use the word advisedly. I don't think you actually slept with any of them, you just gave them your affection temporarily. And it hurt me. But I suppose I did the same thing. Ah yes, that may come as a surprise to you! I did, and still do, daydream about a girl I knew at the Bay. I'm not referring to Winifred; she was always, and still is, just a pal. The other girl broke my heart and it took me years to get over her. I fantasize about meeting up with her, picking up where we left off. And there were others, women I'd meet on a consulting job, at various parties you didn't want to attend. But you were my anchor, I never seriously considered cheating. Was that the way it was with you? I have to know. I'm trying to find my way back to you but I can't do it without knowing the authentic you.

If you want to write, go ahead. If you don't, I'll understand.

I also wanted to let you know that I'm going to France to visit Winifred for a while. It's better than moping around here with nothing to think about but my problems. That way, I won't have to wait for her responses and it will take my mind off my endless problems. I really need to get over myself. M

1 May 2004
From: ruth.blanchard@psychnet.org
To: fractal@netconnect.net
Dear Malachi,

Although I'm far in distance, I'm a mouse click away if you need me. And if the need is pressing, you have my cell number and, of course, the number at Cletus' house.

It's my understanding that your father has periods of wakefulness and relative lucidity that go on, at times, for twenty-four hours or more. He's very old and very ill, and must sense that he's near death. No matter how heinous his crimes or misdeeds against you and your mother, perhaps he'll feel the need or desire to unburden himself and tell me exactly what went on in the early years of your life. If he does, I'll let you know in an e-mail attachment using only initials, of course. I don't want to trust sensitive material to cyberspace and risk the prying eyes of hackers.

During my absence, let your mind wander. Don't concentrate on remembering or try too hard to dredge up the past. Let it happen. It will. A chance encounter with a smell, a sound, a texture is all it will take for the dam to burst and a flood of memories to be released. Be aware that this may be painful in the extreme and you may rush to block it. Use breathing to calm down, and lie or sit comfortably, letting it flow. If you remember something and are afraid you'll forget it, write it down. In fact, keeping a daily log may be an excellent tool. I hope you've been saving your letters to Winifred, and hers to you, in an e-mail folder. If so, they're safe from computer melt downs. You can retrieve them no matter when or where.

Take care of yourself and let me hear from you. Keep me posted on what's going on. Ruth

2 May 2004
From: ruth.blanchard@psychnet.org
To: cmartin@psychnet.net
Dear Cath,

I'm safely ensconced in Cletus' guest quarters and using his computer to stay in touch.

The flight to Phoenix was uneventful. Temperatures were about the same as in New Orleans, but the dryness was quite a change. My eyes are bothering me and will continue to do so till I'm back in the land of great coffee and huge roaches.

I picked up my car and headed north on I-17, then took the Prescott exit and headed up Mingus Mountain to Jerome. I intend to return to Prescott to visit its wonderful city center, an historic county court house surrounded by a beautiful park filled with excellent, and very western, bronze statues. Prescott was the first capital of AZ, hence its imposing aspect. I also must visit the Palace Saloon on Whiskey Row before I leave this part of the world.

I reached Jerome in late afternoon and found Cletus' house with no problem. My map service directions were fine and Cletus' house, built in 1912 and meticulously restored, is fabulous. It's in Giroux Street on Cleopatra Hill, as high in the town as one can get. When I walked onto the back deck, I gasped in wonderment at the view of Verde Valley, but also with a certain unease at the precariousness of my perch. The deck is supported by uprights fixed into the mountainside and seems to float in space. The drop-off on the side facing the valley is precipitous. The deck faces east so the escarpment across the valley was drenched with setting sunlight and ablaze with color. At a moment in the past, parts of the town, including the jail, slid down the hill much to the delight of some townsfolk. I trust the supports of Cletus' house are firmly entrenched in bedrock.

The house is small but quite comfortable. Cletus has collected a few period furnishings and completed the decor with reproductions. I feel as if I'm back at the turn of the nineteenth century and will probably return home in buckskin and turquoise. By the way, silver jewelry in this part of the country is ubiquitous, addictive, and reasonably priced, so let me know if there's anything I can get you. Cletus tells me there's a jeweler in Jerome who makes his own exquisite pieces and sells at lovely prices.

Tomorrow Cletus will give me a tour of the town and fill me in on Parker's condition. He's at a super posh assisted living facility in Sedona, about twenty miles away. Once we're down the hill, the road is flat and we can get there in about half an hour. The staff has orders to call Cletus on cell if Parker seems to be coming around. Meanwhile, I plan to sit back and indulge in some tourism. Prescott is thirty miles away, but gets us farther from Sedona, so I'll probably visit there after I see Parker. You're probably wondering what I'll do if he doesn't come around fairly soon… I've been told that his periods of hyperactivity are becoming more frequent and I intend to wait him out. What else do I have to do? Malachi is plotting a trip to France. And I can always return home and then come back. It's Malachi's money I'm spending, after all.

This is my first real interaction with a man since Liam died and it feels very strange, especially since Cletus and I had some history before each of us married someone else. I'm terrified and exhilarated at the same time. Worrywart that I am, I'm also uneasy about leaving my house in Covington. What if it floods, what if a tree falls on it...? You get the picture! If I could just settle down and be comfortable where I am and with the person I'm near. Why am I so anxious? Ever since I retired, it's been getting worse. But having Malachi's case to work on has surely lifted my spirits. I don't feel so alone and useless. The sight of Cletus gives me butterflies. I feel sixteen again. I have a suspicion my sentiments are reciprocated. I may be old but I'm still female and my intuition isn't completely gone.

Write when you have a chance. I'll keep the e-mails coming to keep you posted, but also to construct a diary and make notes to and for myself. Always multi-tasking... Ruth

2 May 2004
From: Amanda.Greene@worldcom.net
To: Cletus.Hardin@psychnet.org
Dear Cletus,

I know this is a long shot but I have to try. Could I come to Jerome and talk to Malachi's friend Ruth? I've screwed my marriage up badly but would like to try to salvage it. Malachi has put his plans to divorce me on hold and wants to try again. At least I think he does. His most recent e-mail, the first in months, was hesitant and somewhat peculiar. Perhaps Ruth could give me some tips on how to handle a very fragile guy... I'll wait to hear from you before I answer his letter.

Thanks, Amanda

3 May 2004
From: cmartin@psychnet.net
To: ruth.blanchard@psychnet.org
Dear Ruth,

You go, girl! You're doing exactly the right thing. Do you really miss faculty meetings, grade sheets, forms to fill out...? The retirement blues will pass.

This will have to be brief because I have to go... to a faculty meeting!!!!

Keep those cards and letters coming. Tell me more about Cletus when you have a chance. And don't take delay between mails as lack of interest.

Cath

4 May 2004
From: Cletus.Hardin@psychnet.org
To: Amanda.Greene@worldcom.net
Dear Amanda,

Ruth will see you but will reveal nothing of Malachi's past or present situation. As for interceding with Malachi on your behalf, she'll play that by ear. Right now, we're on call to speak with Parker Walmsley should he ever come around sufficiently for coherent dialogue. When Ruth is ready to go back to Louisiana, she'll contact you and arrange something. Don't get your hopes up too much but don't despair either.

Best, Cletus

4 May 2004
From: ruth.blanchard@psychnet.org
To: cmartin@psychnet.net
Dear Cath,

Cletus called Red Rock Springs this morning and was told we should go frolic. Parker is asleep and is likely to remain so. If he has a period of wakefulness, the staff will be only too delighted to let us keep him company. But for now, he's out. Nonetheless, we're ready to drop everything at a moment's notice and head down the hill.

Today we toured Jerome with nary an interruption. The town, an old mining center, is a treasure and not overrun with tourists. There's something about the place that strikes me as distinctly European, perhaps the way it clings to a mountainside like so many villages in Umbria or in the Dordogne region in France. It has several nice B&Bs and some fine old western hotels. There's a terrific artists' co-op and a woman who makes artwork out of papier mâché. Her confections look like they're made of stone; they're light as air. There are many talented and wonderful people here. I'm discovering a vein of "west worship" in myself. My first glimpse of red rock hit me in the gut in a very special way, as if I were meant to be here. It's comforting to know I have a crash pad anytime I want one. Unless Cletus finds someone else. My relationship with him is beginning to consume my thoughts. See how discussion of him and of us creeps into everything I send you?

As I was writing the previous sentence, we got a call from Red Rock Springs and they want us there tomorrow. Parker's not awake, but he's showing signs of incipient activity, behaving as he does before a period of wakefulness. I'll let you know what comes of the trip down the hill as soon as we return and IF I have anything to report. Malachi plans to see his friend in France. I think this is a positive step as any contact with his past and especially with someone with whom he has close ties at the present is good.

Love, R

6 May 2004
From: fractal@netconnect.net
To: gold.digger@netconnect.net
Dear Wump,

I'm alone now. Celestine and Ruben decided they wanted their own quarters, probably because they're not sure about me, how long I'll want them here and so forth. I realize how lonely I am and how attached I've become to Ruth. She e-mails regularly and keeps me posted, but it's just not the same. I thought I'd be perfectly happy as a divorcé and I still don't know if I want to be tied to Amanda, but the thought of living and dying alone is not appealing. I wrote to Amanda a few days ago but still have not heard from her. Perhaps she's lost interest. I had the notion that she wanted to hang on. There seems to be no good way to spend the rest of my life. I wish you didn't live in France… Sometimes I just escape into memories of summers at the Bay. That seems to be my salvation. What was it about that time that was so magical? Was it the innocence of childhood, not knowing all the dirt life could throw at you? It must have been, or at least included, ignorance of the world. I know you play the hand life deals you, but it does seem that I've been hit pretty hard. So here I sit, a poor little rich brat with a good friend across the sea and no friends nearby, a wife who's probably cheated on me forever, time on my hands and millions of questions that will remain unanswered. I'm tortured by doubts and nameless fears, pangs of desperation and longing, for what I know not. I do know that I miss red rock, towering buttes, San Francisco Peaks and the west in general. Having so much beauty a few hours away is addictive. I'll probably console myself with a trip to the Bay. It draws me, tugs at my heart, even though the Bay of my youth, *our* Bay, no longer exists.

Enough of this pity party!! I can hear your brain wondering if I'm on the verge of another attempt to end it all. No. I promised you I'd never do that again and I won't. Help me stay strong. Write when you can.

Love, M

7 May 2004
From: ruth.blanchard@psychnet.org
To: cmartin@psychnet.net
Dear Cath,

The Parker/Buddy/Joanna triangle is much uglier and more grotesque than I could ever have imagined. That is, if I can believe a word Parker says…

Cletus and I arrived at Red Rock Springs at about 8:30 and, as the staff expected, Parker was wide awake and babbling away. I had seen photographs of him at Malachi's house. He was one of the most devastatingly handsome men I've ever seen, of the Randolph Scott type, with a fine chiseled jaw, a regal bearing and a smile that would melt a glacier. What I saw when we were finally face to face truly shocked me. I've rarely encountered anyone who filled me with such revulsion at first sight. It's not his age. I've seen elderly people who were much more physically repulsive, but who managed to convey their former dignity and self-respect. Parker is just loathsome, and, what's more, seems to find joy and pleasure in his disgusting appearance. His face is contorted into a perpetual sneer as if he were a child whose parent had warned him, accurately, about the permanence of nasty faces. He has the nose of a heavy drinker. His gnarled hands are covered with so many age spots, they looked permanently stained or dyed brown. The same could be said of his scalp, which shows through sparse reddish hair. His fingernails are exceedingly long and yellow, and his teeth, the color of tobacco juice. He reminded me a little of Howard Hughes at the end of his life. Since he was in bed when we saw him, his body was covered with sheets and blankets. It was quite warm in the place, yet, according to the staff, he complains incessantly of the cold, the usual lament of those who have lived far too long. All I could see of him was his head perched on a scrawny wrinkled neck; his long arms and his shoulders, outlined through the covers, were pushed forward toward his sunken chest by acute osteoporosis. He looked at me through rheumy eyes, whose color I could not discern, and asked what the f… I wanted. I told him I wanted the full truth about Buddy and Joanna. He laughed, no, cackled, and said they were one and the same. When I asked for an explanation, he went on to another topic. This went on for hours. When he was lucid, he was mean. When he was cooperative and friendly, I knew I wasn't talking to the real Parker. At about four in the afternoon, I think he tired of playing games and, for whatever reason, decided to tell what sounded to both Cletus and me like the truth. It's appalling. It's also pieced together from the semi-coherent rant of a sick old man. Bear that in mind.

The accident that happened in 1950, the one around which this whole saga revolves, was an attempt by Joanna to kill herself, her brother and Malachi. By that time she hated Parker so much, she felt she had no choice but to kill Parker or herself, there was no other means of escape. Parker was a bisexual pimp and blackmailer who used the house on Dauphine Street, the one I am now renting (!), as a house of assignation for people of all sexual persuasions and their lovers. He had set up an elaborate system of cameras that he used to gather his materials; this was the source of his considerable wealth. He got paid for supplying whores to suit every taste and then got paid again for keeping the information gathered from being disseminated throughout the community. Several of his clients were from the highest echelons of New Orleans society, the last remnant in the world of *noblesse d'épée,* a social rank into which one has to be born. It is still the case that no amount of money can buy membership in New Orleans toniest carnival clubs, which constitutes the very essence of status in this town. Joanna hated Buddy because he was both Parker's lover and also available to anyone willing to pay Parker his fee. Parker used him to lure several big fish into his net. For whatever reason, Buddy commanded big bucks, probably because he was a cross dresser willing to get himself up to suit any taste. He was a smallish man to begin with and able to mimic women's ways to perfection. He was also physically and emotionally weak; I suspect his mental well-being hung by a thread. I guess Joanna figured she might as well take Buddy out with her. He was probably easily persuaded to flee with her and then the flight turned into a deadly scheme. As for her son, we may assume that Joanna was close to unhinged by this time and decided Malachi was better off dead than left with a vice-ridden pervert of a father. I have no doubt—and Joanna probably feared the same—that Parker would begin passing Malachi around as soon as he was a bit older. It was purely fortuitous that Joanna and Malachi survived, and Buddy died; I guess she badly miscalculated the crash and its potential impact.

Such is the tale told by a person whose mind is gone and whose malice is immeasurable, so decide for yourself how much, if anything, to believe. Parker never explained his "one and the same" remark but he did give us one last nugget of information before he lapsed into unconsciousness, the name of the facility in California where Joanna had her surgery. I may be able to get more useful information from there, assuming anyone remembers the case and is willing to talk. I'm also assuming Parker remembered correctly and told us the truth, a gamble on the best of days. Once I locate it, if it existed then and still does, I will leave for CA and keep you posted.

Love, R

7 May 2004
From: ruth.blanchard@psychnet.org
To: fractal@netconnect.net
Dear Malachi,

I have discovered what I believe is a large cache of pieces to our puzzle, but would prefer to convey them to you in person after I've uncovered a few more that may be in California. As soon as I can determine if the clinic where your mother was operated on is still up and running, and if I can locate anyone willing to speak with me, I'll go there to try to close the circle. Even though I have the answers to many of the questions plaguing you, I won't feel that my investigation is complete without an attempt to tie up some loose ends. If you find the wait intolerable, I suppose we could talk on the phone. But I truly feel a face-to-face would be more comforting and best for you. I'll abide by your wishes in this matter; after all I'm working for you. I'll have my cell with me in case you or my CA contact calls. If I don't hear from you, I'll assume you wish to wait for my return to hear the news.

I hope you're sleeping well and still enjoying life in Covington.

Take very good care of yourself. Ruth

10 May 2004
From: fractal@netconnect.net
To: gold.digger@netconnect.net
Dear Wump,

Just spent a couple of days in Mississippi. After my usual pilgrimage to the house on Leonhard Avenue, I went to your old place and who do I find in the yard, gardening as always, but your mother. She looks well, especially considering her advanced age, and insisted I come in for cookies and milk. Can you imagine? She remembered my fondness for ginger snaps and apologized for not having a supply. I told her of our correspondence, assuming e-mail has passed her generation by. She is aware that you're in France on a dig, but that's about it. I presume you write about more personal subjects. I had checked into a hotel or I'd have gladly accepted her offer to stay with her. In many ways, she was more a mother to me after the accident than my own mother was. She seems eternal, changeless. You and she were anchors in my chaotic life and I'll always be grateful to both of you for bringing some sanity into my desolate adolescence.

I heard from Ruth. She's discovered something of vast importance that she wishes to convey in person. She's going to try to see the people in California who worked on my mother. I'm not at all certain I wanted all this stirred up; perhaps I should have let sleeping dogs lie. Problem was I couldn't sleep if I had…

Write when you have a chance.

Love, M

10 May 2004
From: ruth.blanchard@psychnet.org
To: cmartin@psychnet.net
Dear Cath,

How about some personal news for a change? After my encounter with Parker I wanted to take a shower, both physical and mental. I needed his information, but found his company indescribably repulsive. So I took some time away from freaks and transvestites, pimps and blackmailers, to see some northern AZ/southern UT splendor with Cletus. But let me first confide that we've rekindled a fire that never really got started when it could have—and perhaps should have—and we're going to face some tough decisions down the road. Each of us has a life, a good life, where we are. Cletus adores Jerome, even with its broiling summers and bleak, frozen winters. There are times when residents are marooned, trapped by icy mountain roads and the hairpin curves of Mingus Pass. Of course, the town is adorable. It's an old mining town that almost died, but is now vibrant and full of artists, feeding off its own colorful history. I'll send you a picture of me behind the bars of the old women's prison. And Cletus now accepts only as many clients as he wishes. Malachi has been his patient for years and I know he'll never cease trying to help him. There are a few others in the same situation and they all live in the area: Prescott, Sedona, Cottonwood, Flagstaff. One man drives up from Phoenix about once every two months, but I suspect it's more social than professional. I'm virtually in the same position in Louisiana. Our summers are just as nasty with slightly lower temperatures but higher humidity. And our winters can be frigid. But Covington is so much my home, I couldn't even think of leaving permanently. I've poured myself, along with my resources, into my house; it's become my nest, my shell, like a carapace to a turtle. So what do we do? We haven't spoken of our future as a couple and I'm dreading the moment of reckoning. In fact, I'm not sure Cletus sees us as such. As my departure date looms ever closer, we'll both get edgier and finally one of us will bring this to a head. Till then, I'll sit back and enjoy the ride.

Now, more about my adventures… We left Jerome and headed north, passing through Cottonwood, Sedona, and Flagstaff before hitting highway 89, which would take us to our various destinations. We went through Sunset Crater and Wupatki National Monuments on our way north, and were soon on the Navajo Reservation. Along the route are numerous roadside stands with wonderful handmade confections for sale, and trading posts at Gray Mountain and Cameron. As we traveled north, the landscape became ever more spectacular, from lunar desolation, to multi-colored mounds of Chinle formation, then on to painted desert near The Gap, Cedar Ridge and Bitter Springs. Echo Cliffs just south of Bitter Springs give a hint of splendors to come. At Bitter Springs, the highway forks. If we had stayed on 89, we would have reached Page and Lake Powell, also on my list of eventual must-sees. We continued straight on 89A—not much imagination in highway numbering. We stayed the first night in Marble Canyon, whose towering vermilion cliffs stretch as far as the eye can see. When the canyon first comes into view, the effect is electrifying. I was speechless in the face of such magnificence; I wanted to melt into the landscape, become one with it. Cletus chose a motel near Lonely Dell, a bucolic yet sinister place infused with the spirits of John Doyle Lee and his multitude of wives. Their descendants are still around and form the nucleus of several renegade polygamous communities of the FLDS Church in northern AZ and southern UT. Lee was executed for his complicity in the Mountain Meadows Massacre of 1857, but the exact nature of the killing spree and the extent of Lee's participation are still hotly debated in some circles. I bought a book about Emma Lee, John's seventeenth wife, and will be interested in reading of life at Lonely Dell from a woman's perspective. It must have been physically hellish as temperatures soar into the 100s in the summer. Today there are primitive farm implements lying about and a one-room schoolhouse for the Lee tribe. The nature of the tools indicates how difficult it must have been to scratch an existence out of such a place. A favorite saying in the west is: pack in plenty of food and water, you can't eat the scenery. How well I understand that saying now. We also got a look at the beautiful Paria River, which meets the Colorado at Lee's Ferry. The ferry, a few miles north of Lonely Dell, was the only means across the mighty Colorado in Lee's time and he is credited with opening AZ to further settlement. However, the choice of this place, very sparsely populated even today, is said to reflect John's attempt to hide from those who considered him guilty for taking part in the massacre.

We saw Lonely Dell first thing in the morning, before the heat was searing. By 9:30 it was in the high 80s and I was ready to depart for Grand Canyon. We drove past Vermilion Cliffs that rim Paria Plateau and then began our climb through Kaibab National Forest to Jacob Lake, then south to North Rim. Thought not an abrupt change, the contrast between the warm, late spring desert of Marble Canyon and the lush cool forest was stark. As we climbed, it got cool and damp, a welcome respite from the temperatures of the canyon floor. I wondered if Emma Lee ever guessed what an oasis was at the edge of her world. John Wesley Powell explored and fell in love with this land. In fact, I believe he interacted with the Lees. Here's what he had to say about northern Arizona: "Here antelope feed and many a deer goes bounding over the fallen timber. In winter deep snows lie here, but the plateau has four months of the sweetest summer man has ever known." I doubt he was referring to summer at Lonely Dell. We reached North Rim at about noon and entered Grand Canyon Lodge. I crossed the lobby, a loft overlooking the Sun Room, and stood looking out through three huge panoramic windows at my first view of the canyon. Cletus told me this is the traditional way of seeing Grand Canyon for the first time. *Shock* and *awe* are the best words to describe my reaction despite their sinister suggestion of war. We were lucky enough to get a table for lunch at a window that seemed to overhang the canyon. I was enchanted. I think often of Powell and his reactions to the overwhelming majesty of this area. You must read his Journal someday. His superb eloquence equals his matchless courage. He was always on the fringes of my acquaintance with the west and I thought of him as a rough soldier, with the grammar and the sensitivity to beauty usual to men of his era. I've had to revise upward my assessment of his attributes in those areas. He's no Daniel Boone.

We had Bright Angel Point, Point Imperial, Cape Royal and their attractions to ourselves. North Rim has far fewer visitors than South Rim, probably because access is so much more time-consuming. Rain was forecast, and alternating sun and clouds gave a most particular quality to the light. There were several rainbows thanks to the atmospheric conditions. A vista would emerge in muted shades, then the cloud covering the sun would shift, revealing a dazzling, blazing array of red, ochre, green and white. How could places with names such as VenusTemple, Siegfried Pyre, Wotan's Throne, or Zoroaster Temple not be marvelous? Angel's Window is a natural cleft in the rock through which the Colorado is visible where it turns at Unkar Delta. We crouched down to get a good photo shot of this feature and I realized after the fact how close to a precipitous drop Cletus had been standing. The extent of my fright indicated how dear he is to me and how hollow my life would be without him. Do I want to be in love again? This is preoccupying me as is my impending departure date. From various spots, Flagstaff's San Francisco Peaks were visible. At Point Imperial, the highest point on either rim, we could look back at Marble Canyon. I thought of Emma Lee, bedazzled by the beauty of Paria Plateau. What would she have thought of North Rim?

We left the Canyon at sunset and traveled through Fredonia to Kanab, the epicenter of Western movie-making in the '30s, '40s and '50s. I must have seen the mountains that surround Kanab in countless B movies when I was a kid. We stayed at Parry Lodge, where some rooms are named after the movie stars who occupied them. It's a charming place.

I leave 15 May for California. Cletus found a nurse who worked at the now-closed clinic where Joanna was a patient and she seems willing to talk. I'll let you know what I find out. Wish me luck.

Love, Ruth

12 May 2004
From: gold.digger@netconnect.net
To: fractal@netconnect.net
Dear Mug,

How's this to pull you out of the doldrums—more text. Enjoy a good read. I'll write more later about life in France. There's this *monsieur*...

Love, W

p.s. Why don't you come see for yourself what I'm about here? You'd love it!

Attachment to mail dated 12 May 2004:

Thomas amazes me. How can he be at once so devious, opaque to himself, and so delightfully frank and sincere in some instances? He and I could share a good laugh over the slut in the forest, for I too was taken in at the sight of her. I too believed her half-witted, even as my loins were responding to her physical aspect, entirely in spite of myself. She did not seriously tempt me; I could not have gotten past the smell of her. But the face was truly extraordinary, not pretty, not pleasing, but totally sensual. As Thomas says, the mouth and the nostrils were wholly lustful. This was to be the last time he and I would agree, especially where women were concerned. His treatment of Ghislaine... But I digress again, and it is important to keep things in order. I want you to understand. If he distrusted his own intended to such an extent even before the exchange of vows, what sort of union could they possibly hope for?

One thing I must give Thomas to his credit is his immediate and wholehearted marvel at the Abbey at Cluny. Of course, arriving at sunset did not hurt, just as the chant of compline was lingering in the air. His characterization of my meeting with Abbot Pierre, like that of long-lost brothers, was, as you may imagine, accurate. Any serious passage of time without a conversation with Pierre of Montboissier is as an age. You know him; do you not agree that he is a font of charity? He loves you and Heloïse, considers your union one of the spirit and blessed for that. As Pierre has so often said, love is love. It matters not who or when or why. He is the least pharisaical man I know. Which does not prevent him from losing patience with some of his monks. He is aware of the Poncians and of their plots to overthrow his abbacy. He has lain awake nights wondering if they mean to murder him in his bed. The ones Thomas took up with are the purest scoundrels masquerading as men of God, true whited sepulchers.

Thomas' reaction to Steven, Pierre's dwarf, should not have surprised me. He saw no value in Mallory and he had no charity to spare for the apparently useless of this earth. Pierre's statement to the effect that he keeps Steven about as a penance was a lame jest on his part, meant perhaps to disguise his tender heart. Steven is at times ill-tempered, especially with those he perceives as the haughty of the earth. Thomas has a way of looking at those he considers his inferiors that quite gives away his prejudices. Steven has a secure place in the palace of the most powerful abbot on earth. Of what concern to him is Thomas' assessment of his talents? Besides Steven is not at all dim-witted, he just looks the fool. His demeanor is at times of the greatest use to Pierre. Guests have been beguiled into saying things in Steven's presence, things that have gone straight to Pierre's ears. The dwarf was most instrumental in keeping Pierre advised of the plotting of the Poncians. They too mistook a crooked body for a defective mind...

As poor as was Thomas' eye for people, so accurate was it for things, carvings to be precise. The tympanum at Cluny is, as you have remarked, a glory of the world. Thomas did love it so. I caught him gazing at it when he should have been working, but I let him go because that too was an integral part of his work. Sculpting for Thomas was not a job but a passion. He could have been sublime.

Thomas' perception of Pierre's distress concerning the Cathar heresy was also accurate. Pierre wanted Orders and the Eucharist reaffirmed at every turn, even at risk of offending the brothers or Holy Benedict himself. There are good and bad at Cluny in both ranks, of course. Pierre is concerned that the Abbey not become a museum but remain a maelstrom of prayer manifested in stone and a fortress against those attacking the sacraments, especially the sacrament of Love Incarnate.

How odd it is to think of Thomas huddled over his text as he was hunched over stone, creating images in both cases. But the written image of what he perceived reality to be was so grotesque, so misshapen, it makes me wonder how his sculpture was not equally monstrous. He claims that I did not see him in what he sculpted. Perhaps that is because his sculpture, though beautiful, was unfaithful and mendacious. Perhaps his vision of his sculpted subject was as deformed as his perception of life. His use of whore in describing my Casilda is abominable. Someday I will relate to you the full story of our love; it almost rivals your union with Heloise in strength and depth, but that is extraneous to Thomas' situation. How easy it is to forget that confessing my sins is what I am about. It is much more pleasant to confess Thomas'!

As angry as I was at Thomas' slanderous rant concerning Casilda, I was nearly so furious at his unspeakable cruelty to Ghislaine of Normandy. A gentler woman has never lived nor one so unworthy of mistreatment. She and her husband Hugh were en route to Compostela by way of Rocamadour to pray for a child. Ghislaine had had trouble carrying a child to term and they were going to Rocamadour to pray to the Black Virgin. They had also visited the shrine of Holy Radegonde in Poitiers, perhaps even crossing paths with Thomas' family there. The first time I saw her in the presence of Thomas I knew she was doomed. Thomas was a handsome man in a rather ordinary way, but he had a quality that many women find irresistible. He seemed not to care at all for their feelings. If you are curious about his looks, he is depicted at Autun. He is the young, beardless magus doffing his crown as he offers his gift to the Christ child, and he is again in the *Dream of the Magi* in the center. You will also notice that I am the older king offering the cask of gold in the capital of the *Adoration of the Magi*. He ignored Ghislaine for days. I should have guessed it was part of his seduction although you must remember that, when I was witnessing all these events, I had not yet been privy to his diary. He gave the impression that she was, at best, a nuisance to be tolerated.

Ghislaine was married to Hugh at her father's insistence to cement some sort of alliance or other in the manner of noble folk, who are, I swear, the least free people on earth. Or rather, the women are the least free, little better than merchandise traded back and forth for profit. She did not love Hugh, or at least was not passionate about him. She was ripe for Thomas' plucking. And he was, at first, enamored of her, in the manner of a frivolous young man who encounters his first pretty wench, ready for love but not forever. In a sense, each was the other's "first," not in the flesh but in the spirit. Thomas, it may be assumed, was no virgin and Ghislaine certainly was not. But neither had ever really been in passionate love before. It is simply that young Thomas' interest waned far sooner than poor Ghislaine's. She took far too seriously what Thomas considered a lark. Thomas never had any notion of permanence in this relationship whereas Ghislaine would have deserted her husband in an instant had Thomas not had the cruel decency to dash any hopes she once had. Hugh also was nearly destroyed by all this. Despite the arranged aspect of their relationship he had fallen in love with his wife —what a droll idea among the aristocracy—and had always hoped that she would one day see him as a lover, chosen and wanted even if after the fact of marriage. Thomas' notion that he and Ghislaine were discreet and their affair, unnoticed was dreadfully wrong; Hugh knew and everyone else knew, and Hugh was aware of the pity that surrounded him, at least on the part of the monks. Not a few others were snickering behind his back and making the sign of the horns at his passage. Hugh and Ghislaine left Cluny under a cloud of gossip; and both looked miserable as they departed. Thomas took scant notice of Ghislaine's absence, having gone already to the bed of a scullery maid who caught his fancy. I wonder if he now recalls so much as her name...

As for those ecstatic Poncians... I wonder how joyful was the Father Hosteller Philippe. For I learned, from that ill-favored gossipy stable hand Crispin, that Father Philippe had not been ill at all during our sojourn at Cluny, but rather had nearly died from the loss of a limb, to wit, his left hand that some robber had brutally separated from his arm in his desire to possess a ring which Philippe had been wearing, a ring the Hosteller had lifted from his own Abbey and had been wearing for God knows what purpose. As you see, Peter, this is delicious to the taste of one who despises Philippe's hypocrisy and endless scheming as much as you do.

It is the moment now to return to Thomas' text.
End of attachment.

13 May 2004
From: fractal@netconnect.net
To: ruth.blanchard@psychnet.org
Dear Ruth,

Wump just sent me some more wonderful text to read. I really hope they find the whole ms. as the story is engrossing. She suggested again that I come visit her. But she also hinted at a romance brewing between her and some French guy. Do I want to witness that? I guess if I want her, I'll have to fight for her. But do I want her that way? How pleasant life would be if one could survive without making decisions.

As for your telling me of your finds, I'll let you and Cletus be the judges of the timing. I'm so anxious and uneasy, as though I'm on the brink of learning something I desperately don't want to know. But I must know the truth or I'll be unable to sleep for the rest of my life. The dreams are awful. Now I see a figure coming out of the woods with a body. The figure always says, "This is your doing." I can't make out the features of either the person carrying the body or the body itself. But just as both begin to come into focus, I wake up. My heart is pounding in my chest and further sleep is out of the question. If the dream comes at 5 or later, it's OK. I can bear an early morning call. If it's at 2 or 3, the night is over and my day begins. Those hours before sunrise are hell. Sometimes I get out of bed and roam around the house. It's very big and empty now without Celestine. (I did tell you she and Ruben decided to move into a place of their own?) Everything looks sinister and menacing. If there's a moon, the rooms are full of shadows and the yard is filled with nameless shapes. The air is filled with delicate sounds—creaks, sighs—as if the house were a living entity sleeping fitfully.

I took another sentimental journey to the Bay; that seems to calm me down. I of course visited my old house, but also went to Wump's house and found her mother working in her garden, just as I had so many times so long ago. She actually remembered my fondness for ginger snaps and worried that she had none to offer me. She's such a dear. I don't recall mentioning in our conversations how much I loved her. In fact, after the accident I nourished guilty desires to have her as my mother rather than Joanna. The Hausers live on de Montluzin Street in the heart of town. We were rather farther away from the center and I wasn't able to walk to her place. But my dad was always more than willing to deposit me there and leave me for as long as I wished. Neither house had a phone so he just guessed when my welcome would wear out. It never did.

I assume you're still enjoying the west and your visit with Cletus. Save me the effort and share this letter with him, and apologize for my laziness. I'll write again when I have something to say.

Best, M

13 May 2004
From: fractal@netconnect.net
To: gold.digger@netconnect.net
Dear Wump,

The text just gets better and better. I await each installment with great anticipation.

I enjoyed my visit with your mom. She's aging but still looks wonderful and says she feels great. She envies me my ability to e-mail you but says she's too old for newfangled contraptions such as computers. The usual lament of the elderly. She sends you her best via me.

I'm very eager to hear what Ruth wishes to tell me face-to-face. I wish she'd just call with the news. But I know she and Cletus have my best interests at heart. I've put myself in their hands and prefer not to second-guess their recommendations.

Write whenever you can.

Love, M

20 May 2004
From: ruth.blanchard@psychnet.org
To: cmartin@psychnet.net
Dear Cath,

I'm back in Jerome after my trip to California. I thought Malachi's family history was incapable of getting any more bizarre, but I was wrong. All along, I suspected Buddy of malicious mischief. But he was, in fact, a tragic and abused person, and far more kind than I could ever have imagined. Let me begin at the beginning.

The nurse involved in this affair was all too willing to talk. In fact, she seemed eager to unburden herself now that all the principals in this soap opera are either dead (doctor and patient) or dying (Parker). We can place her in the latter category as she has bone cancer and is not expected to last out the year.

The patient who arrived at the clinic in 1950 was John Claiborne (I realized while I was at the clinic that I had never learned Joanna's maiden name), a.k.a. Uncle Buddy, not Joanna Claiborne Walmsley, who was in fact killed in the accident of April 1950. This explains the extraordinary secrecy surrounding the accident reports, the inconsistencies, the suspected lies and cover-ups. Buddy and the nurse, whose identity I agreed to conceal, became close friends during the long months of his convalescence and he told her his life story while he was in the process of assuming the features and the identity of his sister, Malachi's mother. He loved Malachi very much and that love explains in part why he accepted this deception and also why he left his nephew such a wealthy guy. He knew the nightmare family Malachi was left with and wanted desperately to take the place of the mother Malachi adored. He carried on the deception as long as he could. But life with Parker eventually became intolerable and he decided Malachi could take care of himself by then.

At the time of the accident, Buddy was considered a hermaphrodite, a term no longer in vogue. He was, in today's parlance, an intersexual, a person born with genitalia and secondary sexual characteristics combining elements of both sexes. He suffered specifically from 5-alpha-reductase deficiency and would ordinarily have been raised a girl. But his father wanted a son and it was decided, almost immediately, that the child would henceforth be "John." The birth and the baptismal certificates were issued as such.

When the children were about fourteen, they became acquainted with Parker who saw a fortune falling into his lap. At the time, Parker had a chic antiques shop on Dauphine Street, the very building I am now renting from the son of a former colleague of his. He was also a twenty-year-old pimp for the New Orleans upper crust and made his fortune by supplying them with whores, then blackmailing them for using his services. He catered to those with unusual proclivities. An intersexual teenager was a gold mine. Parker had sold John—or Buddy— and Joanna's mother, Emma Claiborne, furnishings for her home until she died at a young age, and gradually insinuated his way into the family's inner circle. He often had both Buddy and Joanna for week-end visits in my rental house. It's possible Buddy and Joanna's father, Miles, was one of Parker's clients and Parker blackmailed him into giving up his son for use in his trade. Buddy felt that his father found him loathsome, but dangerously seductive at the same time. What better way to humiliate the boy whose very existence tormented him than by passing him around to his friends? Parker may not have had to do much coaxing to get the father to give up his freakish son. Furthermore, Buddy, to his everlasting shame, enjoyed his exotic sexuality and was fully compliant with his exploitation. Joanna was certainly unaware of what her brother was doing while she was strolling the Quarter with Parker or one of his pals, or she would never have married Parker. However, after the marriage, things probably didn't feel right to her; this general and vague sense of impropriety pervaded the household and was very likely the subject of the incessant quarrels between Parker and Joanna. By the time she had the full picture of the Parker/Buddy thing, she was ensnared in a web of deceit and had a child to protect. Buddy loved Joanna and Malachi, and continued to do Parker's bidding in exchange for a family to which he could belong. His mother died when he was young, his father gave him to a pimp... Joanna and Malachi were the only bright lights in an otherwise miserable existence. He enjoyed the sex, make no mistake about it, but he was intensely ashamed of his activities as well. After the accident, he at first rejected Parker's ridiculous scheme to turn him into his dead sister. But Malachi kept injecting himself into his sphere of consciousness and into his conscience, and he decided the best way to protect the little boy was to go along. When he was of an age to take care of himself more or less, he broke all ties with Parker, telling him basically that there was nothing Parker could do to him, that he'd rather die than continue the charade they'd all been living. Henceforth he led a double life, venturing out, usually at night, as John C. Since everything he had to sign involved "J. Claiborne," getting stopped by the police was all he had to worry about. His driver's license was in the name "Joanna." I guess he could have just 'fessed up to cross-dressing. The cops in Louisiana are pretty tolerant of such stuff, especially in New Orleans. And the rest, we all know. He could do nothing about Malachi's perception of his mother as the person who rejected him. If he had fought Parker for custody in court, the entire sordid mess would have been exposed. He had no idea how devastating the terms of the divorce would be. But I firmly believe that Malachi's problems have deeper roots than what we've uncovered so far, and I intend to encourage him to continue exploring his self, his past, for more answers.

When I return to Covington, I'm going to probe his dreams of the accident. He believes they're inaccurate, figments of his imagination, but I'm not so sure. He may have had moments of lucidity and seen more than he remembers. If what he saw before he passed into unconsciousness did not jibe with what he was told, this may account for a great many of his emotional difficulties since then. I'll probe this possibility gently and let you know what I discover.

Leaving Cletus and the west will be very difficult. But he promises to visit very soon. I'll keep you posted on that. Perhaps you could visit at the same time and meet him.

Write soon.

Love, Ruth

20 May 2004
From: ruth.blanchard@psychnet.org
To: Amanda.Greene@worldcom.net
Dear Amanda,

I'll see you tomorrow or the 22nd if that suits you. I leave for Louisiana the 23rd, so let me know what your schedule is. I believe Cletus has told you I cannot reveal anything Malachi has told me, but I'll be glad to listen to you and interject anything I can that may be of use to you. I'll also ask your permission to communicate to Cletus anything I find that may be useful to him as therapist to both you and Malachi. Just let me know.

Ruth

20 May 2004
From: Amanda.Greene@worldcom.net
To: ruth.blanchard@psychnet.org

Tomorrow will be fine. I'll drive down from Flagstaff and meet you at Cletus' around 10 a.m. unless that's too early.

Amanda

20 May 2004
From: ruth.blanchard@psychnet.org
To: Amanda.Greene@worldcom.net
    See you at Cletus' at 10.
    Ruth

24 May 2004
From: ruth.blanchard@psychnet.org
To: Cletus.Hardin@psychnet.org
Dear Cletus,

What a change! From a sauna to a steam bath… Louisiana is already in full summer weather and they're predicting a heavy hurricane season.

I found Malachi and the house in good shape. He was in frequent contact with his friend Winifred, aka Wump. This woman seems to calm him very much. The story of what she's finding on her archaeological dig consumes Malachi and he looks for new text in every mail. Wump can't e-mail very often, since she's working in France where internet is iffy and expensive. Malachi is thinking of going to France. That may be a very good idea.

Malachi took the news of his grotesque family history with poise and grace. I wonder if he knew all along on a very deep level that the person posing as his mother really wasn't Joanna.

What hasn't changed are the frequency and intensity of his dreams. I'm convinced that something else entirely, some aspect only tangentially related to the Joanna saga, is at the root of his problem and I'm determined to discover what that something else is. I'm going to continue probing into Malachi's past and will, as always, keep you apprised of his condition. I suspect a connection with this town, Bay St. Louis, that Malachi talks of so much. It is there I'll find my answers, I'm sure of it.

How's the progress on the house on the hill of Jerome? I truly love the place. It's so turn-of-the-century, so western. I'm discovering a side of myself I didn't know existed, that I'm so connected with the land, the red rock of the west. It grabs me and won't let go. I imagine myself on a windswept spot of North Rim, gazing at Venus' Temple, or in the blazing morning sun at Lonely Dell, wondering about the woman who lost her daughter the day she was born. Soon the cemetery there will be a furnace. I wonder about the condition of the bones… Are they bleached white, do they still exist? How deep could one bury in the hard soil of Paria Canyon?

Oh, I almost forgot... I taped my session with Amanda and will be sending you the transcript ASAP.

Write soon and let me know how my new home away from home is. And let me know how you are.

Ruth

24 May 2004
From: Cletus.Hardin@psychnet.org
To: ruth.blanchard@psychnet.org
Dear Ruth,

Jerome is not at all the same without you. I feel so fortunate to have reconnected, and I want that connection to last. We'll explore the *why*s and the *how*s of Paria Canyon and Lonely Dell's cemetery upon your next visit.

Trust your instincts about Malachi. I've always felt there was more to his saga than just an accident and the loss of his mother. As grotesque as the whole situation was, it was not quite enough to explain some of the details of his dream. Things don't fit and I'm glad you'll continue your sessions with him. Keep me posted. And encourage the trip to France. Any contact with his past is good.

Love, Cletus

25 May 2004
From: gold.digger@netconnect.net
To: fractal@netconnect.net

You wanted more text, here it is. Enjoy! It just gets better and better. But be warned, Thomas will leave you with more questions than answers...

Are you thinking about my suggestion that you visit?

Love, W

Attachment to mail dated 25 May 2004:

I came to Cluny to work, not to spend all my time plotting to discover worms in the woodpile or wooing old women. Ghislaine was becoming insistent as well as tiresome. Surely she did not expect anything permanent to come of our dalliance. Why would she have ever entertained the thought that I would love her forever—or even that I loved her now? She could not have considered leaving her husband, abandoning her position, her family, her home to spend her days looking after a stone carver? She may have thought she loved me in a way she did not love Hugh. But I know that, had we persisted, she would have grown tired of me and regretted all that she had given up. I did not want this responsibility of having a woman requiring my love who had sacrificed so much more for me than I for her. She would have eventually chided me, grown older and more cross. What would I do with an old woman when I am in the vigor of my life? She sees us living a simple life, content with each other. Ghislaine has always been wealthy; she would chafe under poverty.

In the time left before she and Hugh left for Compostela, we met every night in our usual spot. She was becoming more and more foolhardy. She cried out during lovemaking, hoping, I daresay, that we would be discovered and that Hugh's hand would be forced. She could be absolved from responsibility for the dissolution of her marriage. One night, when Ghislaine was even more insistent than usual, almost incoherent in her begging for my pledge of eternal devotion, someone came upon us in the midst of the act. The man had no light, but when he called out, I recognized his voice. It was Crispin, the stable boy, a sorry lot. He was a filthy, stinking scoundrel, forever skulking about, spying on his betters, a coward who bullied those few beneath him and licked the boots of those in power. I disguised my voice and made him think we were a couple from the village just looking for a little privacy. Fortunately, his bodily needs dampened his curiosity and by the time he came out of the latrines, our ardor had cooled and we had departed for our respective beds.

In addition to Ghislaine's bleating, Gérard was becoming a source of irritation. Something had to be done. He was becoming ever more valuable to Gislebertus, adopting his techniques, following his instructions slavishly. Gérard was forgetting what he himself had seen in the house frequented by Gislebertus and was becoming bewitched by the master's skill. I always stand back. If Gislebertus became lodged in my soul, I would lose my own self in my zeal to become like him. I warned Gérard of the consequences of too much trust, but he would not listen. If he became too close to Gislebertus, his soul would be lost to that woman's fiend and I would lose the place that was rightfully mine. The day of Gérard's freedom was approaching. Someone had to warn the Duke of his presence at Cluny so that Gérard could be returned to his rightful owner before the year and a day were fulfilled. I could not do so. Blaise and Marthe would refuse to lodge me. Gislebertus would be furious and his anger would follow me all the days of my life, preventing me from finding work elsewhere when this task is done.

As Gérard was Gislebertus' client, so was Marcel mine. His devotion to me smacked of the sensual. He may have been one of those men who lie with either sex. In any case, he loved me. That was obvious. Therefore he was of potentially great use. He had to be made aware of Gérard's condition and made to think that I preferred Gérard to him. As I used Germanus' wounded vanity to my own ends, so I determined to exploit Marcel's boundless jealousy. As a first step, I told him the secret I had learned about Gérard all the while adjuring his utmost discretion and knowing he would betray Gérard if need arose.

In the work yard I contrived to use Marcel whenever possible. I was rapidly moving into position as second only to Gislebertus, at least as far as work was concerned. It was clear that the master preferred the company of Gérard just as it was plain that when skill was the issue, I was the sculptor of preference. I decided to adopt the same tactic with Marcel, using him for technical advantage while choosing Gérard for personal reasons. One day, a group of itinerant performers came to Cluny. Gislebertus allowed all the imagers to attend their performance since we might be called upon to execute in stone a tumbler, an acrobat, even beasts. He believed it was necessary to see an object before attempting to render it in stone. That was why I closely observed a hanged man despite the disapproval of those who watched me do so. I asked Gislebertus once if he had ever seen a demon. His reaction to this was sour. One of the acts of this troupe involved a dancing bear. The poor beast was clearly distressed at being tugged this way and that, regretting his life in the forest where he belonged. He emitted little groans and, each time, Gérard groaned with him. At these marks of compassion, I touched him in sympathy, making certain that Marcel observed all this, which he did with the most careful scrutiny. I accomplished much with this action. I achieved my primary objective, that of making Marcel jealous beyond all telling. But I also curried favor with Gislebertus, for whom Gérard had become an icon of virtue, and cast away all hint of suspicion that might have come upon me as a result of Gérard's eventual arrest.

I did not have long to wait for the results of my charade. Marcel lost little time informing the Duke's men of Gérard's status. He was taken into custody the night of the troupe's performance and spirited away without anyone's knowledge. Ghislaine and Hugh left Cluny the day after Gérard's arrest, which threw suspicion on them as possible culprits in the discovery of his status. Once again Ghislaine served me, all unaware of her usefulness.

A few days after these two departures, I became aware that I had not seen the Father Prior in days. Germanus provided me with confirmation of his absence as he triumphantly announced that I had succeeded admirably. Savin had left Cluny for Citeaux, deserting Pierre for Bernard, his critic and rival. What better revenge could there have been than the loss of Pierre's beloved Savin to that thorn-in-his-side of Clairvaux? Germanus, Philippe and the other Poncians were ecstatic. Surely one of them would now be named prior. Their stars were both ascendant.

[There is at this point a break in Thomas' text. Gislebertus' response follows.]

When last we spoke, I mentioned need for absolution. Here is the explanation for that need. About three weeks after our return from Cluny, I awoke to an empty dwelling. I believe you know our practice of living in the ruins of Augustus' theater in Autun, Augustus' own city. Believing Casilda and Mallory to be on a search for firewood, I made my way to Saint-Lazare, where I encountered a large crowd milling about. They were all gazing up at an object dangling from the scaffolding set up for the purpose of putting my Eve in place. At first, I paid no mind, thinking one of the masons in a drunken stupor had hanged a pig or a goat. When I heard someone say, "Surely this was spawn of the devil," I decided further investigation was required. I clambered up to the top of the structure and from there gazed down on my Mallory, naked, his pitiful sex exposed, his tiny sex of which he was so ashamed, his neck broken, swaying in the gentle April breeze. Casilda was directly beneath him and our eyes met in a mutual gaze of such exquisite pain, I thought I would throw myself to my death at the thought of having failed her. This was my scaffolding, my rope, horrifying my dearest wife and killing her harmless, gentle brother. In a corner of the square I spied Thomas and a few of his fellow stone carvers, laughing uproariously, that is until they saw me looking intently in their direction. At that moment, they knew that I knew. How long Thomas had been aware of Mallory's existence, I know not. But anyone watching our comings and goings would have been able to pick off the poor fellow in a trice. Mallory was well named; he knew much unhappiness. But a gentler soul never lived, save my Casilda.

I do not know what the last moments of Mallory's life were like and I care not to imagine them. But I do know how Thomas ended. As I had no proof at all of his culpability, there was no going to the bishop. Neither church nor crown would punish the felon on my hunch alone. So I pretended to forget the whole matter. A whole year went by before I made my move. I arranged for him to climb the very scaffolding he had used for the killing of my wife's brother in order to put in place my Suicide of Judas capital. Is that not a delicious touch, using an image of the betrayer in a scheme of vengeance? Sinful, I know, but delicious nonetheless. I had loosened one of the floorboards and shortened and so arranged the ropes of his harness that, when he fell through the support, the rope slipped around his neck and he, like Mallory, dangled high above the heads of the other workers.

By the time they got to him, he was dead, his neck broken and his soul in hell. I am not sorry. I cannot be sorry nor could I say I would not do this a thousand times over were it necessary. And so, Father
End of attachment.

Here ends the narrative and I have scant hope of finding any more. Every inch of the walls of the hidden room in the ruins of the Roman theater at Autun was covered and, if the text continues, it is in a place we cannot guess. Gislebertus, along with Thomas, appears to have died before his time. His skeleton was the last to be found, at the foot of the wall on which his last words were scribbled. The hand in which the text was written grows fainter and less legible towards the end, and I suspect that he, nearing death, wished to make a confession of sorts even though there was no one to hear it or give him absolution. But considering his "I cannot be sorry...," it is doubtful whether absolution was what he wanted or would have gotten. I think it was rather a need for someone someday to know of his deeds and Thomas' shameful actions. He indicates the narrative was destined for Abelard. Perhaps Gislebertus sent him word about his secret abode and the message awaiting him. I think he especially wanted the debauched Ghislaine to know that her tormentor had met a traitor's end. Whether that desire was granted remains forever a mystery. How would a woman of Ghislaine's status come to know of such an event? Tales of the events of the lives of masons and stone carvers did not find their way to the dinner tables of the well-born. She and Hugh found, I hope, a way to cope with her shame and lived happily ever after.

Of Gérard's fate we know nothing. After his arrest, he disappears from Thomas' text. He was probably returned to his owner.

We also know nothing whatsoever of the manner of Gislebertus' death. We do know that Mallory's pitiful corpse must have been retrieved somehow by Gislebertus and brought back to the home he and Casilda had made for him in the ruins. After Gislebertus exacted vengeance upon Thomas, the couple may have simply walled themselves up in this cave with the remains of her brother and awaited death, Gislebertus writing his story as he waited. Or he may have wished to spare his beloved a slow agony and waited for an opportune moment to end her misery. Her skull shows some evidence of trauma, but whether accidental or manmade is unknowable. If you'd come for a visit, you could see all this for yourself—the bones, the text, the ruins. The story would really come alive for you.

Our work here is nearly done and I don't especially relish a summer in France overrun with tourists, although the tourist trade is considerably down. Apparently Americans aren't the only ones disgusted with the

French. The oil-for-food scandal has seeped—pun intended—into other parts of Europe and many nationalities are staying away. Italy is enjoying a boom and I may make a side trip there before I return. But not if you're coming. I'd stay here and show you Autun.

Write again, dear Mug, and let me know how things are going. W

30 May 2004
From: ruth.blanchard@psychnet.org
To: Cletus.Hardin@psychnet.org

I'm extremely worried about Malachi. He has become very despondent, lethargic almost, and spends a great deal of time at his computer. Perhaps the high of discovering the truth has given way to depression. Celestine indicates that even as a child, Malachi was given to mood swings, one moment full of piss and vinegar, and the next, withdrawn and sullen. He may have a stash of drugs I don't know about. I'm going to stay with him for a while and observe closely his habits. He indicated this would be OK with him, but I didn't notice any marked enthusiasm for my presence. Tomorrow—or next minute—it may be a different story. He received an e-mail from his friend Winifred that seems to have depressed him. I think he wanted closure to the story Winifred was relating or a different ending. He mumbled something about those who destroy those whom they love and about jealousy and revenge and all sorts of other mumbo jumbo that made no sense. Perhaps I'm just not seeing the connection. His family was all about secrets and betrayal, and apparently this rather ancient story was also. I'm going to keep a close eye on him. His case is far from closed.

Celestine is coming to trust me more and more. She visits frequently. What I first took for hostility is just a fierce loyalty to Malachi and his family. I may make her an ally yet. She could really help with details of childhood Malachi doesn't remember or couldn't process at the time. Will keep you posted.

Love, Ruth

1 June 2004
From: ruth.blanchard@psychnet.org
To: Cletus.Hardin@psychnet.org
Dear Cletus,

Here is the transcript of my taped conversation with Amanda, taken the day before I left Jerome. Malachi is as despondent as ever, as if he doesn't know what to do with himself. He also hasn't heard from his friend in a while and that worries him. His attachment to Winifred is unnaturally strong or so it seems to this amateur shrink. I think he's going to go to France to meet up with her. I know you thought this was a good idea. What about now?

Transcript of 21 May 2004 meeting of Amanda G.
and Ruth Blanchard:

A: Thanks for seeing me. I don't have a great deal of hope for Malachi and me, but I'd like one last try.

R: You're welcome. And you may be able to give me some insight into what makes Malachi tick. Even though we've discovered a portion of what was bothering him, there's a large chunk of the puzzle missing, perhaps the most important one. I'd like you to talk and let me listen for a while, then, if I can, I'll answer any questions you may have. Just remember there's a lot I can't tell you.

A: Fair enough. I guess I'll just begin at the beginning, with our meeting. We actually met for the very first time in Bay St. Louis…

R: The Bay again!?

A: What do you mean "again"?

R: Malachi mentions that place a lot. It apparently had some quasi-mystical role in his childhood. But go on. I'll try not to interrupt your train of thought.

A: As I said, we met at the Bay. I was eighteen and visiting some friends, and Malachi came to a party with a friend of his. I didn't see Malachi again until our paths crossed at NAU. I had gotten a degree in law in the meantime and was there as a prof. He joined the faculty shortly after I did but eventually left for a private company. He had been a student there and it's difficult to join former professors on an equal footing. At our first encounter, I fell for him hard and almost instantaneously. I remember thinking when we met that we were somehow destined for each other. We lived together for about two years then ran off to Vegas for a quicky wedding. His father was none too happy but there was nothing he could do about it. I don't think Parker ever approved of me. Maybe he didn't like lawyers. Or maybe I just rubbed him the wrong way.

The early years were wonderful. We shared ideas, had lengthy discussions about art, politics, literature. Malachi was a mathematician, interested in chaos theory, and I was a lawyer, but the similarities in our backgrounds and education made us soul mates, or so I thought. There's lots of chaos in law. And Mal is very interested, as am I, in both art and literature, surprisingly so. Most scientists care for nothing that doesn't involve proof of some theory. Then, as the years passed, we seemed to grow bored with one another. He's right about my little affairs of the heart, but none was so serious as to make me want a clean break, just a temporary one to recharge my batteries so to speak. Falling for another man gave me the oomph I needed to rekindle my feelings for Malachi. Is that a weird thing or does it happen in other marriages?

R: I wouldn't say it's uncommon, but it is dangerous. Counseling, rather than experimenting with your feelings, would have been a better way to go. But counseling then wasn't as common or as discussed as it is now. Infidelity of any sort, even when there's no physical component, is no cure for the marital blahs. This is disputed in some quarters. I've seen articles on the 'net that claim an affair can cure what ails a marriage. I don't buy it. But some pros do.

A: There was only one really serious, threatening relationship and it was rather recent, perhaps a result of my age. I felt my youth, my desirability slipping away and I had a fling of sorts with a male colleague. Brad and I never progressed beyond passionate necking. And some emotional intimacy. Malachi suspected everything; he knew I was falling for Brad before I did. But I broke it off before anything dreadful happened. Odd, that one.

R: Odd in what way?

A: Brad claimed he told Malachi all about us but that Malachi claimed not to be my husband. Brad assumed he was in complete denial and would rather have a cheating woman than no woman at all.

R: That also is not uncommon. Many men prefer the cheating to the humiliation of having anyone know about it. At times, they collude with the spouse to hide the affair. Go on.

A: There's not much else to tell. Right now, I'm in limbo. Malachi claims he wants to try again but sometimes ages go by without a word from him. My last mail from him was April 30th. This is May 21st and I've had no message. He adamantly refuses to talk so I'm a prisoner of cyberspace, awaiting e-mails that never come. If we were really working on marital issues, we'd e-mail a bit every day. My mails to him remain unanswered.

R: I tend to agree with you and I'll gently try to push Malachi into more openness with you. But I cannot stress enough the necessity of his finding wholeness before he can tackle a real relationship. His only intimate contacts at the moment are his friend Winifred and me. And I am most emphatically not suggesting anything of a romantic nature with either of us.

Let's move on. Tell me about Parker. What were your impressions about his relationship with Malachi?

A: Very possessive, very controlling, didn't like much independence in anyone. Perhaps that's why he and I clashed. He was always badmouthing Malachi's mother and, of course, Malachi was none too happy about being abandoned by Joanna. But he didn't seem crazy about Parker either. He didn't talk too much about his family or his past. What little I know—about Buddy, the accident, stuff like that—has sort of dribbled out in bits and pieces. I remember there were times when Malachi was off in a different world, a different time. As I said, he began to have mood swings, accused me of marrying him for his money, of having these infernal affairs. I think my casual—and platonic—fling with Brad was a result of that. I figured I might as well have a roll in the hay since Malachi was convinced of my infidelity anyway. As I mentioned, there was no roll in the hay, but nothing's been the same since. We were thinking of divorce when he received news of Joanna's death but it came just as I was regretting our impending parting and wanted to try yet again to work things out. Malachi seemed amenable to this until he returned to Louisiana and fell in love with the house he grew up in. He wants to stay in Louisiana for a good chunk of the year. I guess I'll have to decide if I can hack the climate. It would be a big change from Flagstaff. But I can get used to just about anything. It's time for me to retire anyway.

R: Cletus and I plan to divide our time between the two states. Perhaps you and Malachi could work out a similar arrangement if you patch things up ...

A: Possible. But only if Malachi will have me. I suspect, but don't know for sure, that he has tried to test me by e-mailing me a proposition under a false name. He doesn't trust me, and rightly so, but cares enough to determine if I'll fall again. What do you think of our chances?

R: To be honest we haven't discussed you or your marriage much. I can tell you this. Unless and until I can find out what's eating Malachi, your relationship—in fact any relationship Malachi attempted—would be doomed. I'll leave it up to him to reveal to you what I'll convey to him when I return with my report on my meeting with his father. It's both shocking and disgusting, and he may want to keep it to himself for a while. After he comes to terms with this aspect of his past, I'm going to try to keep probing till all that's troubling him has been faced and dealt with. Once that happens, and it might never happen, you and he may want to try to pick up the pieces. In that case, you should both start fresh with a new therapist, one that neither of you will feel is on the other party's side in the thrashing out of your differences. Now, I'm afraid I'll have to end our meeting, which I've enjoyed very much. I have packing to do, and Cletus and I have some planning for our future to tackle. Love complicates life greatly, doesn't it?

A: Yes. But it's worth it. Thank you for your time. Would you stay in touch with me?

R: I'll e-mail as much information as I can. I surely hope you and Malachi can work things out. But first Malachi must straighten himself out.

A: Understood! Have a good trip back to the south.

[End of transcript.]

That's it. Thoughts…? Now I must go pay Malachi a visit and let him know the truth about his pseudo-mom. I'll let you know how that goes.
Love, Ruth

3 June 2004
From: Cletus.Hardin@psychnet.org
To: ruth.blanchard@psychnet.org
As you suggested, I called Malachi with news of his father's death and was struck by the lack of affect, something you predicted. In the brief

time you've known him, you seem to have connected with him better than I could in the years I've been treating him. I'm glad the nursing home staff called me; they probably would have been shocked at his reaction—or lack thereof. I guess they preferred that his shrink give him the info. He'll be receiving documents in the mail and will be very wealthy indeed.

Interesting, this woman Amanda. I don't quite know what to make of her. Put her on a back burner and concentrate on Malachi.

Love always, C

5 June 2004
From: ruth.blanchard@psychnet.org
To: Cletus.Hardin@psychnet.org
Dear Cletus,

Malachi's reaction to all the events and revelations of the past few days continues to be troubling. Parker's death on the 3rd did not faze him. His passing was of no interest to his son; he didn't even ask about the fortune Parker left him. It will, of course, take a while to probate his will. But I'm sure he realizes he'll be a wealthy man indeed. I hope this isn't behind Amanda's renewed interest in her husband. He seems withdrawn, in a world of his own. At times, I call out to him and he seems not to hear me. He did say one curious thing: he believes his friend in France, Winifred, has lost interest in him and his difficulties. I'm trying to remember his exact words. Something like, "Wump is too busy for me," or "My problems bore Wump; she has a real life." His last mail from her was May 25th, not so long ago. I find Malachi's discontent with his friend unreasonable. I've e-mailed Winifred and will try again although I realize she's probably very busy, can't get on the 'net, or has some other very good reason for not contacting Malachi. If she knew of Parker's death and all the horrors Malachi has discovered, I feel certain she'd try to contact her friend. I'll keep you posted.

Love, Ruth

6 June 2004
From: Cletus.Hardin@psychnet.org
To: ruth.blanchard@psychnet.org
Dear Ruth,

How I wish you were back here and we were planning a jaunt to Grand Canyon or Kanab or Lonely Dell... I miss you terribly. I'm sorry our correspondence seems consumed by other people's problems.

As I think back, Malachi discussed his friend a lot, seemed very concerned with what Winifred thought of him, what he said and did. Her considerable accomplishments in the field of archeology really impressed Malachi and made him feel inadequate, I think. Malachi lived *through* Wump and depended on her for his own self esteem, strange as that sounds. It was as though the two of them shared a life or rather, as though Wump let Malachi share in her academic triumphs. Apparently she was a prolific scholar. I know that Malachi looked for mail from W almost every day and when W went to France and Malachi knew he'd not hear from her as often, that depressed him. The trip to France is fine but, when he returns, try to get Malachi to "get a life." I hate that hackneyed expression, but it really does describe what he needs—some accomplishments of his own and activities he can throw himself into. Aren't there any clubs he could join? Volunteer work he could do?

I wish I could be more help.

If this weren't an e-mail, I'd make you blush, telling you what I wish we were doing now. But I'll save it for our next encounter, which will be fairly soon. As soon as I can tie up some loose ends, I'll plan a trip to Louisiana, probably in October when the humidity is only 80%.

Take care of yourself. Don't burn out over this thing.

Love always, Cletus

8 June 2004
From: ruth.blanchard@psychnet.org
To: Cletus.Hardin@psychnet.org

Malachi left for France today. I know you find his attachment to Winifred too strong but, frankly, what other emotional support does he have? I'm very fond of him and listen patiently to his sorry stories, but I'm paid to do so. I think a change of scenery and a visit with an old chum will be good for him. I'll keep you posted and forward his mails to you. He promised to stay in touch.

Love, Ruth

9 June 2004
From: fractal@netconnect.net
To: ruth.blanchard@psychnet.org
Dear Ruth,

All is well. I arrived at CDG exhausted but in pretty good shape otherwise. The Paris airport is, as always, a nightmare to navigate. I'm going to spend a few days here then proceed to Autun. I can't face getting on a train without some R&R to see me through the journey south.

I rented a cell phone, called a *portable* here, and managed to get through to Winifred. She always has her cell on whereas e-mail is iffy. She suggested an Ibis hotel so I think I'll just go to the reservations help desk here in the airport. I'm at a 'net café now and will be sure to get a hotel with service or in close proximity to a hot spot. I brought my laptop with me so there should be no problems staying in touch.

I'm about to collapse so will close till tomorrow.

M

9 June 2004
From: ruth.blanchard@psychnet.org
To: fractal@netconnect.net

Will keep mails few and brief as I know time is money. Will contact you only if needed. Send cell number and write as often you can.

Ruth

11 June 2004
From: fractal@netconnect.net
To: ruth.blanchard@psychnet.org

E-mailing isn't the difficult nightmare I expected it to be, so I'll be in regular touch. Feel free to write as often as you wish. Remember how rich I am ;-))

Paris is its usual wonderful self, everything I expected. Mother brought me here when I was thirteen but I don't remember much of that trip. Amanda and I visited a few times and did the usual touristy stuff. So I decided to see some things off the beaten track. I've always wanted to see what was left of Victor Hugo's Paris, the part of the city that was the setting for *Notre-Dame de Paris*, aka *The Hunchback of Notre-Dame*. The Place de l'Hôtel de Ville now occupies the former Place de Grève where Quasimodo was beaten and Esmeralda, executed. The Parc des Buttes-Chaumont has replaced the sinister cave of Montfaucon thanks to the efforts of Napoleon III and Haussmann. Although much of the park is artificial, it's still beautiful. There's a small lake with an island and a bridge—the bridge of suicides yet—leading to the island. I also love to visit Gaston Leroux's setting for his *Phantom of the Opera*. Strange how that awful novel has grabbed the human psyche, refusing to let go. And I never visit Paris without going to Saint-Denis. Although in a miserable slum now, the basilica retains its splendor despite the graffiti that cover many of the recumbent statues of kings and queens. The semi-nude bodies of Henry II and Catherine de Médicis are trashed with names, slogans, etc. It's tragic how France's past is disrespected by the masses. Fortunately, the statues on the upper levels of the monuments are in good shape.

I spoke to Winifred today and she'll be waiting at the station tomorrow when I arrive in Autun. I'll take the TGV. More later, M

13 June 2004
From: fractal@netconnect.net
To: ruth.blanchard@psychnet.org

All is well. Winifred was waiting and whisked me off to a wonderful hotel, a former 17th-century Ursuline convent in Rivault Street bounded on one side by ancient Roman walls. My room looks out on the courtyard and is very quiet. The hills of the Morvan are visible in the distance. As you can tell, I have 'net access. The hotel is very close to the cathedral but it's quite a hike to the theater where Winifred's team is digging up the past. At present, they're working more with the text rather than digging, having satisfied themselves that there isn't any more to be found. All we did today was visit Saint-Lazare. Winifred pointed out the little street near the cathedral, Impasse de la Maîtrise, which just might be the Street of the Thistle where Thomas lodged with Blaise and Marthe. (I printed out and let you read the text Wump sent to me, didn't I? If not, I certainly shall once I return.) The Impasse is at right angles to the facade of the church, a very convenient location for one working on the building. I'll have to look into the name of the street. Perhaps a cathedral school was located there. Or perhaps the street is younger than the church. The notion that it's the former Street of the Thistle may be fanciful.

14 June

I spent the day strolling about the town. Winifred is busy so she suggested I come to the theater tomorrow. It's near the Chapelle Saint-Nicolas, which now serves as a museum of ancient and medieval artifacts. Autun was an extremely important town of Roman Gaul and the museum is apparently crammed with tombstones, sarcophagi, funerary inscriptions and all sorts of stuff I love to examine. I'll do those two sites on the same day. Today was given to the south end of town, the cathedral, the Rolin Museum, the ramparts. Some of the best capitals are preserved in the chapter room of the cathedral and one can see them up close. The exquisite detail of the carvings is visible in a way not possible had they been in their original locations in the church. They're placed too high for anyone without binoculars and a ladder. The Rolin Museum houses Gislebertus' famous *Eve*. What's exciting is that this is the same *Eve* Thomas complains about in his criticism of the Master. It's eery to look upon a sculpture described in a manuscript dating from the time of the sculpture's creation, a ms. I've been reading in bits and pieces. The most extraordinary thing I saw, however, was the *Suicide of Judas* capital, the one that figures so prominently in Thomas'story. I wonder if he had a hand in carving it or if the body he examined on his journey to Autun had any part in its conceptualization. The manner of the hanging is most curious. Judas is suspended from a straplike contraption from which he could easily escape just by lifting his head. And there's a weird bulge on his back that no one has been able to identify. It's too bad the ms. doesn't give any hints about the iconography of Gislebertus' product. Thomas wasted his time and resources complaining about Gislebertus' imaginary flaws. And Gislebertus spent his energy defending himself against Thomas' cruel charges.

I'll tell you all about tomorrow after I have a chance to spend some time with Wump at the dig. I also hope to have a chance to do nothing but talk, especially about the past at the Bay.

As the French say, *A demain*. M

15 June

Good day today, although not as much time to yak with Wump as I would have wanted.

The Roman theater is huge with many nooks and crannies, a perfect place even today for a couple on the lam to hide out. The place where the text was discovered is cordoned off but Wump was recognized and allowed to pass, even with me in tow. The remains of a dwelling are clearly discernible. There are niches carved out in the wall, all done very neatly as if a master stone carver had been at work, which of course he was. There's even a crude bed formed from a natural rocky outcrop smoothed over to accommodate a body. The tiny opening that Mallory must have used is still visible and we managed to squeeze through into his quarters. What an awful life he must have had, always hidden, afraid to show his face or any other part of himself, fearing for his life and that of his protectors.

x

The parts of the manuscript written on the walls are barely visible and I now understand well why photographing, then photocopying the text was helpful. I wonder what will happen to the site once the excavations are completed. The most marvelous places on earth are those we need to protect zealously from human contact, it seems. Gislebertus and Casilda must have been extraordinary people and wonderfully in love. It's nice to know such mutual devotion can exist.

Wump and I had lunch in a charming bistro. But when I broached the subject of our young lives at the Bay, a sadness came over her face and she indicated, not in words but in facial expression, that she really didn't want to dredge up the past. I don't know why. I would have expected her to enjoy talking about that time of our lives.

Her colleagues are very nice and were charming to me. There's a guy she's interested in who strikes me as shallow and self-absorbed, but it's her life and I'll keep my nose out of her affairs. He's French and that may have something to do with my impression of him. He's the guru of Autun, overseeing all antiquities investigations. There are others on the team who impressed me a lot: a British woman, Mary, who specializes in medieval French; Max from Germany, who tells the workmen how to dig without destroying; Wump is the art historian/archaeologist who places all in context for the others. She'd also recognize a fraud if she saw one. There's been a spate of fraudulent objects on the antiquities market lately so everyone involved in that line is very nervous. The one she referred to as the "big cheese" of the dig has returned to the US for a few weeks so I'll not have the pleasure. Mary is also the literary specialist who recognized "Morel" as the name of a character in a novel. I hope our Morel is fine and that Cel and Ruben are taking good care of him. This is his first stay at their house but at least the people are familiar to him. Cats hate change. It took him a while to warm up to me but I think he finally resigned himself to the stranger in his domain and has accepted me. At times, he's even affectionate.

I had to let Wump get back to work so I went to the antiquities museum on my own. Very interesting and in a wonderful, peaceful setting. There are artifacts everywhere, piled against the walls of the former cloister, lying on the ground. I guess it would be impossible to catalog it all but it would be nice to know what I'm looking at. I don't read Latin at all. Wump does but she can't be my tour guide at the moment.

I'm a little disturbed and hurt that Wump doesn't want to talk about the Bay or our past. She's consumed by her work and I wonder if she's really glad I came to see her. Maybe I'm being too touchy, too sensitive. I'll probably stay a few more days to see what else there is in the vicinity.

I don't feel completely welcome and may want to strike out on my own. Wump has been telling me of the attractions of Burgundy. I wonder if she's trying to get rid of me. I also wonder why she urged me so enthusiastically to come for this visit. Perhaps she was being polite and didn't expect me to accept the invitation. M

15 June 2004
From: gold.digger@netconnect.net
To: ruth.blanchard@psychnet.org
Dear Ruth,

I'm sure you've heard from Malachi. How does he sound to you? Since his arrival, he's become more and more despondent. Nothing I show him interests him, and what I say to him just seems to frustrate and depress him. He displays a subtle hostility towards my colleagues, who welcomed him warmly. I'm at my wits' end. I know I'm not responsible for his emotional state but I do so wish I could help. He needs me to an unhealthy degree, or so it appears to one untrained in such matters. Can you give me any guidance? I'd love to help him but I don't know how.

Regards, Winifred

15 June 2004
From: ruth.blanchard@psychnet.org
To: gold.digger@netconnect.net
Dear Winifred,

You read your friend's mental state fairly accurately. His demands on both you and himself are unreasonable and I'm going to write in an attempt to assuage his feelings of depression and loneliness. But I'll probably not succeed until he and I can meet face-to-face. Hang in there! And thanks for being a good friend to him. Ruth

15 June 2004
From: ruth.blanchard@psychnet.org
To: fractal@netconnect.net

I've avoided writing because I know getting e-mail may not be easy and I didn't want to clog your inbox. But I had to comment on your relations with Wump. First, it's very common for us to be let down when confronting a person or place important to us in the past. People seem less loving and friendly, houses seem smaller or shabbier, and so forth. Don't be discouraged. We're making huge progress in disentangling this mess and when you return, I expect to have many of the puzzle pieces put together in a coherent image. Soon we'll have the enigma of Malachi solved and you will be at peace.

In closing, I'll suggest you take notes of your reactions to people, places, images, even odors. All of these may or may not be significant. I'd like to explore them with you when you return. Keep your chin up. And have some fun! Ruth

17 June 2004
From: fractal@netconnect.net
To: ruth.blanchard@psychnet.org

Wonderful last two days! It was a bit of a relief to be on my own and surprising to me that I did so well solo. I managed to get to two other famous Burgundian sites, Brancion, a little hole in the wall that's a real piece of the past, and the former priory church at Perrecy-les-Forges. They're in a section of Burgundy called the Mâconnais. These are two places one really has to want to get to desperately as they're both much off the beaten track. I hired a car and got to Brancion on the evening of the 16th. Fortunately I found a room at the local—and only—auberge. As I entered the town gate, having left my vehicle at the car park some distance from the city walls as required, I felt that I was entering a lost world. A 10th-century feudal castle, refashioned and enlarged by the Dukes of Burgundy, is still there; Catherine de Médicis was a visitor and probably cast covetous eyes on the possessions of the very rich and powerful family that owned the town. The 15th-century market place is still standing. But the jewel of the area is the 12th-century church of Saint-Pierre, decorated with 14th- and 15th-century murals and the funerary monument of Josserand IV de Brancion, who died, as the plaque proudly proclaims, at the side of Louis IX during the seventh crusade. From the yard in front of the church, one has a breathtaking view of a beautiful valley as the town sits on a rocky promontory between two deep ravines. I was the sole visitor. It was wonderful.

Today I visited Perrecy-les-Forges. I got here late and will probably not return to Autun until late tomorrow as I want to revisit the church. I got only a perfunctory glance today (17th).

18 June 2004
From: fractal@netconnect.net
To: ruth.blanchard@psychnet.org

So glad I returned to Perrecy. I saw details in the sculpture I totally missed yesterday because the light was so dim. Of course, seeing anything there is a bit of a challenge. All the sculpture is on the façade and the capitals of the very deep narthex, much of it badly degraded. But what is preserved is lovely. It's much quieter and less exuberant than most depictions of the Passion. At Autun, everything swirls, and everyone shouts and gestures dramatically. At Perrecy, the only really animated figure is Saint Peter as he brandishes what looks like a sword. It's a most unusual carving as he is twisting and turning, not upright, and outsized. If he stood up straight, he would surpass the boundaries of the lintel. The most moving scene is of Gethsemane. Winifred told me the sleep of the Apostles is an infrequent subject in Romanesque sculpture, which makes the one at Perrecy all the more special. The lintel frieze makes a sharp right angle in the middle of the scene, with the sleeping apostles beginning to awaken on the left, Christ at the corner and the angel sent to console him waiting in the wings behind him. And, of course, there's the betrayal scene. But no suicide. The one at Autun and others at towns close to Autun, Saulieu and Vézelay, are the only ones in the region according to Winifred. Her next project, after she wraps up the "dig" text, will be a study of images of the suicide of Judas in Romanesque Burgundy. The three aforementioned towns are all fairly close together and, spurred by the curiosity typical of the true academic, Wump wants to know why they all feature this episode. She figures something in the air or politics or theological disputes caused this scene to be repeated in this part of France in the twelfth century. She has spoken of this project often and I have the sense that she's anxious for the dig project to be over so she can begin her "Judas" quest. The person for whom the text found in the Roman theater was destined is presumed to be Peter Abelard. Wump is a great fan of his and of his theology of evil: sin lies in one's intent. She suspects that Abelard's take on the betrayal, which deeply offended theologians of his day, may have influenced the iconography of the period, especially the suicide iconography. She expects to have a tough time selling this idea since there's not a shred of proof, so dear to art historians' hearts, for this notion. In fact, she's encountered outright hostility.

The central image of the Perrecy tympanum is quite extraordinary also, Christ flanked by two seraphim. His face is unforgettable, gazing out at the observer with an inscrutable look of mystery. Almost enough to make a believer out of me…

I remain frustrated that Wump and I have had so little time together. I know she's frightfully busy but I did come to France at her urging and mostly to see her, not Gallo-Roman ruins or sculptures in churches. I now think she regrets having suggested I visit. Well, I'm here and I won't be coming back to the US for a few days so I'll just try to stay out of her way.

I understand one of Abelard's burial sites is fairly near Paris so if Wump is still unenthusiastic about my presence, I'll make my way towards whatever town is close to the former tomb and poke around there. Then I'll complete my pilgrimage at Père Lachaise cemetery where Abelard and Heloise found eternal rest, IF one can believe the guidebooks. I'll have gotten somewhat close to the principals in the theater text drama and seen the areas connected with the ms., all except the abbey at Cluny. There's not much left there so I don't think I'll bother.

I'll let you know where I am and what I'm doing in my next mail. I will very much hate to leave Les Ursulines. It's a superb hotel and I'll miss the view from my room.

More later, M

20 June 2004
From: fractal@netconnect.net
To: ruth.blanchard@psychnet.org

I'm in Nogent-sur-Seine, having left Autun yesterday. Wump had gotten a bit friendlier, perhaps because she knew I'd be leaving. I was really hurt by her increasing coldness, but I'll discuss that with you when I'm back in Covington. Perhaps I'm just too sensitive. I do wonder what it would take for me to be truly convinced of someone's love for me. Amanda, Wump, my mother… I don't completely trust anyone.

Today I hired a taxi to drive me to a place called The Paraclete. Beautiful! Abelard had originally built it for himself but gave it to Heloïse and her nuns when Abbot Suger chased them out of their convent at Argenteuil. People think of Abelard and Heloïse as the archetypal misbehaving religious, but the facts in the matter are quite different. Heloïse became a nun in obedience to her husband but she struggled to be faithful to her vows, even if it was primarily to please Abelard. I wonder what name she took as a nun and if she was "Madame Abelard" after their marriage… I think they slipped up once after her profession and his ordination, but who's keeping score? Abelard was quite the super star of his day and that got a lot of people angry and jealous. I'm beginning to think that insecurity and jealousy are the bane of human existence. And there's the Judas thing again in the mix. I too wonder if Abelard's writings had any effect on the frequency of the suicide portrayal near Cluny. He pointed out that Judas did the same thing when he handed over Christ for death as did God the Father and Christ himself. His fellow monks were none too pleased. More on the Cluny connection later. Perhaps I should go there after all.

I arrived at *Le Paraclet* on a little-traveled road and finds it almost by accident. A small blue sign says *Abbaye du Paraclet XIIIe et XVIIe*. I followed a small side road at right angles to the highway and reached a disappointingly modern conventual building. But I continued exploring the grounds and reached the grotto where, according to all best guesses, the crypt of the former church was. In it Abelard was laid to rest after Peter the Venerable of Cluny had his remains sent to the woman who adored him throughout her life. Abelard died at St-Marcel-lès-Chalon and there he would have remained were it not for the desire of Peter to reunite the lovers. The grotto is extraordinary. One approaches by a descending walkway into a semi-subterranean barrel-vaulted chamber. There's a white slab marking the spot where Abelard was laid to rest. It's dark, cool, humid and mysterious, very much like Covington when I arrived in the dead of winter. In fact, the surrounding forest reminds me of the St Tammany Parish in which I grew up. The rest of the area is a mishmash of private property, some portions of what could be buildings original to the Paraclete, and a barnyard. Along one side of the *basse-cour* are what appear to be former cells for the nuns but are today used for storing farm implements. I'm still not clear if these are former cells or not. There wasn't a soul around so no information was forthcoming and guidebooks are useless as they generally ignore the site. Even though I have to backtrack to get to Cluny, I'll go just to feel closer to Peter the Venerable. I've been doing some reading about him since TV is out for one who speaks little French and gets tired of CNN in the few places it's available. No wonder Abelard sought shelter near Peter at the end of his life. What he did for Abelard and Heloïse alone would merit a halo in my book. How I wish I could experience a love like that of the pair but it's too late for me. I'm sixty-one, almost sixty-two. And Amanda and I could never create anything like what Abelard and Heloïse had, no one could. It was one of those miraculous relationships that just happen in very rare circumstances and, I suspect, it requires one of the partners—Heloïse in this case—to subordinate completely his or her life to that of the other. It just occurred to me that Gislebertus and Casilda had such a love. And it's possible, I suppose, that the couples knew each other. I'm too selfish for such a love. And Amanda wouldn't be interested. But it must be a sublime experience. Perhaps if I found exactly the right woman, I could give myself completely to her but she would have to be most extraordinary. Amanda would not do and I'm sure it's too late to find someone else.

More from Cluny after I've had a chance to visit. M

20 June 2004
From: ruth.blanchard@psychnet.org
To: fractal@netconnect.net
Dear Malachi,

How interesting that you should have become interested in Peter Abelard! There are some who believe he invented psychology as he was intensely interested in the workings of the mind and the will in the perpetration of evil. His thinking is so very close to that of Jung, my favorite scholar when it comes to plumbing the depths of the human heart. Sin is in the will and this underlay his defense of Judas if I understood correctly what you related about Winifred's assessment of the morality of his betrayal of Jesus. She apparently is conversant with this notion and agrees with it.

You have not given me a copy of this manuscript that has so engrossed you. I look forward to reading it when you return at which time I'll have so much to tell you. And I'll be eager for a face-to-face about the situation with Winifred. It troubles me that a friendship of such longstanding is in trouble. Try to patch things up before you return to the States.

Ruth

22 June 2004
From: fractal@netconnect.net
To: ruth.blanchard@psychnet.org

It took me almost all day yesterday to get from Nogent to Cluny. France is not well set up for trips to out-of-the-way places, but I managed.

Cluny was disappointing. There's so little left of the original splendor of the place, just the right arms of the two transepts. But they give an idea of what the size of the establishment must have been. I had expected to feel something here, but all I came away with was frustration. There are marks in the ground of where this, that and the other were, but the overall sensation is one of a desperate attempt to revive a dead civilization. Of Peter the Venerable there is no trace. He was buried in the church, having died on Christmas day as he had wished, but his tomb was profaned during the Religious Wars of the sixteenth century, then what remained was scattered and lost during the Revolution. I'd like to return to France in a few months to check on progress at the Autun dig and to visit other sites that sound interesting, but Wump certainly didn't give any indication of enthusiasm for another encounter. I'll see her tomorrow briefly on my way to Paris for the return home and let you know how things go. M

25 June 2004
From: fractal@netconnect.net
To: ruth.blanchard@psychnet.org
Dear Ruth,

I saw Winifred briefly on my way north and she was much warmer, but I suspect it was because my visit was at its end. I spent most of the 23rd on trains and that night at an Ibis Hotel at the airport. The 24th was the usual ghastly return, almost twenty-four hours in transit. I fell into bed but couldn't sleep very well. That's always the way, I was too tired to sleep. At least, I was spared dreams. I'll call when I've had a chance to rest a bit.

I wonder if I'll hear from Winifred anytime soon. The dig work is almost over and she has turned her gaze towards the suicide of Judas capitals project that she's been contemplating for a while. I used to open my e-mail every day in anticipation of a letter from her. I have the sense that my trip to France destroyed what was left of the only good thing in my life.

M

25 June 2004
From: fractal@netconnect.net
To: gold.digger@netconnect.net
Dear Wump,

I'm home, I'm exhausted. This will be brief. I sense things didn't go too well for us. Write and let me know what you think went wrong.

One last thing before I tumble into bed… I'm going to go through those newspaper clippings I found months ago under a floorboard in my old room. Perhaps they'll give me a peek into my past. I hope I'm not disappointed.

Love, M

1 July 2004
From: ruth.blanchard@psychnet.org
To: Cletus.Hardin@psychnet.org
Dear Cletus,

What a nightmare! I hope you've been able to come to terms with Malachi's death. When last we spoke, I promised to send more details as I discovered them in my continuing attempt to discover why, after making—or seeming to make—such progress in his journey to peace and wholeness, Malachi chose to end his life. The trip to France and the visit with Winifred apparently destroyed him. As you read in the mails I forwarded, he became increasingly agitated and depressed after his encounters with his old friend. After I make funeral arrangements, I may go to France myself to see what makes this woman tick. What is curious is the method Malachi chose, hanging, the traitor's mode of execution; equally strange is the message he left for us. It was very brief and mysterious: "Who am I? Who is killing me? I am Thomas. MW" The only "Thomas" I've ever heard him mention is the stone carver in the text that Winifred has been sending in drips and drabs. And remember Malachi's e-mails from France? Full of mentions of Judas, specifically his suicide. As for "MW," I suppose Malachi decided he needed both his initials on something as serious as a suicide note. He signed almost everything else with his first initial, M.

To return to Malachi's death… he hanged himself from the rafters of the upper attic. His plan was well thought out and meticulously executed. Although Celestine and Ruben moved out a while ago, Celestine frequently came to the house to fix dinner for Malachi; otherwise, so Celestine surmises, he would have lived on cereal and PB&J sandwiches. And Celestine always telephoned to let him know she'd be coming. If he didn't answer, Celestine left a message on the answering machine. On June 28th around 6:30, Celestine called out that dinner would be ready in about five minutes. She had assumed all along that Malachi was in his room because the door was shut. After waiting twenty minutes for Malachi to appear, Celestine went looking for him, first in his room, then throughout the house, and finally in the yard. When she noticed Malachi's car was gone, she supposed he was out for the evening although he seldom went out, and it was unusual for him to leave without letting Celestine know not to fix dinner for him. At 8:30, Celestine gave up, put away the food, left a note for Malachi, watched TV for a while and then went home around 10:30. When Malachi still hadn't shown up the next morning, Celestine called me and we decided to call the police. Although he couldn't be classified officially as missing, we asked the cops to keep an eye out for his car and I got on the phone with every person I thought he might be with. His cell phone and the addresses it contained were gone so

I was extremely limited in the number of people I could phone. None of the people I called had a clue as to his whereabouts. He had been talking a lot about the Bay and I would have assumed he had decided to take a run there; but leaving without a word to any of us was so uncharacteristic, I couldn't accept that as a real possibility.

By the night of the 29th, we were all dreadfully worried. Worry turned to panic when Ruben came in at 8 with the news that he had found Malachi's car at the far end of the property, parked in the bushes just off a seldom-used dirt road that leads to the spot where the boathouse used to be. The car was unlocked, empty, with no sign of a struggle or of any unusual activity. Ruben popped the trunk, also empty, with nothing out of the ordinary. The key was not in the ignition and none of Malachi's stuff was in the vehicle. All indicated he had left the car there simply to throw us off the track, convince us he was out on an errand, an outing, a visit. He must have pulled down the stairs to the attic, pulled them back up after himself and closed the door in the ceiling. He then placed his wallet, keys and his strange note on the floor, slipped a plastic bag over his head and a noose around his neck, cuffed his hands behind his back, and then kicked over the stepladder he was standing on. It wasn't until the morning of the 30th that we found him, guided by the foul odor emanating from the hot airless space under the roof. It didn't occur to us that we'd find Malachi up there. We opened the door in the ceiling and went up the ladder expecting to find a raccoon that had gotten trapped or perhaps a squirrel. When we caught sight of him, the stench of death indicated that no rescue was possible so we closed the door and waited for the forensics unit to do its job.

I did the official identification of the body and a friendly forensics tech let me see the photos taken of the scene. They still have the note Malachi left but the tech conveyed the message to me in the vain hope I could decipher its meaning. We were all fingerprinted but there was no evidence whatsoever of any involvement other than Malachi's in any of this. Ruben's fingerprints were all over the car, of course, but the plastic bag and the handcuffs all bore Malachi's prints alone. That fact and his history of mental illness have pretty much closed the case. All that remains is finding the answer to the hard question: why? I intend to find it…

Now that Malachi is dead, Celestine may be more willing to part with her knowledge of the early years, what Malachi was like as a baby, a child, a teenager—everything he was until he left for AZ. Celestine's loyalty must now be to me and my attempt to solve the puzzle of Malachi. I know the Buddy/Joanna thing took its toll. But he really seemed to snap out of the shock of first discovery of that strange mess. And as I mentioned, Buddy-as-Joanna was careful to keep himself distanced from Malachi's intimate physical details. Celestine took care of all that. As evidenced by Celestine's revelations to me, she really was the boy's guardian angel and took quite tender care of him. While she was not stunned by Malachi's suicide, she is nonetheless devastated. It's as though she's been punched in the gut and can't quite catch her breath. I'll work on this and see what I can manage to learn. More later…

Love, Ruth

2 July 2004
From: ruth.blanchard@psychnet.org
To: Cletus.Hardin@psychnet.org
Dear Cletus,

I called Amanda Greene with the news. She was very shaken and blamed herself for a great deal of Malachi's chronic angst and depression. I did my best to convince her that ultimately each of us is responsible for his or her own happiness, but there's no reasoning with the grief-stricken. I'll just give her some time and then provide her with a few more details when I deem it prudent. I'll contact Winifred to let her know of Malachi's death and see if she has any insights to offer. Amanda will undoubtedly want to come for the body. He's in the morgue and they want him "disposed of" as soon as possible. Amanda will probably have him cremated and then scatter the ashes here or take them home to sit on the mantel in an urn… though she doesn't seem like the ashes-in-an-urn type to me. If it were up to me, I'd scatter him at Lonely Dell. Perhaps I'll suggest that to Amanda.

Till tomorrow, R

3 July 2004
From: ruth.blanchard@psychnet.org
To: Cletus.Hardin@psychnet.org

Progress! Now that all the principals are dead—Malachi, Parker, Joanna, Buddy—I was able to convince Celestine to talk. Here's a transcript of her story minus my questions. It's enlightening to say the least and, oh, so southern…

Celestine's narrative:

I came to work for the family when I was ten. The twins, Miss Joanna and Mr. John, was only five and my mama, who was their maid, needed another pair of hands. Miss Emma was feeling so poorly, she couldn't do much. And her husband, Mr. Miles, didn't *want* to do much. Then Miss Emma died and my mama and I raised Miss Joanna and Mr. John all by ourselves. If only Miss Emma had lived, everythin' woulda been different... My mama took care of Mr. John. She never let me see him naked. Now I know why but then I thought she was jes' kinda prissy like.

I remember when Mr. Parker came courtin' Miss Joanna. Slick as a sheet of black ice he was. And jes' as dangerous, but the danger was invisible to Miss Joanna. He was so handsome though, and Miss Joanna jes' fell for him and his ways. On Miss Joanna's weddin' day, my heart nearly broke, her so beautiful and so in love with the evillest man I ever knew. She couldn't see what was underneath. She also didn't know the way he'd been lookin' at me since the beginnin'. I knew one day he'd take what he wanted and there wasn't nothin' I could do 'bout it. If I'd said somethin' they'd've chased me away with a whippin'. And maybe even put out my mama. When I was fifteen, Mr. Parker told mama he needed me to do some cleanin' and ironin' in his shop in New Orleans. By this time, the family had moved to Covington, 'cept Mr. Parker spent most of his time in the city. He'd come to Covington to see Mr. Miles on business. But mostly he looked at me and Miss Joanna and Mr. John. My mama didn't want me to go with him. She knew what he wanted. But she also knew if she said no, she might lose her job. And we needed all the money Mr. Parker promised if I went with him. So she told me to be brave and do what Mr. Parker wanted and everything 'ud be fine for us. "Jes' a little pain," she said, "and a lifetime of food on the table..." The man he gave me to didn't want to do anything but watch me take my clothes off. So I got off lucky at first. But then my luck run out and the man who jes' wanted to watch quit comin'. Some of the other girls there was jes' kids, twelve, thirteen... And there was boys too. There was a special room way in the back. None of us ever went back there. That's where they kep' Mr. John only I didn't find out till later. One day in Covington, Mr. Parker was havin' his fun with me in the boathouse and Mr. John surprised us there. Those two had a really bad ruckus. I thought they was gonna' kill each other for sure. Mr. Parker called Mr. John a whore and Mr. John called Mr. Parker a pimp and to think they was kin sort of. That's when I realized it was Mr. John Mr. Parker kep' in that back room. Mr. John was like a great big sandwich, everybody took a bite. There was all sorts of peoples there, men, women, some you couldn't tell what they was. Then I got pregnant with Ruben. My mama must have made a deal with Mr. Parker 'cause from then on, we lived in the big house with runnin' water and 'lectricity, and we ate at the table with Miss Joanna and Mr. John and all the family. For a while Ruben thought he was Mr.

Malachi's part-brother and he might be too. He sure was fond of him and took his death real hard. I guess today we could do some sort of tes', but Mr. Malachi's dead and gone and all... Everybody's gone but Ruben and me, and I don't know if Miss Amanda wants a black brother-in-law. What would be the point of doin' a tes'? I'll jes' let it be. I'm almost ninety and I'm too tired to worry myself with such stuff. Besides Mr. Parker left me and Ruben well fixed—provided we don't cause no trouble. Yeah, I'll jes' let it be...

[End of Celestine's narrative]

There's a footnote to this never-ending saga. I found this prayer (?), incantation (?) buried under a pile of Malachi's papers: "Oh, you gods of the netherworld, Hades, Proserpina, and you the nameless enormous army of those who killed themselves, or who were murdered, or died before their time." A google search revealed that late antique invocations of black magic began with these words. And we both know of the so-called death pull affecting those traumatized by a death. But whose death traumatized Malachi? He already knew his mother was gone. All the garbage swirling around Parker and Buddy should not have pushed him over the edge. There's something else in the mix. I was not able to discover what was really eating Malachi but there was certainly some other event or situation in his life driving the depression, the sleeplessness. I'll keep looking through his papers in hope of finding what it was.

To my stupefaction, Malachi left me all his worldly goods. He drew up an olographic will shortly after his return from France. It is dated June 27th and was placed neatly in a sealed envelope with his other belongings next to his body. The police found and opened it. It will take a while for the legal niceties to be completed so I haven't bought a villa in Umbria yet. His disconnect from Winifred must have been shattering, as I would have expected him to leave most, if not all, of his fortune to Wump. His dissatisfaction with the recent reunion in France must have been profound.

Since I am his heir, I feel free to rummage through his belongings, even those of an intimate nature. If I think it prudent and kind, I'll let Amanda in on more details. If I discover something that would really hurt her, I'll keep it to myself unless there are compelling reasons to disclose it. I also think Celestine has more to tell me. I'll maintain my distance and give her time to decide when to tell me whatever is on her mind.

Much to my surprise, I've heard nothing from Winifred since Malachi's death but in an e-mail dated 28 June, the very day Malachi died, she did indicate she'd be out of touch for a while, doing some research in some village near Autun. (That's the city whose name I couldn't remember, the locus of her dig.) But I would have expected to hear from her by now. The last e-mail from Winifred was dated and timed shortly before Malachi's death but Europe is seven hours ahead of the US, so the e-mail was actually sent several hours before Malachi died. It had not been opened and read; perhaps hearing from Winifred would have prevented her friend's death. What irony!

Malachi mentioned an encounter with W's mother fairly recently. I think I might take a trip to the Bay to visit with Mrs. Hauser to see if she remembers Malachi and can shed some light on this tragedy. I sensed that Malachi was on the brink of a breakthrough discovery; I'd love to know what it was. I'm also going to dig into his computer. I have his password somewhere in my files; he mentioned it in the course of one of our talks.

It's getting very hot and sticky here and the mosquitoes are terrible. But the blackberries are in full fruit and are delicious. There's something special about eating what you grow on your own property. The warblers are fledging late because we had such a dreary and protracted winter. With luck I'll see the little ones pop—or drop—out of the nest.

Off to the cyber salt mines.

Stay tuned.

Love, Ruth

4 July 2004
From: Cletus.Hardin@psychnet.org
To: ruth.blanchard@psychnet.org
Dear Ruth,

Good luck with digging in Malachi's computer. As for your status as his heir, I told you that you and Malachi connected on a very deep level. I'm not surprised that he left you his estate. Besides I bet he thinks you'll share it with me ;-)))

It's getting hot and dry here, and the tourists are beginning to return. July and August will be the worst. Europeans are trickling back, good for business.

I miss you terribly, you know. We keep putting off decisions about our future, and I think we need some long, soul-searching, face-to-face conversations. I'm tied up with patients throughout the summer, but hope to come see this Louisiana you love so much when the weather there cools off a bit.

Keep me posted on the "M" situation.

Love always, Cletus

6 July 2004
From: ruth.blanchard@psychnet.org
To: cmartin@psychnet.net
Dear Cath,

Cletus is coming to Louisiana in the fall and wants some soul-searching talk. I guess that means marriage or a reasonable facsimile thereof. However, there are some details that would need ironing out. We could split our time between Louisiana and Arizona, but many aspects of both our lives would need serious retooling. Cletus would have to give up his practice; he can't accept patients and then ask them to put their difficulties on hold for half the year. I am unwilling to uproot myself permanently and leave family and friends behind. At our age, we must consider the fact that one of us will be widowed, who knows when? However, I must say that his part of the country has taken hold of me by the throat and heart. I think I have red rock dust in my blood now. The memory of the sound of a distant drum sets my heart racing. I sometimes wonder if I'm in love with Cletus or with his abode. I've pestered him to dig into his roots to see if he's descended from John Wesley Hardin, one of the West's most vicious and notorious gunslingers. How exciting that would be! John Wesley once allegedly shot a man through a hotel room wall for snoring too loudly. I think that alone redeems him for all his terrible ways…

Did I ever tell you about the cemetery at Lonely Dell? It's so simple yet so touching. A few souls are buried there, one a girl who was born and died on the same day, perhaps stillborn. Her name was Lucy Emett and her headstone is a simple piece of red rock with "Lucy Emett B&D June 11 194 " on it. The last digit is hopelessly obliterated. The stone isn't even stuck into the ground but is simply propped up with another rock. These memories are really keeping me grounded in the midst of all the craziness surrounding me here. I'm going to begin digging into Malachi's computer for clues to this most mysterious man. Perhaps he kept a diary in a file somewhere. He mentioned his e-mail password in one of our sessions and I have the transcripts. I'll hunt for it. And I'm going to work on the housekeeper, Celestine. I sense strongly there's more vital information she could give me. I think she'd like to tell but is afraid. Perhaps she was complicit in whatever it is.

Write when you have a chance.

Love, Ruth

7 July 2004
From: ruth.blanchard@psychnet.org
To: Cletus.Hardin@psychnet.org
Dear Cletus,

I just called you but the machine picked up and I wanted you to have this information ASAP. I didn't know if you'd check phone messages or e-mail first. How to begin…?

I managed to get into Malachi's computer with no problem. And his e-mail was easy. As soon as I typed the "f" of fractal, his ID, the name and password were completed and I was in. I went through the folders of saved mail and found nothing startling. It had been so long since he logged in, all the trash had been deleted. He had saved all mail from you, me and "Wump." You may wonder why I put the latter name in quotation marks. The reason is simple: there is no such person, at least not now and not in Malachi's life. Malachi had been writing the "Wump" letters himself, including, presumably, the attachments with the story of Thomas, Gislebertus, Casilda and Mallory. All these characters are just that: characters in a fictitious confection of Malachi's own making. If you read carefully all the mails sent in this matter, you'll see that the story of Thomas and his treachery becomes more and more complex and that he shows himself ever more deceitful and devious as Malachi is progressing towards his suicide. This must have been a bizarre journey of self-discovery. The final realization, if indeed there was one, must have been unbearable. And the tales of adventures in France were equally full of fabrications. I know Malachi went to France and visited the places he claimed to have seen. Credit card statements tell that story. But "Wump," her interest in images of Judas' suicide in Burgundy, Mary, the "Big Cheese," Winifred's love interest, and all the other alleged workers on the dig project in Autun do not exist. How, you may wonder, did I determine all this? By mistakenly typing "g," right next to "f" on the keyboard, when I last tried to access Malachi's account. He had set up both accounts to remember ID's and a search through my transcripts of our sessions revealed his password: girlofmydreams. Literal, wouldn't you say? Fortunately he used the same password on both accounts. The "gold.digger" account had all the letters from Malachi and the few from me, and nothing else. Malachi presumably wrote to me and to himself when he was in Wump's skin so to speak. In other words, Wump had no life other than that given her by Malachi. And note the letters, M and W, each the upside down image of the other.

Did Malachi see anyone in France? I wonder if his trip there pushed him over the edge. Did he go in the expectation of finding his friend? The answer to many such questions may be in Bay St. Louis and I plan to go there tomorrow. I'll let you know what I discover.

I'm almost in a state of shock, as you can imagine, and I suppose you are also. I found the "Wump" manuscript riveting; it would have stunned the academic world were it authentic. But it is, perhaps like Wump's very existence, a fiction. We know from Amanda Greene that there was such a person in Malachi's childhood. Does she exist now and, if so, where is she?

I'll let you know what I discover in Mississippi as soon as I can.

Love, Ruth

7 July 2004
From: Cletus.Hardin@psychnet.org
To: ruth.blanchard@psychnet.org

Good grief! What next?? Who's who in this crazy saga? Let me know what you discover in Mississippi. Meanwhile I'll google "Winifred Hauser" to see to what extent this woman was a figment of Malachi's imagination. C

7 July 2004
From: ruth.blanchard@psychnet.org
To: Amanda.Greene@worldcom.net
Dear Amanda,

I trust you're coping as best you can with Malachi's death. Your relationship with him had no closure, no chance to heal, no chance to be decided one way or another. My call must have been a shock to you and caused you much anguish. But now I have further information that only deepens the mystery, the enigma of Malachi, and I must share it with you, not only because you deserve to know but also because we could use your help in trying to solve a puzzle that gets only more complicated just as we think we're beginning to understand.

Your husband and the person he called "Winifred" or "Wump" were one and the same. I discovered this when I mistakenly typed "g" for "f" while trying to access Malachi's e-mail account. Up popped Wump's account, all the mail from Malachi, the segments of the alleged 12th-century manuscript, everything. Malachi had apparently been writing to himself—and responding. All the manuscript segments were in a computer folder and Malachi had clearly written them himself. Since Malachi is deceased, we'll never know if he was playing a game or was severely psychotic or somewhere in between. He may have suffered from Dissociative Identity Disorder, what used to be called multiple personality disorder, although that disorder, whatever it's called, is highly suspect in some mental health communities. It really doesn't matter what it's called; Malachi was in a world of hurt assuaged by a world of fantasy. I plan to go to Bay St. Louis to try to unravel more of this mystery and may need to quiz you further. I'm asking you now, in light of this new development, to wrack your brain in search of anything that could shed light on this situation. Try to remember everything Malachi ever told you about Wump; every detail is important, no matter how insignificant it may seem. Question #1 is: where is Wump now? What happened to her from the time she and Malachi last saw each other? Write whatever you remember, nothing is trivial. I'll keep in close touch with you throughout.

Thanks for any help you can offer.

Best, Ruth

10 July 2004
From: ruth.blanchard@psychnet.org
To: Cletus.Hardin@psychnet.org
Copy: Amanda.Greene@worldcom.net
Dear Cletus and Amanda,

I got to the Bay on the 8th and settled in to my motel room, answered a few e-mails, checked both Malachi's and Winifred's e-mail accounts for any activity and, of course, there was none. I was so hoping somehow there really was a Wump, that Malachi had just hacked into her account, that all this was just a bad dream... Alas, nothing on either account.

Then I got busy with the phone book. No Hauser listed. So I did a white-pages search and again came up empty. On the 9th I set out for de Montluzin Street with Malachi's description of the house in mind, hoping I could find the place and/or someone who could give me a clue as to Mrs. Hauser's whereabouts, assuming there is such a person. I found what I thought was the place and knocked at the door. Silence. Fortunately this town is well supplied with nosy neighbors and the lady next door came out to see who I was and what I wanted. This woman was a close friend of Mrs. Hauser, and was able and willing to fill in many missing pieces once she determined my motives for inquiring were benign. She informed me that it was indeed the Hauser residence but that I was too late to see Mrs. Hauser. She had died around the time of Malachi's visit, in late June. Malachi must have gone to the Bay the day after his return from France. That tidbit knocked me off my feet as I wasn't even aware of this trip to MS, and I began envisioning Malachi as some sort of mass murderer. But Malachi was himself deceased when Mrs. Hauser died—of natural causes, the neighbor assured me, but provoked by Malachi's visit. Here's where the story as related by the neighbor gets really interesting. Winifred Hauser did exist and was an acquaintance of Malachi's, but she disappeared in 1950 while she and Malachi were at the movies together. The two had met in town to see some picture and while the film was playing, the railroad bridge, which was located within easy view of the theater, caught fire. The whole town turned out for the spectacle as word spread of the incident and at some moment during the conflagration, Winifred vanished. The police, her family, the whole town searched for her for days, weeks, but finally the case went cold and everyone forgot about the little girl including—or so it seemed—Malachi. The Hauser family found it odd that Malachi, Parker and household staff left town the next day without even saying "good-bye," but then everyone found Malachi and his entourage strange. The following year, when Malachi and family returned, he deeply offended Mrs. Hauser by asking if he could take Winifred's place. He didn't put it exactly that way. What he said was that his mother was gone and so was Winifred, so why not adopt each other. He was apparently quite insistent and a still grieving Mrs. Hauser asked him to leave and not return. It took the intervention of the police to keep Malachi from haunting the Hauser premises. So when Malachi showed up and identified himself to her, it was too much for the very elderly, and still grief-stricken, woman to take and her heart gave out a few days after Malachi's return to Covington.

What to make of Malachi's co-option of Winifred's identity? That may be impossible to unravel. But I don't plan to leave town without speaking to the local constabulary. There may be records of the case, newspaper articles, people who saw or remember things... I'll keep you posted. Perhaps you could take a crack at Parker's caregivers. Remember, he gave us the truth about Joanna and Buddy in a very oblique manner. We thought he was out of his head or lying. But it was the truth after all. See if he babbled something his caregivers thought was the raving of a lunatic, something about the Bay, Winifred, a child who disappeared. Anything...

Amanda, continue thinking about Malachi and his friend, everything Malachi said about her or that period of his life. Something that seemed nonsensical or meaningless to you at the time may be crucial now that we have a context. Stay tuned...

Love, R

10 July 2004
From: Amanda.Greene@worldcom.net
To: ruth.blanchard@psychnet.org
Dear Ruth,

What a shocker! I'll wrack my brain for anything that could possibly be of significance, but don't expect too much. One thing I can tell you is that, even though Malachi spoke of Winifred occasionally, I never saw her or spoke to her, even on the phone. It didn't occur to me that Winifred was a figment of Malachi's imagination, but now it all seems to make sense. The times when Malachi was out of himself, so to speak, almost someone else, were perhaps fugue states when he became Winifred in his own mind and had no real connection with me. I'm no shrink and may be talking nonsense, but I think you understand what I mean. I'll ask my friend's sister, the one who knew Malachi and introduced him to me, what she remembers of all this and forward to you any response I get.

Best, Amanda

12 July 2004
From: Amanda.Greene@worldcom.net
To: emily.daspit@connect.net
Dear Emily,

The chances of your remembering me are slim to none, so allow me to reintroduce myself. I'm a friend of your sister Ann. We were just little kids that summer I visited your family in New Orleans. You may remember the weekend your folks took all of us to Bay St. Louis for a stay at your family home. While I was there, you had some friends over. Malachi Walmsley was one of them. I ended up marrying him after we re-connected several years later.

Unfortunately Malachi had a very troubled childhood and recently died. In fact, he ended his own life. His mother left him property in Covington LA and Malachi decided to remain there in apparently perfect contentment until some unsavory material from his past bubbled to the surface. Some of the troublesome matter involved his own family but there remains considerable mystery surrounding the fate of Winifred Hauser. A woman named Ruth Blanchard was working with Malachi at the time of his suicide and Ruth believes that Winifred's fate is heavily implicated in Malachi's depression, which was the principal factor in his demise.

As we understand it now, Winifred disappeared the night the railroad bridge at Bay St. Louis burned. However, all throughout his life, Malachi acted as if Winifred were alive and a very close friend of his. He spoke of her and to her on the phone, e-mailed her, showed me some of the e-mails. I'd love to know who was at the other end of the line when Malachi was talking to "Wump," his pet name for her. A telemarketer? Dead air? A dial tone? And, at the time of his death, Malachi was receiving by e-mail attachment portions of a medieval manuscript of sorts that pseudo-Winifred and her team of archaeologists had uncovered in France. We now know that Malachi *was* Winifred, writing the medieval ms. himself. This explains why I never actually encountered Winifred; "she" was always too busy to come to our home, out of town on a dig, etc.

Since you knew both my husband and Winifred as children, you are in a unique position to provide Ruth and me with information that may help us understand what was going on in my late husband's head and also unravel the mystery of Winifred's disappearance.

I realize I'm a total stranger asking for information you may not want to give up. I got your e-mail address from Ann; she has indicated her willingness to vouch for me. If you'd rather keep your memories to yourself, I'll understand and respect your wishes. If you choose to divulge anything about anyone, rest assured it will go no farther than my eyes and Ruth's. All we're looking for is answers.

All best, Amanda Greene

p.s. My late husband's last words (written) were "I am Thomas." If you have any comments about that, I'd be glad to have them.

14 July 2004
From: emily.daspit@connect.net
To: Amanda.Greene@worldcom.net
Dear Amanda,

Indeed I do remember you. I'm extremely sorry to learn of your recent (and past) difficulties and am more than willing to help.

Winifred was one of my best friends. She liked your late husband but also felt very sorry for him. She was aware of a rather bizarre family situation and may have befriended Malachi more out of pity than because of any real affection. These are harsh words, but you seem to be on a quest for truth, and sometimes the truth is ugly. Malachi spent the time the three of us were together trying to keep Winifred and me apart. He seemed intensely jealous of our relationship, possessive to an unhealthy degree, and there were moments when I saw what I perceived as rage in his eyes. It was as though he wanted to possess Winifred, not in a physical, but rather in a spiritual sense. I am most emphatically not suggesting that Malachi harbored erotic feelings for Winifred although I realize we are sexual beings from the moment of birth. On the contrary, the desire was to become one with her in an almost mystical way. Of course, there are erotic undertones in even the most religious experiences of this sort.

The night Winifred disappeared, she and I were at the movies; Malachi was also there and sat with us. About halfway through the film, someone came running into the theater screaming the railroad bridge was on fire. Naturally the ridiculous film—that's all we got at the Bay in those days— was forgotten in favor of a real life drama. We all got separated and the rest you know. The only noteworthy thing I remember was Malachi's strange detachment from the event. He seemed totally unconcerned about Winifred's disappearance. The police questioned both of us that night and all Malachi would say was that he had seen Winifred going off down the street to her house and that he was sure Winifred was all right. I know the cops would have preferred that the family stick around, but Malachi's father insisted that he had urgent business in New Orleans. Since there was no evidence of foul play, much less of any involvement of Malachi's family in Winifred's vanishing, the police had no choice but to allow them to leave. I know they made at least one trip to the city to question Malachi further, but that apparently went nowhere. To this day, the mystery of Winifred's disappearance remains just that, a mystery. I never saw Malachi again. I believe his family returned to the Bay but they kept to themselves and I confess I didn't seek him out. Mrs. Hauser harbored deep suspicion of and resentment towards the Walmsley family, but nothing could ever be proven and there was no real evidence of Malachi's involvement in the affair.

As for Thomas, I'm clueless. There was a cute little boy who lived a few doors down from the Hausers but I don't believe that was his name. I think he and Winifred had discovered each other at one point. It was totally innocent, just one of those little kiddy crushes. Malachi may have been jealous of his relationship with Winifred also. But that's as far as my memory reaches. If I recall anything further, I'll let you know.

Good luck to you in your quest.

Best, Emily

17 July 2004
From: ruth.blanchard@psychnet.org
To: Cletus.Hardin@psychnet.org
Dear Cletus,

As you can see from the correspondence I've forwarded from Amanda and Emily, no one seems to know or remember anything. I'll take another crack at Celestine. She was there and might know what happened. You stick with Parker's caregivers and see if you can get any info out of them. I think the kiddy crush shared by Winifred and the neighbor boy may have taken hold of Malachi and bubbled to the surface when he was concocting the ms. story of betrayal and unfaithfulness. He may have felt W and her little boyfriend were cheating on him. On the other hand, the fact that "Thomas" means "twin" may also have factored, on a subconscious level, in Malachi's use of that name in his ms., if indeed it was as Malachi that he was writing. If the Winifred persona confected the ms., then Malachi would not have made the choice. It would have been Winifred. Confused enough? Or the whole Thomas/twin thing may have been connected to the fact that Joanna and John were twins. Buddy in fact became Joanna, or tried to; Malachi knew this subliminally but could not accept the burden of certainty recently imposed upon him. We'll never understand Winifred/Malachi's choice of "Thomas" as her/his villain's name or her/his identification with him. As for Malachi's death, did Winifred execute Malachi? Or did a repentant Malachi, following the lead of Judas with whose story he was clearly obsessed, condemn himself to a traitor's death? And, if so, what was he repenting and whom did he betray?

More later...

Love, Ruth

19 July 2004
From: Cletus.Hardin@psychnet.org
To: ruth.blanchard@psychnet.org
Dear Ruth,

It took some searching but I found a bit of information on Winifred, who, as you know by now, did exist however briefly. The Rock Springs staff recall Parker's babbling on about a little girl named Winifred but assumed she was either a figment of his imagination or one of his son's friends in whom he took an unseemly interest. When patients are admitted to the facility, the people who run the place do a background check. Some unsavory suggestions were part of Parker's file, but nothing definite. Parker was strongly suspected of involvement with a child's disappearance, but nothing stuck to him and with no witnesses or physical evidence, the police eventually had to let the case grow cold. Apparently, all the kids Parker offered to clients were teenagers who, astonishingly, were all too willing to go along with Parker's schemes for drug money, clothes money, make-up money or whatever. His clients' tastes ran to jailbait rather than children. Keep at Celestine; she's our only hope of discovering the truth in the matter. With everyone dead, she shouldn't be too reluctant now to give up her secrets. Unless she was implicated in the crime... I'm assuming there was a crime committed. Children don't just vanish, not at the tender age of eight. But I'd find it hard to believe that Celestine was a criminal after what you've told me. She sounds like the typical southern black servant of her generation, utterly devoted to the family she cares for but completely honest and unwilling to participate in unlawful activity. Yet willing to keep her mouth shut... This thing gets stranger by the day.

I miss you and wish I could be with you. I'm slowly weaning my patients from me. Most seem happy I've found you and are willing to continue therapy with other shrinks in the area. However, several come in

166

mostly to shoot the shit on an occasional basis and we can continue that during the periods when I'm in Jerome. It will work and we'll be happy. I'm happy now, just knowing you're in my life.

Keep me posted.

Love, Cletus

25 July 2004
From: emily.daspit@connect.net
To: Amanda.Greene@worldcom.net
Dear Amanda,

This may or may not be of any use to you. The Thomas I mentioned in my previous mail was not the little boy who lived down the street but rather his older cousin, who lived a few blocks over and came to visit his family with some frequency. I remember him as a nice kid who kept watch over us with some diligence. I don't remember the boy's name but the cousin made an impression. I have no idea what became of him or even if he is still alive. Your friend may want to check on this, but I doubt that this man had anything to do with Malachi's fate or any of the matters involved in this affair. On the other hand, Thomas may have been more perceptive of Malachi's intense, overzealous attachment to Winifred than we kids were. Perhaps it troubled him and he wanted to keep an eye on things.

Please keep me posted. I'm really curious about all this now.

Best, Emily

26 July 2004
From: ruth.blanchard@psychnet.org
To: Cletus.Hardin@psychnet.org
Dear Cletus,

Now I have it all. The whole story, the big picture. I know why Malachi was so distressed all his life. It's almost more than anyone could possibly have borne. Grab a Scotch and take a deep breath.

Malachi loved Winifred and, more importantly, Winifred's family. It was everything Malachi's was not: sane, wholesome, one of those "'50s families" that supposedly didn't exist. Malachi wanted it; he wanted Winifred's family to be his own. As we found out from Emily Daspit, Winifred didn't like Malachi very much, she just felt sorry for him and hated to send him packing. She tolerated Malachi, that's the best one can say about the relationship. Malachi tried very hard to insinuate himself into the family circle, but this just made him all the more irritating. He frequently asked Mrs. Daspit to be his mother. This broke the dear lady's heart but, of course, the answer was always a sugarcoated "no." Unfortunately, her excuse was that she already had a daughter. She apparently repeated this too often for Winifred's good. Malachi processed that statement in the following way: if I make Winifred disappear, her mother will need another child.

The remainder of this story is from Celestine's recollection of the events surrounding Winifred's death. She finally consented to tell me everything and I'm convinced there's nothing left to unravel.

The night of the railroad bridge fire, Malachi, Winifred and Emily left the theater together and were watching the spectacular disaster unfold when Malachi talked Winifred into seeking a better vantage point. Emily stayed put. Malachi knew the location of an exterior staircase to the roof of the theater, one at the rear of the building to be used by authorized personnel only. When the two reached the roof, Malachi pushed Winifred to her death and then dragged the body into the woods. At that time, the Bay was not nearly so developed as it is now. Wilderness abounded and there was plenty of space for hiding whatever one wanted to hide. Add to that fact the attention of the town riveted on the burning bridge and you have an explanation why Winifred's screams went unheard as she plummeted to the ground and why Malachi could drag her into the woods unnoticed. Malachi returned to the Hauser home and told Winifred's mother that Winifred was lost; he again asked if Mrs. Hauser would be his mother. This triggered a phone call to the police and a massive manhunt began for Winifred. How they managed *not* to find the girl's body remains a great mystery to all who know the story. Malachi simply hid her in the bushes; she should have been easy to find. The police must have concentrated on sex offenders—or whatever they were called in those days—and assumed she had been abducted. As weird as Malachi seemed, no one suspected him of any involvement. He was not even closely questioned by the police. His obsession with joining the Hauser family was well known and no one connected the missing child with Malachi's odd request. All assumed he wanted to join the family precisely because Winifred was part of it. When Malachi returned home and matter-of-factly told Parker and Celestine what had transpired, the two waited till the wee hours of the morning, retrieved the body from the underbrush where it lay hidden, and returned to Covington with Malachi in tow and Winifred's corpse in the trunk. Malachi then assumed Winifred's identity in his own mind, invented a life for his murdered friend, and went merrily on his way. The substratum of deceit and selfishness in his own home must have deeply influenced his personality development. Winifred Hauser's remains are buried under the slab of the now-destroyed boathouse. Her bones will be disinterred and returned to whatever relatives may be found. If there are no relatives around, I'll see to it that she gets a decent burial.

Now it is all clear, including the suicide note left by Malachi. As he was preparing his own death, since he had killed the child whose identity he had assumed, he must have switched back and forth between his two personae and been terribly confused about who was about to die: Malachi or Winifred. His statement, "I am Thomas," reflects his feelings of guilt about betrayal of his friend, so perhaps at the last moment it was as Malachi that he died, especially since he signed the note "MW," with the M first. It was Thomas the betrayer, the sadist, the killer in the manuscript that Malachi identified with at certain moments and this explains his "I am Thomas" message. Notice the dates of the ms. attachments. The emotional upheaval Malachi was experiencing in the very setting of the events of his childhood must have provoked this extraordinary spate of creativity. His Thomas—artist, schemer, lover, traitor—embodied all his emotional traits. Unless it was Thomas the twin… I have to let this go and accept that there are some things I'll never, ever know for certain.

This also explains completely Malachi's dreams. They had nothing to do with his mother's accident, Buddy's alleged death or what happened that night in April 1950. Remember his telling you of a dream in which he saw a figure coming out of the woods covered in blood and saying, "It's the wrong one. You must never tell." It was the wrong one of his own two personae he had killed and that's what his mind was trying to convey. He may have adopted Winifred's identity well before he killed her and that's who he wanted to be. But that was impossible; everyone knew he wasn't Winifred Hauser. That's also why both his father *and* Buddy were in the dream. It was accurate, only Malachi didn't realize it at the time. They were not both involved in Joanna's death but they did both know of Malachi's crime and both cooperated in covering it up. Buddy was in the hospital at the time of the crime but he knew what had happened and, on some level, Malachi knew he knew. Malachi knew exactly what the boathouse was for and it wasn't for Buddy or his boat. Buddy spent his entire life protecting Malachi from himself, from the law, from his dreadful family. And he never knew this. He died before the truth could be revealed to him. Of course, one may wonder if this was a truth he'd have cared to know. His life seemed to revolve around loathing his uncle.

All along I've withheld my trust from Celestine, assuming she was somehow guilty of something. Instead she was zealously protecting a man she obviously loved as her own child. She could have spilled her guts the moment I arrived on the scene but instead she waited until everyone who could be prosecuted was dead. She even protected that old pirate Parker. Dear Celestine—I must apologize to her.

One last item: Malachi had some childhood trinkets hidden under a floorboard in his former room, the one Celestine was in when Malachi moved back to Covington. Celestine showed them to me when she knew Malachi was safe. Among the items were newspaper clippings, including all write-ups concerning the death of Winifred Hauser. I wonder if he ever looked at them and how he would have processed such information. If he did read them, it must have been terribly confusing. Celestine was probably occupying that room in order to protect Malachi. And I thought she was being stubborn and selfish when she didn't offer to give it up to him.

Write when you have a chance.

Love, Ruth

26 July 2004
From: ruth.blanchard@psychnet.org
To: Amanda.Greene@worldcom.net
Dear Amanda,

I'm afraid I have some shocking news for you. I neglected to get your phone number or I'd have called rather than sending this news via e-mail. Your late husband killed his friend Winifred and that event, and the guilt he bore all these years, caused all the problems in his later life. Of course, the causes of the murder are multiple and complex: what he witnessed as a child; his mother's depression, genetics—these are all in the mix. I'm forwarding by attachment the transcript of Celestine's recounting of the affair. Celestine, you may know, was the family housekeeper for years and was still here when Malachi and I arrived. She and her son Ruben have both departed, unwilling to be implicated (possibly) in a homicide. This will be made clear when you read her account of the death of Winifred. I'll send it as soon as it's transcribed.

I know your marriage was a troubled one; you will better understand why after you read Celestine's narrative.

I wish I could have told you this in person. If you wish, come to Louisiana and we can have a long heart-to-heart. Or wait till I return to AZ and you can meet with Cletus and me. That, I believe, would be fruitful.

If there is anything at all I can do for you, don't hesitate to write or call. I'm sure the same goes for Cletus.

Good luck to you, Ruth

27 July 2004
From: Cletus.Hardin@psychnet.org
To: ruth.blanchard@psychnet.org
Dear Ruth,

In addition to digging in Malachi's computer, toss the house. You never know what you might find. Malachi kept a diary as a child. Perhaps he kept some sort of journal as an adult, although I'd expect to find it in his computer. You might also find something from Buddy. After all, his effects are all over the place. Try digging in his computer too although I don't think there's any more to find—or that I could bear to learn. Honest to God, I don't know whether to refer to the person who died in February as Buddy or Joanna. Creeps me out. I'm sure there are nooks and crannies you haven't explored. Good luck and keep me posted.

Love, Cletus

28 July 2004
From: Amanda.Greene@worldcom.net
To: emily.daspit@connect.net
Dear Emily,

I know this will cause you much grief but you did ask to be kept informed of the Malachi-Winifred affair, so here it is. The night of the railroad bridge fire, Malachi enticed Winifred to the roof of the theater and pushed her to her death. In his twisted mind, he saw this as a means of taking Winifred's place as Mrs. Hauser's child. Malachi's father and the family maid transported the body back to Covington, buried her and covered the body with a cement slab on which a boathouse was eventually constructed. Thomas had good instincts; he must have sensed that all was not right with Malachi, who obviously had major psychological issues. My friend Ruth, who has been sleuthing these things out, has tactfully avoided calling my late husband a sociopath. Ruth prefers "troubled," "depressed," and similar expressions. But I'm sure someone who loved Winifred as you obviously did might have trouble being so charitable.

I'll understand if you choose to have nothing more to do with me and with this sordid mess. But if you're so inclined, I'd like to stay in touch.

Let me know if there's anything at all I can do for you or anyone else touched by Winifred's terrible fate. Ruth will see to it that Winifred's remains are disinterred and receive a decent burial. We believe there are no relatives of Winifred left.

Fondly, Amanda

28 July 2004
From: ruth.blanchard@psychnet.org
To: Cletus.Hardin@psychnet.org
Dear Cletus,

I've gone through every shred of paper in every drawer in every desk, chest, or piece of furniture and there's nothing to be found. I realize now that what Malachi took for evidence of male companionship was Buddy's men's clothes for moments when he could be himself rather than what Parker made him become. If there's anything, it's in his computer. If I can't hack into his files, I'll seek a pro. But there's a good chance nothing is password protected, so I'll tackle that job tomorrow.

The heat and humidity today are simply unbearable; I wish I were in Jerome for so many reasons. I walk outside and my glasses fog up. The river is no longer visible except from the upstairs windows because of the density of the vegetation in the yard. The only happy creatures are roaches and lizards! Everything else is in a stupor, moving as little as possible. All social life here has ground to a halt and will not resume until the weather gets decent, sometime in November. Hurricane season promises to be very active. We've already had a few near misses.

I'll write again if and when I find something. Perhaps I'll find files I can e-mail as attachments. If Buddy kept a diary or journal and the file is huge, I'll divide it into manageable portions and send them piecemeal.

Love always, Ruth

30 July 2004
From: Cletus.Hardin@psychnet.org
To: ruth.blanchard@psychnet.org

If dry is what you want, we've got plenty! Jerome is full of tourists, especially Europeans, spending money like mad. I've done some work on the house, shoring up the deck foundations and expanding it a bit. I live out there in the evening when the sun is about to give us a break and light up the facing escarpment. No matter how often I see it, it's new every time. The colors seem different and the cliffs more sculpted. If you think this is designed to make you homesick for your newly adopted state, it is. And the guy waiting for you has a dog in this fight as well.

I await news of what you can find of Buddy with impatience. C

172

30 July 2004
From: emily.daspit@connect.net
To: Amanda.Greene@worldcom.net
Dear Amanda,

What a shock! For both of us… Please don't take any of this on yourself. The sins of the husband are not to be visited on the wife.

The whole affair is sickening, but it is all sufficiently in the past that I can get through it.

I'd be happy to stay in touch and even get together. I've kept the family house and spend winters at the Bay, returning to New Mexico for the summer. I have a place in the mountains so it's cool and nice when it's sweltering in Mississippi. And since you're in Flagstaff, we could see each other fairly often.

I hope you can deal with the situation. If there's anything I can do, any further information I can offer, let me know. I'm more than happy to help, especially now that all principals are deceased.

Stay in touch.

Cordially, Emily

1 August 2004
From: ruth.blanchard@psychnet.org
To: Cletus.Hardin@psychnet.org
Dear Cletus,

Buddy's computer was relatively easy to explore. However, what I wanted, a diary or self-explanation of sorts, was hidden in a rather clever way. He tacked it on to the end of a long file of class notes and I had to examine every page of many files to find it. After searching fruitlessly for a file with a promising name and finding nothing, I began combing through ones that were very long. When I finally had my Eureka moment, I divided the text into parts and saved them as separate files, which I'll e-mail to you as attachments. Buddy didn't date any of his entries so we can only surmise when and why he wrote what he did. He mentions someone who's demented, so I suppose he wrote that portion before Parker's death. I suspect it was quite recently since he mentions the war in Iraq. We can also wonder about its intended audience. It's oddly similar to the medieval dialogue Malachi invented when he was in Wump mode. Here's the first part; the second will follow:

Part I (sent 1 August 2004)

How and when did it all begin? I have no recollection, of course, of my life as a girl although I am told that is how I began. My family was of old southern stock and hermaphrodites as we were known then did not happen in "good" families. Besides my father wanted a boy, so that is what I became. It wasn't too hard. I had enough of a penis that I could pass, but hid when I undressed as much as possible. Celestine's mother and my parents were the only people who saw me nude. My father, despite fulfilling his desire for a boy, avoided looking at my nakedness as much as possible. When my mother died, Celestine's mother alone took care of me and then I was able to care for my own hygienic needs.

My mother was the strangest woman I ever knew, although this is all in hindsight and based on the recollections of a very young child. I was only ten when she died. She was very prim and proper, a real southern lady. But underneath the surface simmered a severely suppressed sexuality. I recognize that now. In a different time and in a different place, I think she would have given in to her passions with quite wild abandon. My father was a rake, given to roaming the Quarter with his friends and picking up whatever was available. But when it was a question of marriage, nothing but a Soniat or a Duplessis would do for a Claiborne. He proposed first to Melba Duplessis, but she had the good sense and the good taste to say no. Father and Mother were married at the cathedral and all of New Orleans' finest gathered to fête their nuptials. I have no idea how many children my parents desired, but after she had two for the price of one pregnancy, I suspect Mother put the brakes on because she was afraid of picking up a disease from my father, whose proclivities were well known to her. She also may have decided that two children were quite enough for a southern belle. And *belle* she was, a great beauty.

She had a nearly neurotic desire to please her parents, who wanted nothing more for her than a debut no one would ever forget and a suitable match, "suitable" meaning well-connected and wealthy. Of course, Mother was not averse to such events. As to the marriage, Miles Claiborne fit the bill. I have no idea if love entered into the match at all. I never heard an affectionate word pass between them. It was all about how to hide my deficiencies so Joanna could marry someone worthy of the family name. This required a fabulous debut and a reign as queen of some tony carnival club as well as keeping me hidden from the proper branch of polite society. There is another segment, of which I'll have more to say later. Mother died far too young to attend to such matters and Father had no interest in such, so Joanna missed out on these events, all except the marriage. This also will be discussed in due course. Of course, these are the memories of a young child whose mother died when he was ten. Who knows what I experienced or what I imagined? Of my paternal grandparents I remember nothing. They also died young, before I was born or shortly after. My mother's father is my only ancestral memory, and even that is sketchy.

What would and should have been Joanna's debut year came and went without any mention of it. She seemed not to care. I, on the other hand, had watched with great interest while Mother got ready for various carnival balls. What a wonderful daughter I would have made! I've often thought that Joanna and I should have switched identities long before we did. I even remember some of Mother's gowns. My favorite was pink with vertical panels of black lace. She wore that when the daughter of some friend was queen of some ball. As you see, details are not my forte. I know she had similar plans for my sister. I believe Father attended, in his white tie and tails, primarily to scout out clients and to keep an eye on those already ensnared in his coils. He and Mother were in the carnival circuit from birth. Every detail of every carnival club member's private and professional life was bruited about at club gatherings. This was forbidden by the club rules but no one paid attention to such infractions. See and be seen, learn as much as possible, find clients. This is what it was all about. The most important thing was to discover a client's enemies. With that information, plus a few well-chosen photographs, Miles Claiborne could—and did—do anything. He got whatever he wanted, lucrative contracts, invitations to join other clubs, names of others who might be interested in what he had to offer, i.e. me and others like me. Of course, this was all information he was storing for future use. He didn't pimp me out until I was almost fourteen.

My sexual situation would become apparent to people with whom my dad had to feign respectability so we had to leave New Orleans when I was very young. We moved to Covington when it was a sleepy vacation hideaway for city folk who wanted to pretend that they were country folk. The air was pure and the land was thick with pine forest. If those lovers of all things rural could see the place now... covered with shopping malls, oversized garish mansions, subdivisions everywhere. Developers are having a field day. When we came here, it was paradise. Now... but I digress.

The place I really loved, as did Malachi, was my maternal grandparents' house at Bay St. Louis. I have no idea when they acquired the property; I just know it was in the family from the time I was born. It was furnished in the most eclectic manner, with all sorts of mismatched pieces. There were old—and dreadfully uncomfortable—iron beds, no easy chairs at all, hence no spot to curl up with a good book, beautiful marble-topped chests-of-drawers, an old water heater that had to be lighted with a match, an ice box to which an iceman delivered a huge chunk of ice every other day. He had to use a giant pair of tongs and he could sling that ice into the icebox with a deft twist of his arms. Joanna once left the hot water heater on over night. Damn near blew up the house. The entire back of the house consisted of a small kitchen and a huge screened porch that served as living room, dining room, and anything else other than a bedroom. Directly behind the porch was an old storage shed full of rusting tools. Everything smelled of musty, humid old wood. The only locks for the house were hooks on the screen doors and wooden doors that locked with skeleton keys. Crime wasn't much of a problem. Besides most of the stuff in the house wouldn't have tempted even a semi-respectable burglar. My mother's father lived to a ripe old age and on occasion he would come to the Bay with us. I can still see him in my mind's eye, making a pitcher of Old Fashioneds on the back porch before Sunday dinner. Every family event with us was liberally watered with alcohol. He had a huge bushy moustache that tickled and scratched when he kissed us. He died when Malachi was six and I believe those scratchy kisses were all Malachi remembered of him. He was a sweet old man and, I hope, totally unaware of the turpitude permeating his descendants. The idea that his son-in-law was pimping out his grandson to New Orleans' finest would have killed him. My mother remains a great mystery to me. She died so young; but perhaps the realization that she had a fast-acting cancer came as a relief to her. After eleven years of marriage, she must have realized what trash in a tux her husband was. Could her position, her social standing have been of such importance? I guess her weekly gatherings with the girls at Corinne Dunbar's had great symbolic meaning to her. Did she even suspect the husbands or brothers or fathers of some of her table companions would someday be fucking her son with the connivance of her husband and future son-in-law? That's the first question I'll ask her when I see her in hell.

We spent every summer at the Bay from the time I was born till the death of Winifred. After that event, we felt less and less comfortable until finally, we ceased going there altogether. When Parker and I split, I sold the place. Hurricane Camille finished off what was wonderful about it so I guess I sold at a good moment. I know Malachi was greatly attached to it and unhappy to see it leave the family. Another reason for him to detach from his "mother." I guess this was the only desire of his I was unable to grant. I wanted to keep him and his alter ego as far away as possible from the scene of the crime. Suppose he had shown up around town, especially at Winifred's home, in Winifred's personality? When Parker took him to Flagstaff, I breathed easier.

Parker and Joanna moved into the family home when they married and I sort of came with the place. Joanna had a hard time with that. I had a sense that she loved me as a sister loves a brother but my sexual ambiguity troubled her. And I'm sure she sensed that all was not exactly kosher between Parker and me. After the birth of Malachi, the two ceased sexual relations. But Parker wanted me to dress up like Joanna, look as much like her as possible. All of this had to be kept under wraps, of course. There was an old house down river from the house, and Parker and I would meet there when the main house wasn't safe for our coupling. He had bought it for a song, intending to fix it up for sale but found it more useful for assignations. I was by no means the only one. Parker had a harem of all ages and sexual persuasions. Malachi was intensely curious about all this. He would watch us with closely guarded eyes, and I know he questioned Celestine about what Daddy and Buddy did in the spooky house, as he called it. One day when he was on the river with Celestine's son Ruben, he spied us walking in the woods and we weren't able to duck out of sight quickly enough. The story we put out was that we were inspecting the property with the thought of subdividing. My principal goal was to keep the truth from Malachi. In spite of all my vice-ridden practices, I adored that child from the moment of his birth. He was the only truly pure person in my life for a while, until he reached the so-called age of reason and became capable of lies, disobedience, and, yes, cruelty. He sometimes made fun of my effeminate ways, mannerisms that escaped my consciousness or control. I loved him still, even though he did not reciprocate.

Joanna and I met Parker when we were about fourteen, all seemingly very innocuous. He had been selling antiques to Mother till she died and had struck up a friendship with Father. I had no idea he was his pimp; I also had no idea that the people Parker asked me to be friendly with were pedophiles. I didn't even know what a pedophile was. I just knew they spoke to me in unctuous tones, did things to my body that felt good and gave me many expensive gifts and lots of money. I learned no trade since I imagined I could go on forever living off of satisfying other people's cravings. Perhaps I could, but Parker began badgering me about my future, urging me to learn something. Joanna was becoming quite proficient in French so I decided I should do that also. Little did I know that I would eventually be able to simply step into her shoes as a teacher. Parker sent me to France the same year Joanna was there to spy on her. I managed to watch almost every move she made without her having an inkling of my presence. I also picked up the lingo with a certain ease. Parker had an ingenious method for keeping Joanna unaware of my whereabouts. He would send her letters to me from France back to France, I'd reply, and then he would post my responses back to France from the US. He had no notion that one day I'd simply step into my sister's shoes, assume her identity… At least, I assume he did not. God, what if he planned something along those lines and Joanna's suicide just handed him what he needed? In any case, I didn't want to leave Malachi in Parker's hands. I couldn't. I had no idea what plans he had for his son so I used his own old tricks on him and blackmailed him into letting me become Joanna. At this point the tables were turned and I went from being Parker's slave to being his master—or mistress. I had too much on the crapulous old bastard for him to refuse me anything. And if he had said no, I could have gone to any one of his prestigious clients, who would then have persuaded him by any means possible to do whatever it took to keep me quiet. But I don't think Malachi was fooled. He knew his mother was gone, in spirit if not in flesh. How else to explain his killing of Winifred Hauser? That happened while I was away taking on the identity of my sister. Celestine told me the whole story when I returned, how she and Parker took Malachi and Winifred's body back to Covington in the middle of the night, buried Winifred in a remote section of the property and covered it with a concrete slab the very next day. Parker had people who would do anything for him, no questions asked. Who in his right mind would build on a slab on a riverbank? That was against both building code and common sense, but nobody cared in those days, especially when Parker Walmsley was the one breaking the rules. It's taken me years to fathom the depths of that man's depravity…

Part II (sent 4 August 2004)

After the accident, life with Malachi was an adventure. I had to remember constantly that I was his mother, not his uncle; I never quite fell into the role. Slips of the tongue could be fatal. If Malachi ever discovered the truth, my hold over Parker would be gone, my inheritance from our father would be in jeopardy, and everything would be turned upside down. I believe that, deep down, Malachi did know. After the accident he would stare into my eyes and that was when I realized that my eyes were the only element of Joanna's face I couldn't fake. All the other differences could be explained away—the jaw line, brows, even ears were different because of the surgeries. Hair color can be adjusted especially since Joanna had been tinkering with hers for years. However, eyes are not negotiable. They are much more than the mirror of the soul. Mine were the same color as Joanna's but there's more to the uniqueness of an eye than the color. I wonder why Malachi didn't expose my fraud. Perhaps he couldn't admit on a conscious level that his mother was dead. He was, at times, very cruel to Joanna but, at other times, his devotion to his mother was boundless. I wonder if Malachi is capable of love... Or is he a little sociopath? He never did anything but tolerate me. My presence was a constant thorn in his side; that was plain. I waited patiently for him to come to terms with me at least but finally gave up. So I satisfied myself with fraudulent love, seizing the pseudo-affection destined for another and taking it for myself. When no one loves you, it's better than nothing. I found true love in my old age, but that is a story for another day.

How furious my father would have been had he known the fortune he left to Joanna ended up in my perverted hands. He hated me and would never have left the family fortune to such a monster as I. Even though he had wanted a boy and saw to my various treatments and surgeries, he nonetheless felt that I was twisted, dirty, not quite a man. I was small in stature and effeminate despite the quantities of hormones I took. Reverting back to a female state should have been a relief and would have been had I been able to be myself and not Joanna. I'm the creature who could never be itself: a boy when I should have been a girl; a woman, but not the woman I was born, another one with a different name and personality. If only today's science of gender reassignment had been prevalent when I was born, how different my life might have been.

Malachi's childhood and adolescence were difficult. When he was born, he was so reluctant to be held, it was difficult to feed him. Even as a tiny infant, he hated to be confined in anyone's arms as if that were a form of imprisonment. He would push away from the person holding him with his tiny arms, and his head would bobble on his little neck as he looked around for a means of escape. It was impossible to get him to sit still long enough to be read to. Joanna finally despaired of bonding with him. Yet Joanna's accident affected him deeply. It was as if the child didn't know how much he cared for his mother until the latter was compromised. He coped with the death of his friend Winifred by refusing to accept it as fact, even going so far as to pretend to be her. She would slip in and out of Winifred's personality with great ease, carrying on conversations with her using two different voices. If I intruded, either Malachi or Winifred would vanish and, at times, I would find myself conversing with a total stranger. Then he would snap out of it and Malachi would return, completely unaware of what had just transpired. Gradually, Winifred showed up with less and less frequency. So he lived in the strange world of a pretend mother and a fictitious friend. Neither the person he took to be his mother nor the friend he thought he was communicating with was real. Winifred was a figment of his imagination and I was Joanna. No wonder he had such difficulties later in life.

He dated infrequently and I was surprised when he decided to marry Amanda. I didn't think he had enough of a sense of self to make such a momentous decision. What, I wondered, if he became Winifred at a critical moment, failed to recognize his wife? Apparently he had ways of coping with identity issues just as I coped with always having to be other than what I was in reality. Amanda contacted me a few times when she and Malachi were having problems in their marriage but I could be of little help. At times, I wanted to confess all, tell her who I really was, what Malachi had done to Winifred, what sort of family she had married into, but what would have been the point? The sins of the father and the mother and the uncle should not be visited upon the child. When Malachi killed his friend, I doubt that he understood completely what he was doing or that he was capable of consent to such a vicious crime. I don't remember what an eight-year-old mind is like, but the permanence of death may not be part of the landscape. All I could ever think of was protecting him, from himself, from Parker. Perhaps Winifred vanished altogether after his marriage. I'll never know...

Before I close this narrative, I must mention Brother Luke whom I met when I began to think of last things and started hanging around an abbey nearby. The monk is an odd-looking man, utterly lacking in charisma to the casual observer. I found out after we had been meeting for a while that his nickname is "The Sphinx." Even his brothers in religion find him inscrutable. Perhaps that's what I find most attractive. His eyes are most striking, of a blue so pale as to be nearly colorless. Of his hair I know nothing; what little he has is shaved. He is of medium height and, since he never preached, I didn't even know what sort of voice he had. When finally we did speak, I discovered that his voice, like the rest of him, was unremarkable. Yet there was something about him that drew me to him. So what was it? I'll never know. After Parker's dementia began to set in, I decided it was safe to reveal myself and my wicked ways, and I determined that Luke would be the recipient of my confession. It was then I discovered he was not a priest, so I had to seek another to receive absolution. I so much wanted to confess to Luke, to reveal myself just to see his reaction. Would he find me repulsive? He understood but did not condone the life I had chosen. Nonetheless words of chastisement and condemnation were not offered, just sympathy, and a firm "Go now and sin no more." He shared other details of his life, enough that I felt he was a close, even intimate, friend, a Platonic lover in the most literal meaning of the term. We met many times and what we shared far transcended the bonds of the flesh. I loved him with my whole being, totally and completely. The mere thought of him filled me with delight, and being in his presence brought me intense spiritual and intellectual solace. I don't know if he will ever fathom how deep were my feelings for him.

My friendship with Brother Luke was probably the best relationship in my life. He was truly a brother to me in every sense of the word. You who are reading this, do a poor man a service. Print out my words if you have the means and give them to my brother Luke. Tell him my last thoughts were of him.

9 August 2004
From: ruth.blanchard@psychnet.org
To: Cletus.Hardin@psychnet.org
Dear Cletus,

I have already taken care of Buddy's last request. Brother Luke is exactly as both Buddy and Malachi described him. He has asked me to stay in touch, to let him know of our plans and life together, and to introduce you to him one of these days. After I handed him the printed ms., I got up to leave but he motioned for me to stay. I think he wanted to see if he had any questions I might be able to answer. As he read Buddy's narrative, the sphinx's colorless eyes filled with tears and this "impassive" man looked at me with gratitude I'll never forget. What a cliché about appearances being deceiving! Never was its truth brought home to me with more clarity and force. I now understand Buddy's and Malachi's fascination with this man. He does indeed draw one to himself. In fact, I think I'll print out some of Malachi's letters and give them to him. I think he'd be astonished by the story at whose fringes he's been living.

All is fairly well at the zoo I live in. I've been cleaning out the remaining debris of the various lives lived at Cypress Shadows. How I wish I could contact Celestine… I know she and Ruben fled in fear of going to jail for complicity in covering up Winifred's death. But no one has the slightest inclination to prosecute this case. No one knows about it but me and the few to whom I've revealed it. And they have no plans to talk. I've also decided to meet again with Brother Luke. Our last encounter was far too brief. He may be willing to answer some questions that linger. I'll let you know what comes of that.

Love, Ruth

10 August 2004
From: Cletus.Hardin@psychnet.org
To: ruth.blanchard@psychnet.org

Don't get too fascinated! Seriously, I think meeting with Br Luke is a good idea. You're clearly still emotionally involved with all the characters in this event and anything that will give you better insight into Malachi and your own participation in mapping his personal hell is worthwhile.

I love you. C

15 August 2004
From: ruth.blanchard@psychnet.org
To: Cletus.Hardin@psychnet.org
Dearest,

I had lunch today with Br Luke at one of Covington's restaurants. It was delightful; I wanted the conversation never to end. Luke is fascinating. Turns out he also is a "Bay" person, a native in fact. He was born there and spent his earliest years at Saint Stanislaus. I shall definitely keep in touch. Once you get to know him (and vice versa), the colorless eyes begin to twinkle with a droll sense of humor and affection begins to show in his face. He decided on the religious life early, far earlier than the Church approves now. But his parents refused to let him go until he was twenty-one. So he finished college, Loyola I think, with a major in philosophy. More about him as I learn it.

Other than that, there's not much news today. Still no sign of Celestine. More to follow...

Love you, R

16 August 2004
From: ruth.blanchard@psychnet.org
To: Cletus.Hardin@psychnet.org

I'm glad Buddy had Luke in his wretched life. As I reflect on his situation, I now understand Malachi's dream, the one in which Buddy and Mallory were twinned, so to speak. They were both freaks, outwardly repulsive, but truly loving people in the depths of their souls. Luke seems to have been the only person who loved Buddy well just as he was, without holding back or passing judgment. Someday you will meet Luke and you will love him too.

I'm meeting with him again in a few days and will report to you every shred of the conversation. I gave him some of Malachi's correspondence to read and will be interested in his take on things from Mal's perspective. I'll be especially eager for Luke's opinion about his reaction to our twelfth-century lovers. Entirely yours, Ruth

20 August 2004
From: ruth.blanchard@psychnet.org
To: Cletus.Hardin@psychnet.org
My Dear,

My latest encounter with Luke certainly proved fruitful. We've gotten together several times and he has provided me with much needed and useful information. He was a "Bay" person, as you already know. And he knew Malachi and Winifred better than I could have imagined. This became obvious as he talked about the two as children with far more familiarity than he could have gleaned from reading Malachi's letters. And this was even clearer when he told me that "Luke" was his name in religion; his given, and legal, name is Thomas Jacob Wilson. He's the cousin of the boy on de Montluzin Street mentioned by Emily. He was in his teens when the railroad bridge incident took place, suspected that Malachi was implicated but was far too young to fling accusations at a family as powerful as Parker Malmsey's. He's been an actor in this play from the beginning. And all along, he was praying peacefully on the banks of the Bogue Falaya, upstream from the very house I'm now occupying. How many clues he held in his heart without suspecting it! And without any knowledge of the drama being enacted in this household. Buddy withheld all details of Malachi's life and discussed only his own situation. In fact, I don't know if Luke was aware that there was any connection at all between Buddy and Winifred or Malachi until Malachi showed up with the picture of Buddy in his Joanna persona. I suppose he kept his counsel assuming he had nothing to offer the troubled man whose "mother" had just died. He must have realized then that Malachi was the same person he had suspected in the disappearance of Winifred, but decided there was no point dredging up the past. Without a shred of proof, whom could he have found to listen to him?

Love, R

29 August 2004
From: ruth.blanchard@psychnet.org
To: Cletus.Hardin@psychnet.org

You've probably heard that New Orleans took a direct hit from Hurricane Jean and most of the metropolitan area is destroyed or heavily damaged. When the storm was first predicted, I grabbed Morel, jumped in the car and drove north as far as I could go. I don't even recall where I finally landed. I remembered Hurricanes Betsy and Camille too vividly to take any chances. I did not care to drown in my attic or spend the night clinging to my roof. I would have called before I left but didn't expect such a catastrophe and thought I'd be home in a day or two. I also didn't expect the devastation to go as far north as it did. As I mentioned, my free cell call was timed by the agency offering the service to evacuees. Hence, my brief and breathless (and probably incoherent) message on your answering machine. At least I had a chance to let you know I was safe but would be out of touch for a while.

I have no idea when or how I'll be able to contact you again. Know that I'm safe and will be back in touch ASAP.

Love, R

p.s. Please don't try to contact me. It's hopeless and I don't want my mailbox to explode.

13 September 2004
From: ruth.blanchard@psychnet.org
To: Cletus.Hardin@psychnet.org
Dear Cletus,

I'm finally back home and living under conditions less than ideal. But it's home!

People who streamed out of the way of the storm are slowly dragging themselves back to scenes of desolation and despair. Buildings hundreds of years old are no more. Hundreds are dead, many are missing and many more are homeless and living any way they can. Archives, documents, texts not evacuated are gone forever. Or perhaps they live in cyberspace. One can only hope. There were many more dead than there needed to be. New Orleanians are notorious for pooh-poohing hurricane warnings and most stayed to have hurricane parties. So when the full fury of Jean was unleashed on them, they were too drunk or stoned to do anything even if they had wanted to. People drowned in their attics, some in attitudes indicating they had tried to claw or batter their way out of the roof. Others made their way to the Superdome or the Convention Center, which quickly took on the aspect of a hellish nightmare. With no electricity, no water or provisions, and no escape, people turned into desperate animals, urinating and defecating anywhere they could. Their predicament was indescribable.

And there were horrors uncovered by the storm. A child's corpse was discovered in a room hidden by a false wall. I use the word *room* loosely. It was more a large closet and the severely malnourished youngster was chained to the wall, clearly a victim of abuse. It will take ages to figure out who lived there, who the child was, his or her sex and how long he or she had been locked up there, and who was responsible for his/her pitiful

184

condition. Most records of such information are gone and chances are great the perpetrators are dead or as far from New Orleans as possible. And there's the usual price gouging and long waits for overpriced goods and services. Since I was without electricity the whole time I was gone, I've had to buy two new refrigerators. Even though the ones I had started up again when power was restored, the stench was unbearable and one can never get it out. I had grain, rice and the like in my freezer. Weevils took over the machine, got into the icemaker. Disgusting!

And then there's the macabre... All of New Orleans' deceased are buried above ground, either in private, and sometimes very elaborate, tombs or in what I call safe deposit boxes in mausoleums. The older tombs crumbled and broke apart, sending coffins and bodies into the swirling waters. Some were freshly buried and looked like waxen figures out for a ghastly swim. Others were mere bones. After the floodwaters subside completely, it will be a monumental task getting all the dead or remnants thereof back to appropriate safekeeping. I suspect a mass grave somewhere far from any other flood's reach. Minnesota perhaps...

I'm back in Covington now, but the city is not in quite bad enough shape for free cell phone service from any agency and my home phone is out, so e-mail from the one internet café up and running will be it for a while. The place is making a fortune selling coffee to desperate geeks. The coffee's good, so it's not much of a penance. But it is a pain, having to leave the house to reach you. It's also a major pain living without air-conditioning. When I awake in the morning, I'm bathed in perspiration and the sheets are damp. Sometimes the wet bedding wakes me up. Then I have to search for a dry spot or move to another room. At least I have a roof over my head.

My own home is OK, but my rental in the Quarter, which I hadn't used for months, is gone. It was almost empty, just a few pots and pans were left there. Wind, not water, took it. Cypress Shadows is a floor on pilings surrounded by a pile of splinters. The roof and walls are gone. All that remains are the wonderful heart of pine floors on the first story, warped and soggy but probably salvageable. I couldn't get back there for a while because of all the downed trees, power lines, etc. Roads were completely blocked. Malachi's wonderful artwork is scattered all over the yard, and uprooted and broken trees surround what used to be a house. Furniture, bedding, dishes, everything that constitutes a household are cast about like so much trash in a junkyard. If the stuff were in better shape, it would look like a garage sale stood on its head. Clothing is draped in what few trees are still standing; it looks like a more substantial version of the toilet-paper prank of adolescents. I can't even think straight enough to decide what to do with my inheritance. The setting is lovely, but knowing what is possible in the way of catastrophes, I'm undecided as to what to do with it. It's been the scene of so much bizarre—disgusting really—activity… In a way I'm glad the site of Parker's perversions, Joanna's desperation, Buddy's fraud, and Malachi's suicide is gone with the wind—literally. I'll continue living in my own somewhat tattered home and decide in a very leisurely fashion what to do. In fact, I'll be forced to take my time as all building contractors are booked solid for months if not years. I have a friend whose contractor gave her an estimate of a six-month delay in getting her place fixed up. And she doesn't need much. Since I have alternative accommodations, I'm far down the list of those needing assistance with rebuilding.

I hope Celestine and Ruben made it through OK. I believe they have relatives in northern Mississippi and may have gone there temporarily or permanently. If they happen to return, I'll let you know their fate. But I suspect Celestine, like the others in whose lives I've been immersed lately, is gone forever. This saddens me. I had grown very fond of the pair and hoped they would stick around to help me sort things out. Celestine could have given me so much more information on all the characters in this saga.

I miss you and the west very much. The last few days we spent together were spectacularly wonderful. Our return to Lonely Dell touched me very much. There's something about that place that grabbed me and won't let go. I think it was the cemetery. Situated in that gigantic bowl of red rock, those little markers, especially Lucy Emett's, were pieces of the past to which I feel a connection that transcends mere interest in historic places. How simple the life of those folks must have been, hard but simple. If we manage to work out our complicated lives and situations, I'd like to get married there—at sunset on the banks of the Paria River or perhaps near Lucy Emett's grave as a symbol of eternity.

It's just about the time of day when I know the setting sun is striking the cliffs across the Verde Valley from Jerome and it makes me happy to know you have that beautiful view to revel in.

Finally, always remember I love you, man of my dreams… Love, R

About the author:

Kathryn Wildgen taught French for over thirty years at the University of New Orleans. She has published three academic books and numerous articles for scholarly journals, but now writes for fun and personal enjoyment. Happily retired, she and her husband travel extensively. As a native of New Orleans, she has always enjoyed the Southern Gothic thriller and this is her chosen genre. She and her husband split their time between Covington, Louisiana and Flagstaff, Arizona and thus have close ties to the places involved in the action of *fractal*, her first novel. Visit her website: www.fractalthenovel.com